KW-169-111

THE AFRIKA KORPS

Cairo, June 1942. Tobruk has fallen and the British are desperate – the only way to win the war in North Africa is to eliminate the Afrika Korps commander, Field Marshal Erwin Rommel. However, one commando raid has already failed disastrously and Rommel is now at the Egyptian frontier. Captain John Warrey MC, Army Intelligence, is caught up in the most dangerous mission of his life, trying to persuade the Arabs to carry out an assassination attempt. Can vital information be passed through to the new British commander, General Montgomery, in time to prepare the final desert onslaught – the battle at El Alamein...?

Please Note: *This book may contain material which may not be suitable to all our readers.*

THE AFRIKA KORPS

THE AFRIKA KORPS

by

Alan Savage

Magna Large Print Books
Long Preston, North Yorkshire,
BD23 4ND, England.

British Library Cataloguing in Publication Data.

Savage, Alan
    The Afrika Korps.

    A catalogue record of this book is
    available from the British Library

    ISBN   0-7505-1528-7

First published in Great Britain by Severn House Publishers
Ltd., 1998

Copyright ' 1998 by Alan Savage

Cover illustration by arrangement with Severn House Publishers
Ltd.

The moral right of the author has been asserted

Published in Large Print 2000 by arrangement with Severn
House Publishers Limited

All Rights reserved. No part of this publication may be
reproduced, stored in a retrieval system, or transmitted in any
form or by any means, electronic, mechanical, photocopying,
recording or otherwise without the prior permission of the
Copyright owner.

Magna Large Print is an imprint of Library Magna Books Ltd.

Printed and bound in Great Britain by
T.J. (International) Ltd., Cornwall, PL28 8RW

All situations in this publication are fictitious and any resemblance to living persons is purely coincidental.

Contents

Contents

'Come away, come away,
Hark to the summons;
Come in your war array,
Gentles and commons.'

Sir Walter Scott

PART ONE

The Desert

'My sentence is for open war: of wiles
More inexpert, I boast not!'

John Milton

One

The Sea

'Captain Warrey?' The ATS sergeant looked and sounded efficient, as she ticked the name off her list.

'The very man,' John Warrey said, and smiled at her. In early June it was still daylight at Northolt Airfield, and he envisaged his wife standing there; Aileen was also in the ATS, and had only just returned to duty from their honeymoon. While he was going far, far away. But it would have been too much of a coincidence for Aileen to be stationed at Northolt.

'Number Eight,' the sergeant said. 'Sir.' She was taking him in as well, appreciating his height and breadth and good looks, noting the white and purple ribbon of the Military Cross on the left breast of his khaki tunic to indicate that he must be a fighting soldier. The medal ribbon was a recent addition, but the rest of him had been around for his adult life, and had attracted female attention for most of that time – he was beginning to wonder if such constant admiration was a good thing, certainly for

15

his concentration on his duties.

'Thank you, Sergeant.'

He left the shelter of the bus and walked across the tarmac to take his place in the line waiting to board the aircraft. It was a Wellington bomber, he was pleased to note, and should therefore be able to take care of itself on the flight down to Gibraltar. After that ... in this early summer of 1942 the Mediterranean was very much a battleground.

They were boarding. Nearly all were officers. The interior of the aircraft had been equipped with seats, and they took their allotted places. 'Name's Hartley,' said the major sitting beside John.

'Warrey.'

'Do you know where you're going?'

'Gibraltar, I'm told.'

'And then?'

'Cairo, eventually, I'd say.'

Hartley considered. 'Bit of a flap on, what?'

'So I believe, sir.'

The engines were roaring, and conversation became difficult. The daylight was just starting to fade as the huge bomber rumbled down the runway and lifted off. It was only the second time in his life that John had flown; the previous occasion had been some six months earlier, when he had been returned from Egypt, wounded, following

16

Auchinleck's successful counter-attack, named Crusader as he remembered. That had been intended to end the menace of the Afrika Korps forever, and when last he had heard, the British had recaptured Benghazi, the city in which he had been held prisoner for most of 1941, before he had managed to escape, with the help of his friend Colonel Umberto of the Italian Military Police. But since then something had apparently gone wrong.

Although why he was being recalled ... he had not supposed he would ever return to Egypt or the desert again. To so many memories. Margo Cartwright, enigmatic and tantalising, who had led him such a merry chase, both personally and on behalf of the British Government; Sandy Carmichael and his typewriter firm which had been a cover for British Intelligence; Arsinoe, his landlady in Cairo, who had had only one thing on her mind, and who still had quite a few of his belongings; Roberto Quesmi, his contact in Tobruk – he wondered what had happened to Roberto, who had got out with him? Sheikh Ali, the Senussi sheikh who had died so savagely ... and Soroya. He would never forget Soroya. And of course Colonel Umberto, so sadly torn between Italian patriotism and opposition to Mussolini's grandiose plans.

Now he was being called back. How many

of those old friends, and enemies, were still around? The thought of meeting any of them again made his blood tingle.

The bomber droned into the night. It carried no lights, and was hopefully invisible to any watcher from below, although as the flight path was mostly across water, there weren't going to be too many of those, save perhaps a U-boat in the Bay. But John reckoned they were too high to be hit by a U-boat's gun. 'What's your outfit?' asked Major Hartley.

John had been nodding off, but he jerked awake. The idiot had no business asking that. But he was a major. 'Intelligence,' he said.

'Ah! Cloak and dagger, what? I'm RASC.' He spoke a trifle diffidently, having also identified the ribbon John was wearing.

'Couldn't do without you,' John said cheerily, and nodded off again, to awake when they landed in Gibraltar.

Here again there were ATS girls, efficiently ticking their names off lists and allotting them to cars. 'First time in Gib?' Hartley asked.

'Second. I was here six months ago. Overnighting.'

'First time for me,' Hartley said. 'Any action?' He wore a moustache and clearly considered himself God's gift to any itinerant woman.

'That depends on how long we're here for. Are we staying at the Rock?' John asked their driver, more in hope than expectation.

'You're for the docks, sir,' the soldier replied. 'You sail at dawn.'

'Shit,' Hartley commented. 'Sail? Where the hell are we going?'

'I don't know, sir. It's all very hush-hush. But I would say Malta.'

'Isn't that a very rough ride?' Hartley muttered.

'I believe it can be,' John agreed.

'Ladies and gentlemen,' said Captain Grimes. 'Welcome aboard HMS *Torquay*. For the record, this convoy is codenamed Harpoon. I'm afraid we were not designed as a passenger ship, even for service personnel, but we will do our best to make you comfortable. We should be in Malta in about eight days. If that seems rather a long time it is because we are limited to the speed of the slowest ship. I have to tell you that we shall almost certainly have to fight the whole way, and we must expect heavy casualties. We estimate we're ahead if half of us get there. But it is necessary to resupply the island, without which matters in North Africa would be worse than they already are.'

'How bad are they, sir?' someone asked.

'We know that Rommel has launched another counter-attack and retaken Benghazi,' Grimes said. 'For the rest, we'll know more when we reach Malta. Thank you.'

'Did he say ladies?' Hartley asked, looking around the light cruiser's crowded wardroom.

'Over there.' John indicated the small group of uniformed ATS and Wren officers on the far side of the room. 'You going to chance your arm?'

'Must, old fellow. Challenge, what?'

'And the best of luck.'

John made his way through the throng, now broken up in groups discussing the meaning of what the captain had told them, and reached the deck, to take long breaths. He had done a great deal of ocean yachting before the War, but he had found the air in the wardroom oppressive. No doubt the heat had something to do with it. The day was Mediterranean perfection, the sun almost directly overhead, the wind light, the seas calm and very blue. As was the sky. Gibraltar was already hull down behind them, just the great rock sticking up out of the sea. And in front of them, nothing. Or so it appeared. The most deadly of nothings.

To either side the merchantmen, the tankers, the destroyers, even an aircraft carrier, steamed steadily forward. He supposed he should feel both proud, and safe, to be part of such an armada. But he wasn't. He found the services' way of doing things more remarkable every time he became involved. He had been summoned back to Cairo, most urgently, but to get there he stood a fifty per cent chance of being torpedoed, or bombed. Fifty per cent! The situation had indeed to be desperate.

He brooded at the water. He didn't think he was actually cut out to be a soldier. Soldiers needed one important asset: the ability not to think beyond the next order. Unless one was a general, of course – in which case, presumably, one had already gone through the period of not thinking beyond the next order. He was always trying to look ahead.

And it had not done him a lot of good. When back in the spring of 1939 as a trainee architect, but more a dedicated deep sea yachtsman with a yen for adventure, he had answered the advertisement for a navigator to accompany a photographic expedition across the Sahara, it had seemed nothing more than a jolly. Which had turned into the most desperate adventure of his life, up to that moment. When he had survived that, he had really supposed adventuring on such a scale was behind him for good. He had reckoned without Margo Cartwright, who had led that expedition, and had, apparently, recommended him to various important people in England, amongst them his father's old friend, Brigadier George Brand. Until their virtual arrest by the Italians, John had not suspected Margo, with her curling auburn hair and cold features, her dominating figure and personality, to be a British secret agent. Now he was sucked into her world.

The remarkable thing was that it had been rather fun as well, at first. Before Italy had come into the War. Pretending to sell typewriters in Cyrenaica, while secretly meeting agents on the ground, trekking into the desert to hold equally clandestine meetings with Senussi sheikhs who hated the Italians, had been straight out of the *Boys' Own Paper*. War had been different. War had been blood and guts and terror. Trapped when attempting to escape Cyrenaica, he had exploded with a violence he had not known was in his system, and killed seven men. However much an instinctive reaction to a grim situation, that had earned him an enormous reputation, not to mention the medal ribbon he wore so proudly – it had also cost him the life of the only woman he thought he had ever loved. But only Margo knew that. His relationship with Soroya was their secret. Certainly it was one his wife could never know about.

What a way to begin a marriage, with a lie. But he had a part to play. England, Home and Beauty could never mix with the Desert, Sand and Slaughter. The two worlds could never come into the slightest contact. Attempting to mix them up, to make Aileen understand about Soroya, would have been no more successful than attempting to make Soroya understand about Aileen ... and it would not have brought Soroya back to life.

'Captain Warrey?'

He half turned his head, then turned his entire body, to lean against the rail and take in the young woman standing before him. She wore the blue uniform of a Wren officer. Her figure was full enough to be interesting. Her features were somewhat clipped, but still attractive. Her dark hair was gathered in a tight bun on the nape of her neck, on which her cap was neatly perched. Her eyes were amber. There was something vaguely familiar about her, although he couldn't imagine ever having met her before. 'That's me,' he agreed.

'What a surprise,' she remarked. 'I could hardly believe my eyes when I saw your name on the passenger list.'

'I'm afraid you have me as regards names,' John said.

'Rosalind Carson.' She held out her white-gloved hand.

23

John hesitated for a moment before taking it. 'Did you say, Carson?'

Rosalind Carson smiled. 'Samantha Carson is my sister.'

John gulped. 'It's a small world.'

'In the services, yes.'

Samantha Carson, he thought. She had been secretary at the establishment where he had been trained as an operative, three years before. He had thought they might have something going ... but it turned out the only thing she had wanted to keep going was herself. 'Sam talked quite a lot about you,' Rosalind confided.

'Did she now. I had supposed Blitton Hall was top secret.'

'It was. And is. She talked about the social side.'

'Ah. And is she still there?'

'No. She's been posted. She always wanted to get out into the field.'

'I remember. So ... I suppose sisters have no secrets from each other.'

'None at all. Sam always felt she sort of let you down.'

'Perhaps I wanted more than she was prepared to give.'

'Men normally do,' Rosalind Carson said. They gazed at each other. She knows I have slept with her sister, John thought. And would like to have a go herself. But it simply wasn't on. Not because of any suggestions of incest, but because he was done with that. He was a happily married man, only forty-eight hours away from the end of his honeymoon – and he had a lot of making up to do as regards Aileen. 'It's going to be a long eight days to Malta,' she remarked.

'So I understand. So we'll need all our strength. And as I had virtually no sleep last night, I'll have to ask you to excuse me. It's been a great pleasure. And do give my regards to Sam, when next you're in contact.' He left her standing by the rail, looking quizzical. She supposed time was on her side, and if she was anything like her sister, she'd be quite prepared to wait.

Next morning the wind had freshened from the north-east, as a summer mistral swept out of the Gulf of Lyons, bringing with it some mist. 'Best thing possible,' remarked Lieutenant Wharton at breakfast. 'If the Eyeties can't find us, they can't shoot at us.'

The tables in the wardroom were sparsely attended; John had left Hartley being violently sick. But Rosalind Carson was very evident, on the far side of the room. She flickered her fingers at him, and he gave her a smile. After breakfast he went up on deck, where it was quite chilly enough to wear a coat; the sun came and went through flickering clouds, and the convoy bucked and plunged through a white-capped sea.

'How long do these last?' he asked Wharton, when the officer passed him.

'In June? Only about twenty-four hours, worse luck.'

John saw Rosalind emerging from the after companionway, and went below to see how Hartley was getting on in the cabin they shared, which had been evacuated for them by a junior lieutenant. The major's attempts at playing Don Juan had been abruptly ended by his stomach.

That evening the wind dropped, and the motion became more regular. 'You should try to eat something,' John recommended, as he dressed for dinner.

'Couldn't even think of it, old man,' Hartley groaned. 'I'm really not up to this.'

'You'd be surprised,' John said. 'In a couple of days you'll be as right as rain.'

Dinner was a better attended meal, and after it John got himself involved in a poker game; Rosalind was looking more quizzical than ever. It was midnight before they finished, then he went for a stroll before turning in. The convoy was entirely blacked-out although the ships could see each other well enough, he supposed; the white-crested bow waves streamed away to either side, and the wakes were similarly sparkling with phosphorescence. Overhead the stars twinkled out of a moonless sky.

'I think you're avoiding me,' Rosalind said, standing at his shoulder. She was well wrapped up in her navy greatcoat, and was wearing a chin strap to keep her cap in place.

'Oh, good lord, no,' John protested. 'I'm just finding my sea legs, that's all.'

'How is your cabin mate? Major Hartley.'

'Sick as a dog.'

'Hm. Mine isn't, unfortunately; she does like her sleep.'

'I thought you were part of this establishment.'

'Chance would be a fine thing. They don't let women serve on board His Majesty's Ships. Tradition says it's unlucky. Logic says it would lead to an unwanted number of pregnancies.'

'Which do you believe?'

'Oh, the second. Although there is something in the first. Men don't fight so well if there happens to be a woman lying about spilling her guts all over the deck.'

Definitely Samantha's sister, John thought. 'So where are you bound?' he asked.

'Malta. I'll join the shore establishment there, and wind up underneath some overweight admiral.'

'Does that have to follow?'

'It invariably does. How do you refuse an admiral? But I suppose you've never been in that position.'

'No,' he agreed. 'Well, it's past midnight...'

'There may not be any cabins available,' she said. 'But even warships have nooks and crannies.'

'To be used for what purpose?'

'I'd like to get to know you better.'

'Why?'

'Because I think it might be fun. And I don't suppose you're stopping in Malta long enough to do more than change ships.'

'I'm afraid so.'

It was her turn to say, 'Well?'

The temptation was enormous. But ...

'Sorry. I'm a married man.'

She regarded him for several seconds. 'Some girls have all the luck,' she commented, and went below.

John allowed her ten minutes to reach her cabin, just in case she had a change of mind. Then he inserted himself past the black-out curtain into the companionway, and went down to his own cabin. Hartley was asleep, lying on his back and snoring. As the cabin doors were required to be kept ajar, on a single hook, John was able to undress by the light in the corridor. He went to the bathroom, which was at the end of the corridor, started to return, and listened to the jangling of alarm bells.

'Enemy attack,' commented the tannoy. 'All hands report to action stations. All hands will don lifejackets. This applies to passengers as well. Passengers will assemble in the wardroom.'

John ran to the cabin, pulled the door open, switched on the light. Hartley was sitting up and scratching his head. 'What the hell...?'

'Seems the Eyeties have found us,' John said, throwing Hartley his uniform and dressing himself.

Now he could hear the *brrt-brrt-brrt* of the anti-aircraft machine-guns. Speed had also been increased, and the cruiser was throwing herself this way and that as she altered course again and again. 'Jesus!' Hartley started to vomit once more.

John's every instinct told him to get up top, at least to the wardroom, where he might be able to see what was going on. But he couldn't abandon Hartley, just in case they were hit. 'You'll just have to manage, old man,' he said, helping the major into his pants. 'Can't stay down here.'

He got Hartley dressed, in a manner of speaking, helped him along the corridor and up the ladders. They were the last; below decks the ship seemed deserted. But the wardroom was crowded and there was a buzz of excited conversation. As the ports were blacked out they couldn't see what was happening, but the noise was tremendous, the engines racing, the guns firing, the sea now stirred up and thumping against the thin steel hull, the sirens wailing... 'Thank God! I wondered where you were.'

Rosalind, needless to say, also somewhat irregularly dressed, huddled against him. He couldn't really push her off. 'Good thing we didn't, well ... go looking for your cubby hole.'

'You reckon? If we'd been there we could have stayed there until this attack finishes.'

'Will it finish?'

'They always do.' She had her arms round his waist, hugging him, and they were both leaning against Hartley, who was slumped in a chair. John didn't reckon there was anything he could do about the situation; most of the other passengers were in a similar state of agitation; several of them, like Hartley and himself, were in the Army, but none of them was used to being in action either at sea or quite unable to tell what was happening.

But remarkably, Rosalind's prognosis was proved correct – after about an hour the shooting ceased and there were several bugle calls. 'Passengers may stand down,' said the voice over the tannoy. 'But keep your life jackets handy.'

'Think you can get back to the cabin, Major?' John asked. Hartley grunted, heaved himself to his feet, and staggered towards the companionway. 'He really has a problem,' Rosalind commented.

'He really *is* a problem,' John pointed out. 'I'm going on deck. Coming?'

'You bet.'

So much for good resolutions, he thought. But they had already shared more together, in terms of real feelings, in the last hour than he had the whole of his week with Aileen. A rating allowed them through the curtain, and they took deep breaths of the night air, and gazed in horror at the burning wreck of what had been a tanker, only a few hundred yards away. She was already disappearing astern as the convoy kept on its way, but John thought he saw the dark shape of a destroyer hovering to pick up survivors – if there were going to be survivors. The sea for some distance around the sinking ship was also on fire as the burning oil spread. 'What a ghastly way to go,' Rosalind said. 'Have you ever seen people die?'

'Yes,' John said grimly. 'I was seconded to the Seventh Armoured Brigade in Cyrenaica, for a while.'

No need to tell her about his own exploits. But she would press. 'Grim,' she said. 'Do you reckon you personally have ever killed anyone?'

'Yes,' he said again.

She looked up at him, eyes wide, then threw both arms round his neck and kissed him on the mouth. Gently he removed her.

'I'm sorry,' she said. 'No, I'm not. Excitement, fear, I suppose, always makes me randy as hell. But it has no effect on you at all, right?'

'You'd be surprised,' he said, shifting her entire body so that she wouldn't feel him hard against her. 'I'd better go and see how Hartley is getting on.'

Predictably, Hartley was being sick. 'I wonder if I shouldn't get the MO to prescribe something,' John said.

'I'll be all right,' the major asserted. 'A couple of days will do the trick. You said so yourself.'

'Meanwhile you're suffering a severe liquid and salt loss,' John pointed out. 'General dehydration. He should be able to give you some immediate replacement.'

'Tomorrow,' Hartley said, and fell asleep.

John found sleep difficult. Of course the adrenalin was still flooding his system. He had thought going into battle in the sealed-up coffin of a tank discomfiting enough, but at least he had been part of the action, had known what was going on. He had never been a passenger in a battle before. And then there was the woman. She wanted him, so very badly. And if he was not very careful, she was going to get what she wanted. Because he wanted it too? Not for the first time he asked himself why he was married?

Because it had been the thing to do, and Aileen Southern had been the girl picked by his parents, as they had virtually grown up together ... but that kind of relationship had been, and belonged, and could only have happened, in the heady days before the War, when Hitler and Mussolini had seemed a very long way away, and England had bathed in a kind of eternal twilight of peace, and even slowly returning prosperity after the depression years. When death had been something that happened to other people, never oneself.

Well, he supposed, that was the only way to exist in a war, as well. But he had seen so much death. It was never pleasant, or even acceptable. The thought that had they been hit a gorgeous girl like Rosalind Carson might be floating round the Mediterranean, face green, arms and legs bloated ... he had to shake his head to get rid of the image. Christ, he thought, I'm suffering from some kind of battle fatigue, and I haven't been in a battle for six months. Before last night.

Blue skies and brilliant sunshine. But two less ships. And a certain grimness. 'Came at us out of nowhere,' Wharton told him, as they breakfasted. 'How the hell they found us–'

'At least there were no subs,' John ventured.

33

'Oh, now they've found us, there'll be subs,' Wharton said. 'If they join up with the aircraft, we may have a problem.' He grinned. 'Then there's a rumour that the Eyetie surface ships are at sea. Do you know that they have a couple of battleships that are bigger, faster, and better armed than anything we have?'

'You're not a happy man,' John said.

'At sea, nowadays,' Wharton told him, 'it's what you have that counts. The days when seamanship could beat equipment and size are done, unfortunately. Even old Nelson would have had a problem with that.'

Rosalind was in their cabin sitting beside Hartley, who was looking much better. 'I think I may be able to stomach a bite of lunch,' he said. 'More than one. I'm ravenous.'

'That's what a pretty girl does for you,' John agreed.

Rosalind made a face. 'I couldn't come up. It's all just too depressing.'

'And likely to get more so,' John agreed.

Hartley had been taking in the situation, and remembering other things. 'I'm going to take a walk,' he said. 'Freshen up, eh?'

They helped him wash his face, shave and clean his teeth, and into his uniform. Then, as he left the cabin, Rosalind closed the door behind him. 'He really is a dear,' she said.

'We're supposed to leave the door on the hook,' John pointed out.

'Fuck that. If we're to go, I'd rather go fucking you,' she said, and took off her tunic.

'I wish you'd tell me just what is really on your mind,' he said, but he was taking off his tunic as well. It was hot in the cabin, and the adrenalin was still pumping through his arteries – hers as well, he guessed. Aileen would just have to forgive him. He wondered if she would.

'I don't know.' Skirt, blouse and tie followed tunic. In bra, knickers and stockings she was any man's dream of the ideal woman. 'Like I said, I'm frightened. We still have six days to go. And, well...'

He unclipped her bra. 'You're not going to tell me you're a virgin.'

She gave a little shiver as his hands slid over her nipples. 'Don't be daft. It's just that–'

'You have a death wish. Sit.'

She sat on his bunk, and he slid his hands up her stockinged legs to reach the suspender belt. 'Oh,' she said. 'You've done this sort of thing before.'

'Would you believe you're the first woman's suspender belt I have ever undone? But I've dreamed often enough.' He lowered his head to kiss the gently throbbing, sweet-smelling flesh.

'It's a common feeling, where there's trouble.' He slid down the other stocking. Now there were only the belt and the knickers left. No army drawers, these.

'Oh, Johnnie,' she said. 'Oh, Johnnie...'

Whoop, whoop, whoop, went the alarm, followed immediately by the bugle call. 'Action stations,' announced the tannoy. 'All hands to action stations. Life jackets will be worn. Passengers will assemble in the wardroom...'

'Shit!' Rosalind declared. 'Shit, shit, *shit!*'

John handed her back her stockings. 'We'd better hurry.'

She caught his hand. 'Fuck them. No, fuck me. We have time, Johnny. We're not going to be hit first time. We're not going to be hit at all.'

John hesitated. He was certainly on the verge. But the verge was already fading. And before he could think of getting it back the door burst open, and Hartley was in their midst. 'Up top,' he said. 'There's talk of surface craft...' he goggled at Rosalind. 'My God,' he said. 'I beg your pardon, madam.'

Rosalind sighed, loudly, and put on her bra. 'We'd better get up there,' Hartley suggested to John.

'We'll wait for the lady,' John decided.

'We?' Rosalind demanded, scathingly, as she pulled on her skirt. She had apparently

36

decided to ignore the stockings ... or her knickers.

'Safety in numbers,' John suggested.

She put on her tunic, peered into the mirror to look at her hair, and made a face; there was no way she was going to be able to restore her official bun in the time available. She thrust her feet into her shoes, laced them up. 'Let's go.'

'Ah...' Hartley gazed at the discarded knickers.

'They'll be there when we come back,' she pointed out. 'When you, Major, are going to take another walk, right?'

He gulped. 'Of course,' he agreed.

By the time they reached the wardroom, Rosalind had recovered her good humour. 'Like a French farce,' she remarked, huddling against John.

The cruiser was again throwing herself left and right, her guns blazing. 'I wish we had some idea of what is going on,' he grumbled.

'Do you know how randy it makes me feel to be standing here amidst all these people with no knickers?' she asked.

'Just don't broadcast it, Listen, I'm going to try to get outside and see what's happening.'

'I'll come with you.'

'No, you won't,' John said. 'Suppose the

breeze blew your skirt up? Just stay here and keep the major company. I have a notion he's feeling just as randy as you.'

Hartley was pressed against her other side, and was clearly having great difficulty in keeping his hands to himself. She made a face. 'Hurry back. You have to have something to confess when you see Sammy.'

John turned his head, sharply. 'What do you mean? Just where is Sammy?'

Rosalind giggled. 'Didn't I tell you? She was posted to Cairo. '

'Shit,' he muttered to himself, as he wriggled through various people and reached a doorway.

'Passengers aren't allowed on deck, sir,' said the rating outside the door.

'I'm not a passenger,' John pointed out. 'I'm in Intelligence.'

The boy considered this, and while he was doing so John stepped past him and reached the deck, staring at a scene he supposed he would never forget. Some distance away a merchantman was sinking; both from her angle and from the absence of damage to her upper works John guessed that she had been torpedoed. But there were planes about as well, Italian bombers flying menacingly through the sky while being challenged by fighters put up from the aircraft carrier, which was also blazing away with its pompoms. The destroyers and cruisers were firing too, *Torquay* trembling beneath his feet as she reacted violently to the recoils as well as the changes of course.

Even as he watched, fascinated, a white streak could be seen in the blue water, making straight for them, but at the last moment, it seemed, the cruiser altered course and the torpedo slid under the stern. He looked at the horizon, and gulped, his attention caught by a deep ripple of smoke, some fifteen miles away, he estimated. A moment later there was a cascade of water where the shells had entered the sea, very close to the cruiser. 'You really should go back below, sir,' the rating said at his shoulder.

'Have we no big stuff, apart from the carrier?' John asked.

'It's on its way, sir. Be here any minute,' the sailor assured him.

'I hope you're right.' John allowed himself to be shepherded back inside, where he was besieged by everyone in the wardroom.

'Quite a show,' he told them. 'But our big boys are on the way to clean it up.'

'You're all wet,' Rosalind complained, freeing herself from Hartley's attentions.

'Spray,' he said. 'Didn't you feel it in here? A salvo landed very close. Hell, there it is again.' This time the cruiser heeled so sharply they were all thrown across the room. And she remained listing. 'They've opened a seam,' John said.

'Shouldn't we get out of here?' Hartley asked.

'And go where? Without orders?'

There was another huge gush of sound, and the lights went out, while the cruiser was definitely heeling; pressed against a bulkhead, John had both Rosalind and Hartley in his arms. Someone screamed. The tannoy had also gone dead. But a door was opening, letting in both some light and air. 'Please come on deck.' It was Wharton, his voice remarkably calm. 'Single file would be best.'

His presence restored the discipline of the army personnel, and they filed towards the doorway, holding on to the table anchored to the deck in the middle of the wardroom. 'Off you go,' John told Rosalind.

'Forget it. I'm sticking with you,' she told him.

But eventually it was their turn. John did not suppose it had taken more than a few seconds to evacuate the wardroom, but it had seemed a few hours, as every second the list grew more apparent. He grinned at Wharton. 'Is the water warm?'

'Should be, this time of year,' the lieutenant agreed.

They reached the deck, sliding across it to the rail – there was already quite a steep incline. Looking down, the water seemed very close. 'Oh, gosh,' Rosalind said. 'Are we really sinking?'

Above their heads a siren was still going whoop whoop, but where the bridge had been there was just smoke and twisted metal – and twisted bodies, John supposed. There were also unpleasant gurglings coming from below them. But the ratings unshipping one of the boats on the superstructure above were working with unhurried precision. 'Aft,' Wharton told them. 'Move aft, to the quarterdeck.'

This was higher out of the water and gave an impression of security. Here a gun was still firing, making a deafening noise, and the propellers were still turning, causing some wake but more noise; they were half exposed as the bows were now well down. John looked left and right. Where the merchantman had been was a huge swirl of white water, but further off another ship was sinking, while overhead the planes still moved to and fro trailing lines of vapour, and slashes of tracer bullets criss-crossed the sky.

That apart they were alone! The convoy, as it had to do, was fighting its way onwards with no time to stop for those in trouble. If we lose less than half of our ships, the captain had said, we'll call it a success.

'God, they're taking a long time,' Hartley grumbled, as the boat was slowly swung

41

out. Now the ship seemed to be going very fast.

The commander appeared on the superstructure aft. 'I am sorry,' he shouted. 'Abandon ship! Abandon ship! God bless you all!' Then he was gone again.

For a moment the passengers seemed stunned. Then someone screamed. And another jumped, hitting the water with a great splash, and disappearing. The chorus of shouts and screams grew. The gun had ceased firing.

John looked forward, to where the boat had been let go, prematurely. It shot downwards, struck the rail, shattering it, and then entered the water, upside down. 'Shit,' he muttered.

'Rafts!' Several of these, bright orange in colour, had been released from their position along the superstructure sides, and were tumbling into the sea, some upside down, others right side up, but all floating.

From beneath them there came a rumbling explosion. 'There go the engines,' John said. The water was now very close, and several more people had jumped. 'Come on,' he said.

'Hold my hand,' Rosalind begged. 'Please.'

He lifted her over the rail to preserve as much of her modesty as was possible to the end, then climbed behind her. 'Coming, sir?' he asked Hartley, over his shoulder.

'I can't swim,' Hartley said.

'Your life jacket will keep you up,' John assured him, and jumped, carrying Rosalind with him.

On the way down he caught a glimpse of the still turning propellers, now entirely clear of the water as the cruiser began her last dive. Then they hit the water, and went down, but only a few feet. Their life jackets brought them back to the surface. 'Swim!' he bawled in Rosalind's ear. 'Get away.'

He was still holding her hand. Now he threw it away from him, and she began to breast stroke through the water. He rolled over to look back in search of Hartley, but didn't see him. All he saw was the stern of the ship, high now, and then racing forwards and downwards, while other explosions rent the surface of the sea. He turned and swam behind Rosalind, had just caught her up when he felt the immense tug at his feet. He went down, reaching for the woman, saw her legs flailing in front of him, felt his lungs seeming about to burst, and was then propelled forward again, and upwards, seeming to eject from the sea like a cork from a bottle of shaken champagne. He gasped at air and came down again, once more plunging beneath the surface, but kept buoyant by his life jacket.

He turned his head to and fro. All around him were heads, and bodies. And oil! The surface was covered with a layer of oil, some of which had got inside his mouth and was making him vomit. My God, he thought; if someone drops a match in this lot...

'Rosalind!' he shouted, coughing and spitting.

'Rosalind!'

She wase actually only a few feet away. She was lying back in her life jacket, staring at the sky. He caught her arm, and at the same moment spotted a life-raft floating upside down, and quite close. 'Come on,' he said, and dragged her towards it.

Others had seen it as well, and there was quite a cluster. Amongst them was Lieutenant Wharton, who naturally took command. 'Please take it easy,' he told them. 'First thing, let's get it over.'

Several of the men helped him get it right side up. 'Now,' Wharton said. 'It's very important not to capsize it again. Three of you chaps hang on to this side, and we'll board from the other. Ladies first. Ladies!'

A bedraggled ATS girl reached the side of the raft; she had no hat and her hair was a wet mat on her shoulders. The men pushed and heaved, and she rolled over the low gunwale and landed in the rubber bottom with a little shriek. 'Good girl,' Wharton said. 'Who's next? Ladies!'

'Here.' John pushed Rosalind towards the raft, where she was received by willing hands.

Wharton was next to the raft, keeping command. Now he peered at the Wren officer. 'This woman is dead,' he said. 'Next!'

Two

Cairo

'How do you feel?' asked the MO.

'I'm fine,' John lied.

'Then you'll be anxious to get on. We'll be in Valletta tomorrow morning. God willing.'

Fine, John thought, staring at the bunk above his. It was quite remarkable after what the convoy had gone through – apparently six merchantmen and six warships had been sunk – the destroyer that had picked up the survivors from *Torquay* had not seen or heard an enemy during the past five days. And he was fine. Physically, certainly. Mentally, he was not so sure. He was not sure he would ever wish to go to sea again. Nor could he get the image of Rosalind Carson out of his mind. She had been going to get together with her sister in Cairo, for a wing-ding. No doubt he had been intended to share in that.

Now she was floating around the Mediterranean, being eaten by fish. He would never forget the feeling of sheer disbelief as the men had pushed the dead body away from the side of the life-raft to make room for the living. Her face had been covered in oil – he presumed it had suffocated her – but the rest of her had looked so very alive. So very much a waste, as she went off to join Hartley, also presumably drifting about the Mediterranean – he had not been seen again. All for the succour of Malta. But Malta both needed and deserved succouring. Only a few months earlier the gallant defence of the island against round-the-clock bombing had earned it the award of the George Cross, a unique honour for an entire community. Now the evidence of just what the population had undergone, and was undergoing, was all around the destroyer as she steamed into Valletta Harbour. Houses were half collapsed, streets were filled with rubble. Yet the mighty fortress of the Knights of St John still towered above the sea, and the harbour itself was filled with craft, some being repaired, others loading, others unloading...

'Where do you go now?' John asked Wharton.

'I have no idea. I'll be assigned to another ship. But whether it will be here or someplace else, God knows. I say, old man, I never had the chance before, but ... I've been told you were fairly close to that Wren.'

'Now who told you that?' John asked.

'One of the other survivors spotted you doing a bit of canoodling.'

'Just a bit,' John admitted. 'I was a friend of her sister's, before the War.'

'Ah. Damned bad luck. She was a good-looking woman.'

'I thought so, yes,' John said. What was he going to say to Samantha? He did not suppose there was any chance of avoiding her. Supposing he ever reached Cairo.

'Well...' Wharton held out his hand. 'The best of luck.'

'And to you.' He wondered if they'd ever meet again. There were so many of those relationships in wartime, he had discovered. They had been intensely intimate for about three days on that liferaft before being picked up, half dead from dehydration and lack of food. Two others had died, and there had been only five survivors. They had not spoken a lot, after initial attempts to organise a sing-song and generally try to keep themselves going. Exhaustion and weakness had left them doing nothing more than waiting for death. But they had all – four men and one woman – been very aware of each other, and for that reason had not sought each other out after they had been rescued and restored to a semblance of life.

He had had the same experience with Margo Cartwright, when they had been forced to escape Tobruk across the desert, on the outbreak of war. They had survived for several months, sharing every intimacy

49

in their determination to stay alive – and neither had really wanted to see each other again afterwards. Save that the requirements of war had again thrown them together. He wondered where *she* was now.

'The MO says you're fit for duty,' remarked Colonel Chalmers. 'You don't look it.'

'It's probably the uniform,' John said. 'They knocked it up in rather a hurry. I lost all my gear with the ship, you see, sir.'

'Yes,' the colonel agreed, somewhat drily. 'Well, you may be pleased to know that you won't have to go to sea again. You're being flown out.'

'That does please me, sir.'

'Well, don't count your chickens until you land in Alexandria. You'll go at night, and there'll be an escort – you're going to be keeping company with a general – but there is a lot of enemy activity between here and Egypt. Not all of our planes get through.'

'Yes, sir.'

'So, report to the airfield at seven this evening. And in the meantime, not a word to a soul.'

John looked at his watch as he left the office: it was twenty past ten in the morning. They had docked the previous morning, and he had spent most of the rest of the day at the army tailors, being fitted out. 'They'll equip you fully in Cairo, sir,' suggested the sergeant in charge. 'But at least you'll be decent.'

In a manner of speaking. Now he had several hours to waste.

He went to the mess, and found it deserted, save for a somewhat morose Maltese barman. He had a pink gin, and felt slightly better. 'Tell me a good place to have lunch,' he suggested.

'You can have it here, Captain,' the barman said. 'Maybe.'

'Chef not in?'

'I am the chef. Listen.' The siren cut across the morning. 'They're regular,' the barman said. 'We go downstairs, eh?'

John followed him into the cellars, where several women, who he gathered were the cleaning staff, had already gathered. Soon conversation was interrupted by the thud of bombs. 'They won't reach us here,' the barman said, reassuringly.

The building shook as something landed quite close, and some plaster fell. John studied the ceiling; there was quite a bit of plaster gone. 'Italians?' he asked.

'Luftwaffe,' the barman said. Ten minutes later the all clear went. 'You lunching here?' the barman asked.

'Seems like a good idea.' He had absolutely no wish to go outside and look at rubbled buildings, more dead bodies. 'But first, I'll have another gin.'

51

The barman poured. 'You have no duty?'

'Passing through,' John said.

'You stay the night?'

'Ask me that tonight,' John said.

A couple of other officers came in, but they did not appear interested in John. He ate alone, and found the food surprisingly good.

'Navy brought this in,' the barman-cum-chef explained. 'They too are very regular.'

'I'll say,' John said, and smiled at the pretty dark-haired girl who was serving him.

'You go somewhere this afternoon?' the chef asked.

'What I would like to do this afternoon,' John said, 'is have a good long nap.' He was quite exhausted, just by being up and about for a few hours.

'You do that here,' the chef said. 'We have rooms. You wish company?'

'No.'

'This girl is my cousin,' the chef explained. 'She will keep you company.' The dark-eyed girl smiled at him, and gave a little shimmy, causing her black hair to flutter away from her shoulders.

'Doesn't she speak English?'

'Oh, yes,' the chef said. 'But she likes me to speak for her.'

'You mean you're her pimp,' John said, finishing his meal.

'I am her cousin,' the chef said with

dignity. 'But she is a young girl and needs looking after, or people would take advantage of her.'

'Absolutely.' John drank his coffee.

'She is not expensive,' the chef explained. 'For ten shillings she will spend the afternoon with you. The night too, if you wish.'

'Doesn't she have to serve at dinner?'

'I will give her the evening off.'

'I think I'll take a raincheck on this one,' John decided.

'You don't like this girl? She has a sister, who is even prettier.'

'I've no doubt of it,' John said. 'The fact is, old man, I spent most of last week paddling around the sea out there, and right now I couldn't raise a twitch.'

Just to be sure, he locked the door of the small bedroom to which he was assigned. Presumably the man was only trying to make him happy. He didn't know how uphill was that task. John wasn't sure he would ever be happy again. Until he could get back to fighting, killing, himself. And perhaps even being killed.

He felt like a man through whose hands had passed several jewels of extreme value, each of which had fallen from his grasp and shattered on the floor. He was being fanciful, and less than fair to himself, he knew. He had not deliberately dropped any of the jewels, neither had he thrown them down; he had just been unable to retain hold of them.

But he surely had retained hold of the most precious of them all, his wife. Aileen! Yet as she hadn't known where he was being posted or how he was travelling, she wouldn't have anything specific to worry about. And he couldn't tell her.

He listened to gentle fingers sliding over the door, smiled, and went to sleep.

'You sleep four hours,' the barman told him. 'Now you are all refreshed, eh?'

'Yes, I am,' John agreed.

'So, my cousin is most disappointed. But she will come to you tonight.'

'Brilliant,' John agreed. 'But I am just going out for a while first.' An army car picked him up at six-thirty, and drove him to the airfield. Here a transport waited, and several important-looking officers, wearing red tabs and hat bands.

'Warrey, sir.' John saluted the one with the most brass.

'Hm,' the general said. 'You're coming with us.' He seemed surprised.

'Yes, sir.'

'You can sit at the back. McLean will keep you company.' McLean was an ATS officer, who saluted smartly. Everything about her was smart, but she reminded him too much of Rosalind. Not that they looked the least alike, because this one was blonde, but simply because of the smartness. 'They must need you pretty badly,' she remarked, as the machine thundered down the runway.

'What makes you say that?'

'Simply that you're travelling with all this brass.'

'And who are you travelling with?'

She arched an eyebrow. 'General Gott. I'm his secretary.'

'Ah,' John said.

'Who is interested only in beating Rommel,' she added.

'I should think so too.'

He got the impression she hadn't taken to him, which suited him well enough. Soon she was making tea while they flew through the blackness. As the ports were covered he had no idea where they were and whether there was any enemy interest. But then he was invited up to sit with the brass. 'Intelligence,' General Gott remarked.

'Yes, sir.

'Captured, weren't you?'

'Yes, sir. When Benghazi fell the first time.'

'But you escaped.'

'I was lucky.'

'Useful, to be lucky. You know there's a flap on?'

'I know that Rommel is counter-attacking, sir.'

'He has just won a major battle. A week ago the Eighth Army lost one hundred and thirty-eight tanks, They have only seventy-five left serviceable.'

John swallowed. 'Then—'

'They're pulling back. Well, they have no alternative. And reinforcements are being rushed from England. But they have to go round the Cape. It would simply be too risky to send a couple of hundred tanks through the Med. You saw that for yourself.'

'Yes, sir.'

'Tell me, did you ever meet Rommel? I mean, when you were a prisoner.'

'No, sir. I saw him fairly close to, just after we had been captured.'

'So you'd know him again?'

'Oh, yes, sir. He had the sort of face one doesn't easily forget.'

'He's also a brilliant general. We can only hope he runs into supply problems sooner rather than later. Or that something else turns up. You'd better see if you can get some rest.'

'Yes, sir.' But John hesitated. For the life of him he couldn't figure out why he had been selected for this little chat by an army commander. But then, he had not yet figured out why he was being hurried back to Cairo in any event. Now he felt sufficiently emboldened to ask, 'Are we really winning this war, sir?'

Gott turned his head, sharply. 'Of course we are going to win it, Warrey.'

'It's just that, well ... the Germans control all Europe. They're beating the hell out of the Russians. Singapore and the Phillipines are gone and the Japanese are running riot in the Pacific. And now we have Rommel running riot in North Africa—'

'They're all chickens with their heads cut off,' Gott said. 'They're running out of everything they need to make war with. Sooner or later they are just going to keel over and lie there with their legs in the air, I'm not saying it won't be later. They've been preparing for this war for some time. But it'll happen. And if it'll make you feel any better, we heard the news just before leaving Malta – the Americans have just about destroyed the Japanese carrier fleet.'

'Is that fact, sir?'

'Confirmed. The battle was fought quite close to the Hawaiian Islands. Now it's just a matter of rolling them back. Sleep easy, Warrey. Our job is to make sure Rommel doesn't get to Cairo.'

'Well, what do you know?' John asked, when he seated himself beside McLean in the rear of the aircraft. 'I may just kiss you.'

'Don't chance your arm,' she recommended.

'Well, maybe we'll meet up in Cairo.'

57

'Chance would be a fine thing,' she said, and appeared to go to sleep.

John did also, sleeping more soundly than for some time. It was so reassuring to think that an Allied force, somewhere, had won a resounding victory. But to think of the Seventh Armoured Brigade being virtually destroyed, all his old pals like Blanchard and Plessey and Layton, strewn around the desert beside their burning tanks ... although seventy-five tanks had survived. Maybe some of them had survived as well.

They landed at Alexandria with the dawn. Gott shook hands. 'I'll say goodbye, Warrey. And good luck.'

'And to you, sir.' He smiled at McLean, but she didn't respond. All around him, in fact, the faces were grim. The news obviously wasn't getting any better.

'Captain Warrey?' The lieutenant saluted. 'Clive Dexter. I've a car waiting.'

'To go where?'

'Cairo, sir. Ah ... your gear?'

'I don't have any gear,' John told him, 'save for what is in this washbag.'

'Good lord, sir. You did leave in a hurry.'

'Not that much of a hurry. My gear is at the bottom of the Mediterranean.'

'Good lord,' Lieutenant Dexter said again, and began threading his way through the congested streets, the shouting people, the grunting camels, the barking dogs, the squadrons of bicycles, and the soldiers and officials hurrying anxiously to and fro. 'I'm afraid there's a bit of a flap on.'

'I can see that,' John said.

'We've had to retreat, you see, sir. Right back to the border.'

John turned his head, sharply. 'They haven't got Tobruk?'

'Oh, no, sir. Tobruk will be held. But we've had to allow it to be isolated, again. It's a thorn in their side. Just like last year. It'll be relieved just as soon as we can counter-attack and advance again. But people here are a little nervous.'

'Yes,' John agreed. They were on the open road now, driving south as fast as they could. 'What are we going to counter-attack with?'

'Oh, well, new armour is expected any day now.'

'Of course. Have you any idea what I am doing here?'

'None at all, sir. But you are to report immediately to General Auchinleck.'

Curiouser and curiouser, John thought, as he was driven straight to military head-quarters. Cairo was exactly as he remembered it from the previous December, with the pyramids standing calmly across the river, Shepheard's Hotel as massively

59

opulent as ever, the streets crowded ... but here too there was a sense of nervous excitement. Sentries saluted as John was ushered upstairs and through an outer office into the commanding general's inner sanctum. 'Captain Warrey, sir,' an aide announced.

Auchinleck had been standing by the window. Now he turned. 'Glad you could make it, Warrey.' He was a big man, with strong features. He looked tired.

John had met him the previous year, just before he had returned home, wounded. 'Glad to be here, sir.'

'You've met Commander Jones.'

John had not realised there were other people in the room. Now he turned, and his heart gave a curious pitter pat. 'Yes, sir,' he said. 'I have met the commander.'

Jones had been the secret service officer who had sent him off into the desert on a mission that had all but cost him his life. And *had* cost Soroya hers. Now he came forward to shake hands. 'Glad to see you fit again, Warrey.'

But John was looking past him, at the uniformed woman behind him. 'And Major Cartwright is an old acquaintance, is she not?' Auchinleck suggested.

'Yes, sir.'

They gazed at each other. It was more than three years now since they had first

60

met. In that time they had adventured together, time and again, in the line of duty. They had shared a great deal, if never their bodies; there had never seemed an appropriate moment for that, and besides, there had been Soroya. As now there was Aileen.

But Margo remained as compelling as ever, her red hair caught up in a precise military bun, her somewhat gaunt features relaxed as she smiled at him, her body as slender, and as hard and tough, no doubt, as he remembered. They shook hands, only the slightest increased pressure in her fingers revealing that she was actually pleased to see him.

'Yes,' Auchinleck said, having observed the silent interchange. 'I think you should know, Warrey, that you have been recalled at the suggestion of Major Cartwright.'

John looked at Margo again, and she waggled her eyebrows.

'This is because you know the desert, and you know the Senussi, and Major Cartwright is about to return there on a very special mission. Thus she needs a very special aide, and it seems that you are that man.'

'Yes, sir.' The desert! And Margo! And too many memories. Their last mission had also been very special, and it had cost Soroya her life.

'Now,' Auchinleck said. 'I don't know how

61

au fait you are with the situation, Warrey, but Rommel appears to have done it again, and caught us on the hop. I am flying up to the front this afternoon to assess the situation for myself. Things always sound worse than they are from too close, and the situation is by no means irretrieveable. In fact, it may well react to our advantage.' He gestured at the map on the wall. 'I have authorised a withdrawal east of Tobruk. This is much the situation we were in when I took command last summer. Once again we may expect Rommel to settle down to besiege Tobruk; he cannot possibly advance into Egypt with such a thorn sticking into his side. This will give us the time we need to build up our forces and restore morale. I am hopeful of being able to counter-attack within a couple of months, and drive him back again. However, the fact remains that as long as he is in command it is going to be very difficult for us to gain the victory we want and need to drive the Germans and the Italians out of North Africa.'

He sat down behind his desk, and gestured the others also to chairs. 'What I am now going to tell you is top secret, just as are the orders I am about to give you. Very few people know this, but it was decided some time ago, in England, that Rommel was too dangerous to live.' He looked across their faces. 'I am sure this concept of warfare will be as distasteful to you as it is to me. However, it is the way the Germans wage war, and if we are not prepared to play as rough as them, we are going to lose the War. Thus a commando raid was authorised on the Mediterranean Coast, to, as they say, take him out. Unfortunately, the raid was a fiasco. Rommel was not at the house we had been told was his command villa, it was more heavily guarded than we had been told, and our people were shot to pieces. Only one or two escaped, and where they are nobody knows.'

Once again he looked across their faces. 'I'm afraid London is now more than ever convinced that he must be disposed of. This task has been given to Commander Jones, as head of the Cairo Branch of the Secret Intelligent Services, and he has selected Major Cartwright as the agent to bring this about. Major Cartwright was told to pick her own team, and she chose you. Commander?'

Jones cleared his throat. 'It is not as crazy an idea as it may sound off-hand. And your mission will have a dual purpose. You have already made certain contacts with the Senussi.'

'Unfortunately, sir,' John said. 'The Senussi with whom I was dealing were wiped out by the Italians at the beginning of the War.'

Jones nodded. 'However, Sheikh Ali had a son, who was not in their village when the Italians attacked; he was south in the desert. This man, Halim ben Ali al-Fuad, is very anxious to avenge his father. He has contacted us, and offered to lead a Senussi uprising against the Italians, which means the Germans as well, if his people can be properly equipped. He has, in fact, mentioned your name, Warrey, as the man he would like to deal with, as he remembers you were a friend of his father's.'

'With respect, sir, such a project will take a good deal of organisation, and time. I had thought the situation was urgent.'

'It is,' Auchinleck said. 'Nor are we in a position to equip a Senussi army, even if such a thing were desirable; it is very unlikely that, when we have overthrown the Italians and their Germans friends, the Senussi would give those weapons back. There is, however, a way in which the Senussi can help the Allied cause, very importantly.'

'It is up to you to persuade them to take on this task,' Jones said.

'To assassinate Rommel,' John said.

'Exactly.'

John looked at Margo, while the senior officers waited.

'I know Halim,' Margo said. 'I met him on one of my pre-war expeditions into the

Sahara. He trusts me.'

'To send some of his people to their deaths? It was the Italians, not the Germans, who wiped out his village.'

'It is Rommel who is the commanding general of both the Italians and the Germans,' Jones pointed out. 'Margo thinks he will do it. But that is not your business, Warrey. You will merely act as Major Cartwright's second-in-command, her bodyguard, in the carrying out of this duty.'

John looked at Auchinleck. 'It is an order I am very reluctant to give, Warrey,' the general said. 'But it is a direct command from London. What needs to be done needs to be done. We have a war to win. Now, time is obviously of the essence.' He gave a dry smile. 'I understand that the last time you and Major Cartwright went wandering off into the desert together you were gone for six months. This matter needs attending to in six days. You will therefore be flown to Ali's encampment.'

'There is no airstrip, as such,' Jones said. 'But we are assured there is an area of hard sand on which a light plane can be put down. This area will be marked by the Senussi the moment they are informed you are on your way. They have a radio.'

'I think that's about it,' Auchinleck said. 'You take off at dawn tomorrow. I repeat, this is absolutely top secret, and of course, if you were captured, we should deny having given you any orders other than to contact the Senussi. Understood?' He stood up and held out his hand. 'Good fortune.'

'You're booked in at Shepheard's,' Margo told him as they went down the stairs together.

'All thought out. I presume you are staying there too.'

'Of course.' She raised an eyebrow as they got into the command car driven by an MP. 'It's a place where we have a lot of un-finished business. But that was before you got yourself married.' She was poking fun at him.

'True.'

'Where is your gear? We can pick it up.'

'At the bottom of the sea.'

'Oh, dear! You've been adventuring again.'

'In a manner of speaking.'

'You *are* fit? It never occurred to me that you'd get yourself blown up.'

'I'm improving.'

'Oh, well, we'll be wearing Arab gear anyway.' The car pulled into the forecourt of the hotel. 'Lunch,' Margo said.

They gazed at each other across the table. 'I really am chuffed that we're working together again,' she said. 'I wish you were.'

'Oh, I am,' John protested.

'Then try looking it. I really do value you,

66

you know. Oh, I know we've had our ups and downs, but we made a pretty good team. Now we'll make an even better one.'

'You reckon?'

'More experience,' she said.

He couldn't argue with that, when he recalled some of the mishaps she had been forced to undergo. 'So tell me,' she said. 'How is married life?'

'I haven't tried it yet, so I'm not qualified to give an answer. I have honeymooned, and that is extremely pleasant. Tell me something: have you been in Cairo all the past six months?'

'I was allowed a furlough. But yes, most of the time.'

'And I suppose you various women get together.'

She frowned. 'Sometimes.'

'Do you know someone called Samantha Carson? She's in intelligence too. And I understand she was posted to Cairo.'

'If she is in intelligence, how do you know she's in Cairo? People aren't supposed to know things like that.'

'Her sister told me.'

'I see. Another of your doxies, no doubt. You really are the ultimate MCP.'

'I would dispute that. Her sister happened to be a passenger on the same cruiser as me.'

'So you spent a few pleasant days floating around the Med, stimulating each other.'

'You really are the ultimate bitch, Margo,' he remarked. 'Yes, we did. Only she happened to be dead at the time.'

She gazed at him from under arched eyebrows. 'You serious?'

'Very.'

'God! Yes, I do know Sammy Carson. She's staying in this hotel.'

'Shit! Does she know her sister is dead?'

'I very much doubt it, if you were on the same ship. That was just a week ago, wasn't it?'

'A shade more.'

'Yes. Well, the full report on that convoy won't have been assembled yet. And as even the brass are not supposed to know the whereabouts of intelligence officers unless they actually happen to be employing them, the news of her sister's death will in the first instance be sent to the parents in England. Are you going to tell her?'

'Call me a coward, but I'd rather not.'

'I don't think I will either. But you're almost certain to see her tonight. Tell me, was *she* ever one of yours?'

'Ah ... briefly. We trained together. In a manner of speaking.'

'I think anyone who associates with you deserves danger money.'

'You sent for me, remember?'

'I'm beginning to wonder if I did the right thing. Now, I suggest you have a bath and a shave,' Margo said. 'And that we meet up in the lounge for tea. You *do* have shaving gear?'

'I have a razor, yes, courtesy of the Navy. And I think we should make that drinks, a little later on,' John said. 'I mean to have a nap. I need all the rest I can get.'

She gave him a quizzical look, then shrugged. 'Okay, drinks at six. We'll hope Sammy isn't there.'

John was shown up to his room by a rather snooty bellboy, aghast that the client did not have a suitcase. 'I assume, in a war, that one does not have to dress for dinner anymore?' John asked.

'It is not necessary, effendi. Although many people do.'

'They'll have to accept me as I am,' John said. 'Now, you can do something for me.' He showed some of the English money he had been paid in Malta.

'Yes, effendi.'

'I am going out for a short while, but I do not wish anyone to know that. So, if anyone asks, I am in my room sleeping. Understood?'

'Yes, effendi.'

John gave him a generous tip, then went downstairs. There were always taxies available in the forecourt, and he gave the address, then asked himself what he was

69

doing. Why, getting hold of some of his gear, of course. And Arsinoe was at least genuine. He needed a bit of that. Besides, he had an idea she, or at least her husband, owed him a bit of money.

The house hadn't changed in the slightest. He rang the bell and waited for several minutes before it opened. Arsinoe hadn't changed in the least either, a little gem of a woman, pert-featured, with good breasts and legs, dark-haired and skinned, wearing a very short skirt and high-heeled shoes ... all of which, he had a feeling, had been rather hastily put on.

She gazed at him for several seconds in total consternation, then gave a high-pitched squeal. 'Warrey! Warrey!' She threw both arms round his neck and kissed him with all the passion he remembered from when last he had been here. 'I did not think you would come back!'

'To tell you the truth I didn't either. Mustafa home?' Mustafa was her husband, a man totally lacking in jealousy, at least where his wife was concerned.

'You come in.' She held his hand and dragged him into the house, kicking the door shut. 'Mustafa! He is away. You know he is with the transport, now. He was conscripted.'

'I remember.'

'Well he is up somewhere on the coast.

70

One of those villages, El Alamein or Mersa Matruh, driving trucks for the British. Are you not glad he is not home?'

'Not exactly. You see–'

'Arsinoe? Arsinoe?' The man's voice, coming down the stairs, was plaintive.

'Ah, get dressed, you asshole,' Arsinoe bawled. 'Get dressed and get out. I have a *man* here. A man! He couldn't do it anyway,' she explained.

John sighed, and watched the man come down the stairs, cautiously. He did not suppose Arsinoe would ever change. But then, did he really want her to change? 'Sorry for the interruption, old man,' he said.

The man gave him a dirty look, Arsinoe an anxious one, and sidled out of the door. 'Asshole,' Arsinoe repeated. 'You come upstairs, eh?'

'No, no,' he said. 'I didn't come here for sex.'

'No sex? Ha! You come, you go, all the time, no time for sex! What you come here for, then?'

'Well of course I wanted to see you again–'

'Ha,' she commented, only slightly mollified.

'But what I really would like is my gear.'

'Gear?'

'I really haven't the time for games, my dearest girl. When I was wounded, last

71

December, I was shipped out, remember? In a hurry, remember? I left quite a lot of my clothes here. A spare uniform, certainly. Now I need it.'

'You go, you come, how am I to know when you come? I did not expect you.'

'Arsinoe,' John said. 'You haven't sold my uniform?'

'Well...' she assumed her sulky look. 'When you go, back to England, your army stop paying me rent for the room. What am I to do? How am I to live?'

'You little bitch,' John said, but it was more in sorrow than in anger. Arsinoe was not a woman one could be angry with. 'Couldn't Mustafa provide?'

'Mustafa is never here.'

'Which suits you down to the ground, as I well know. Okay, you sold my uniform. What about my money.'

'Money?' she demanded, eyes flashing. 'What money?'

'The money you owe me.'

'I owe you money? Ha! You want coffee? I make you coffee.'

John recalled that Arsinoe's coffee made his hair stand on end; but he felt he might need that much stimulus. 'That would be very nice. I am not suggesting you owe me money, sweetheart. But Mustafa does.'

'Mustafa?' She was fiddling with various brews on her stove, waggling her hips provocatively as she did so. 'How Mustafa can owe you money? Mustafa never has money.'

'Listen,' John said, 'do you remember when I had to go off into the desert with Soroya—'

'Soroya!' Arsinoe turned round and threw herself into his arms, sobbing into his tunic. 'I loved that girl. You know I loved that girl?'

'I'm sure you did. I loved her too.'

'And you took her off into the desert to be killed? That is love?' Arsinoe disengaged herself and returned to her stove.

'It wasn't my idea that she get killed,' John said. 'Anyway, listen, remember, I had a car?'

'That beat-up old wreck?'

'It worked. And Soroya and I drove the car to Hamdi, the camel dealer, and left it with him while we went into the desert.'

'And you did not come back for six months,' Arsinoe complained. 'You come, you go, and I am keeping your room always ready, and you no come.' She placed two mugs of steaming black liquid on the table.

'But I did come, eventually,' John reminded her. With Arsinoe, as he well remembered, one had to proceed with great patience towards one's goal.

'And then went again, straightaway,' Arsinoe pointed out. 'With those soldiers.'

'Well, I am a soldier, and we were fighting

a war. We *are* fighting a war.'

'What you are doing,' Arsinoe said scathingly, 'is *losing* a war.'

That was a difficult point to argue. 'Anyway,' John said, 'when I had to leave again, so quickly, Mustafa said he would go to Hamdi, reclaim the car, and sell it for me. Did he do this?'

'Ha!' Arsinoe commented. 'Hamdi say, you never returned his camels. So the car is his.'

'That bastard reckons his two moth-eaten camels are worth my car?'

'It was a moth-eaten car,' Arsinoe argued.

'Arsinoe, my dearest girl,' John said. 'I hate to call you a liar, but I think you are one. I think Mustafa did get the car, and sold it. So, give.'

'I know nothing about this,' Arsinoe protested, contradicting herself. 'Mustafa does the money. You must ask him.'

'But he is up on the coast.'

'He will come back, when the British surrender. You come, you go...' her eyes were suddenly enormous. 'This time you stay, eh? I have the room, all ready.'

John drank some coffee. 'Doesn't it belong to that gentleman? The one who just left?'

'Him? You think I would rent my room to such as him? He just came in off the street.'

'Ah. I'm afraid I can't take the room right now. I have to go away tomorrow morning.'

74

'You come, you go. You do not stay.'

'Perhaps, when I come back,' he said.

'You go too long, I tell you who will have the room when you come back: a German officer. Or an Italian.'

Once again, it was a difficult point to argue. 'I'll have to take a chance on that. However, when I come back I'll expect to find my money waiting for me. Right?'

'Ha!' Arsinoe commented.

John walked back to the hotel, although it was a fair distance. But he enjoyed the heat after the cool of England, and even more the cold of the sea in which he had spent those traumatic days and nights. Not that he wanted to think about them. They were merely another load of memories to add to those he had already accumulated over the past three years. The only sensible approach to life for him was to march resolutely forward, fight this war and hope to emerge on the victorious side, and then get back to his father's architect's office, build a career, and make Aileen happy and, hopefully, a mother.

But the War, it seemed, was going to be fought, and won or lost, in the company of Margo Cartwright, who was an eternal bridge to the past. He wondered if taking her to bed would exorcise the almost sinister influence she seemed to have over his life. When two people had been thrown together as often, and as violently, as they, it was quite impossible for thoughts of bed never to enter the equation. He recalled that he had been very keen when they had first worked together; here was a woman, if not beautiful, certainly compellingly attractive, always at his side, sharing the most intimate surroundings ... it had very rapidly dawned on him that Margo was entirely her own woman, who regarded men very much as most men regarded women, to be there when she wanted them, and to fill in the background when she did not. She had only once ever wanted him *there*, to his knowledge, and on that occasion he had not wanted her at all.

No doubt their relationship would always be coloured by his memory of the time she had invited him to her room in this very hotel now looming above him, only for him to discover it was merely for him to be introduced to and instructed by the man Jones, her boss. He crossed the lobby and got into the lift, without anyone giving him more than a second glance. He had the impression there was a new flap on, or merely the original flap had merely gathered pace.

He went up in the lift, hurried along the corridor – there was just time for him to have a nap before meeting Margo downstairs – opened the door, stepped inside, and saw her lying on the bed, smoking a cigarette.

John closed the door behind him. 'How the devil did you get in?'

'I bribed the floor waiter. Where the devil have you been?'

John was slowly gathering that whatever she had come for, it was not sex; she was fully dressed and had not even removed her shoes. 'I went for a walk.'

'Looking for another of your women, I suppose.'

'As a matter of fact, yes,' he said, becoming nettled. 'As I think I told you once before, Margo, you may be my commanding officer when we are in the field, but when I am not in the field, I reserve the right to be my own boss.'

She sat up, violently. 'Not when it breaches security.' She stubbed out her cigarette. 'I don't suppose that's important, now. I don't suppose you know what's happened?'

She was certainly agitated.

'Ah ... Rommel has died of a heart attack, so our mission is aborted.'

'Rommel has not died of a heart attack,' Margo said. 'He's taken Tobruk.'

Three

The Desert

John took off his cap and threw it on a chair. 'I hope you're joking.'

'I never joke.' Margo got off the bed and lit another cigarette.

'Well somebody has to be. Tobruk withstood a siege of several months last year. It's only been isolated for a week this time.'

'I know.' Her hands were trembling as she struck a match. 'There is one hell of a flap on. Nobody can understand how it's happened. But it has. Twenty-five thousand men lost. A hundred tanks. God knows how many guns. The Eighth Army is in full retreat across the border.'

'Jesus! How do you know all this?'

'Jones called. He wants us both to see him at headquarters.'

'When?'

'Now! Which happened to be an hour ago. While you were fucking some Egyptian bint.'

John didn't bother to argue. 'What is Auchlinleck saying about it?'

'Nobody knows. He's gone up to the front, remember?'

'You mean he may be in Rommel's can as well?'

'If he is, God help us all. Let's go.'

The news of the disaster was by now filtering through to the inhabitants of Cairo, and crowds were gathering on street corners. Not all of them were anxious; John suspected that a majority of the Egyptians would be very pleased to see the British go, in happy ignorance of what being ruled by Nazi Germany and its Gestapo might involve. It took their taxi nearly an hour to get them to military headquarters, where their passes were carefully inspected by the MP on the gate. 'Commander Jones is waiting for you,' he told them.

Inside the courtyard they paused in consternation at the sight of the bonfires being erected, onto which boxes of files and various other papers were being dumped. 'They're ready to leave,' Margo said grimly.

Sentries saluted as they were shown up to Jones's office. 'Not so good, eh?' the commander said.

'What exactly is happening, sir?' John asked.

'I believe we're going to try to make a stand at Mersa Matruh,' Jones said. 'But I'm afraid there has been some breakdown

80

of morale, following the collapse of Tobruk. We have to expect the worst, that Rommel will gain another victory, in which case he could well be in Alexandria by the end of the week. In *which* case, there is of course no hope for Cairo; we have no decent defensive position between here and Alexandria, and once he holds Alexandria he can have his people on both sides of the Nile, so that won't prove much of an obstacle either.'

'So we're abandoning Cairo.'

Jones gave him a dirty look. 'Orders have been given to prepare an evacuation, yes.'

'Just who gave those orders, Commander?' The voice was tired, but still crisp. They all turned to face the door, and the Commanding General. Auchinleck's uniform was crushed, and his face was as tired as his voice. But there was no lack of decision in either voice or face.

'Ah...' Jones hesitated. 'They were issued–'

'Cancel them. There will be no evacuation.' Jones gulped. 'We were sent here to fight, and beat the Germans. Well, I don't know if we can beat them,' Auchinleck said. 'But we can certainly fight them, and this is what I intend to do. I have taken over command of the Eighth Army from Ritchie. That means I shall be returning to the front this evening. We are going to attempt to hold Mersa Matruh. If we cannot, we are going to retreat along the coast, to...' he prodded the map on the table. 'Here. El Alamein. It is a good defensive position, with flanks that cannot be turned, as Rommel so likes to do. You'll see that our right flank will rest on the sea, and our left on this thing they call the Qattara Depression. I understand you two have explored this area,' he said to Margo and John.

'Inadvertently, sir,' Margo said.

'But you'll agree that it is impassable to large bodies of men and vehicles, even tanks.'

'Quite impassable, sir,' John said.

'And the distance between Alamein on the coast and the start of this depression is less than forty miles. We should be able to hold that. I have already given orders for defensive boxes to be constructed along that line. Because it will be our last line of defence. We either hold Rommel there, or we die. I wish that clearly understood. And I wish it understood by everyone in Cairo and Alexandria, as well.'

'Yes, sir,' Jones said.

'I make that your responsibility. Now, you two. I said you might have six days. Now you have less than that. Understood?'

'Yes, sir,' they answered together.

'So, good luck. To all of us.'

'Feel like that drink?' Margo asked, when

they regained the hotel.

'Why not? What time is the off?"

'Four o'clock tomorrow morning.'

'I could be back sailing, trying to catch a tide.'

'Maybe that's what we're doing.' They sat at the bar and drank whisky.

'Have you got the feeling that we're rushing at the end?' Margo asked.

'The end of what, specifically?'

'Well ... the end of the British in Egypt. And if you believe old Auchinleck, the end of us as well.'

'Pre-Operational Tension,' John suggested.

'Which you do not feel?'

'Oh, I feel it all right. But there's no use brooding on it. I think we want an early dinner, followed by an early night, if we have to be up at three or whatever.'

'What were your ideas on sleeping arrangements?'

'Oh, don't start that again. You always come on at me just when I don't even know where my willie is, much less whether or not he'll respond to command.'

'Then you *are* tense.'

'I just said I was.'

'John Warrey, as I live and breathe!'

John turned on his stool. He had forgotten the other hazard. 'Sam Carson!' he said, appearing totally surprised.

She looked even better than the last time he had seen her. She was a short woman, very compactly built, with black hair which she wore cut at ear-level. Her features were crisp and strong. As was her mind. As part of his training he had once had to shoot at her, or just miss her – as had a dozen other trainees – and he recalled that she had not batted an eyelid. Of course she had been wearing bullet-proof body armour and a visored helmet, but it must still have been an ordeal. This evening she was wearing a pink frock, and looked entirely unmilitary.

She had also, he recalled, given him one of the most unforgettable experiences of his life ... and then slapped him down by telling him she generally took her pick of the recruits who passed through her hands. Now he felt only pity for her; she clearly still did not have any idea what had happened to her sister. 'Do you know,' she said, 'I had an idea we might meet up. Cairo is your stamping ground, right?'

'It would seem so, as I'm here.'

'Hello, Samantha,' Margo said.

John turned his head, sharply; Margo's tone indicated that she was not pleased at the interruption. 'Nice to see you, Margo,' Samantha said, without great interest. 'You know what, I think I am going to borrow your lad here, for a chat. We have so many things to chat about.'

'Ah...' John said. 'You have heard the news?'

'Oh, yes. Everyone has heard the news. It seems that we are soon to be shot by the Germans. Which makes a little chat all the more necessary, don't you think?'

'John and I are going somewhere, at the crack of dawn tomorrow,' Margo said. 'It is therefore *more* necessary that we get our sleep.'

'I won't keep him long,' Samantha said.

'What are you going to talk about?' Margo asked, more coldly yet. 'Rosalind?'

Samantha frowned, while John mentally cursed. Trust Margo to let him down. 'Margo—' he ventured.

'Do you know Rosalind?' Samantha asked.

'They were passengers on a cruiser from Gibraltar to Malta,' Margo explained. 'Only a fortnight ago.'

'Good lord,' Samantha commented. And then gave a little shriek of laughter. 'You didn't get on her? You did! Rosalind would sleep with anyone.'

'I did not, as you put it so succinctly, get on her,' John said.

Margo gave a happy smile. 'He meant to. But the Italians got there first.'

A frown slowly gathered between Samantha's eyes. 'Would you explain that?'

'They were torpedoed, darling,' Margo

said. 'Boom, boom. Our hero here spent the next week swimming around the Med. Didn't you, Johnnie?'

'One of these days–' John said.

'You are going to break my neck,' Margo agreed. 'Promises, promises.'

'Where is my sister?' Samantha asked, her voice low but charged with anxiety.

'She's dead, darling,' Margo said. 'Dead, dead, dead. Food for the fishes.'

Samantha stared at her for several seconds. Then she shrieked, 'Bastard!' and swung her hand. John wasn't sure whether she was aiming at him or not, but he stepped backwards and Samantha's swinging blow struck Margo's hand and glass together. The whisky shot back in a huge splash down the front of Margo's tunic, and the glass shattered on the floor.

The barman appeared like a startled pheasant, heads turned all round the room. 'Bitch!' Margo snapped, looking down at herself.

'Whore!' Samantha riposted.

'Sammy,' John ventured, and had to avoid another blow, this one definitely aimed at him. He ducked and her body cannoned into him, throwing him against the bar.

'Ladies,' protested the barman.

'Why didn't I know?' Samantha screamed, once again swinging.

Margo hastily got out of the way, and

encountered a large man in uniform. 'This is disgraceful behaviour,' he announced. He was wearing the insignia of a colonel.

'She's just learned her sister is dead, sir,' John explained.

'Bastard!' Samantha shrieked again, and launched herself at him.

This time he caught her wrists, and held her away. 'For God's sake, Sammy,' he said. 'Control yourself.'

'Sorry about the sister,' the colonel said. 'But she must get out of here. This sort of thing doesn't do morale any good. Stiff upper lip, woman. Stiff upper lip.'

'Oh, go fuck yourself,' Samantha suggested. He stepped back, already red face turning puce.

John managed to turn Samantha round and get his arms round her waist. 'I'll see you to your room,' he said in her ear, and began pushing her towards the exit, draping her handbag over his arm.

'Don't forget to come back,' Margo said. 'In one piece.'

Someone clapped. 'Look here,' said the colonel.

'Tell you what,' Margo said. 'Buy me a replacement drink and I'll explain. Then I really have to go and change.'

Samantha was by now struggling and kicking, and cursing, but John got her into the lobby, where he was approached by an under-manager. 'Do you need assistance, sir?'

'I think I'll manage. This is Miss Carson.'

'So I see, sir.'

'Tell me her room number.'

'Ah—' the assistant manager hesitated.

'Bastard!' Samantha shouted as she got her breath back. 'Let me go, you shit!'

'Perhaps one of the housekeepers—' the assistant manager ventured.

'This is a personal matter.' John began carrying Samantha towards the lifts.

'Second floor, number two hundred and seventeen, sir,' the assistant manager said.

'Thank you,' John panted, as he finally got Samantha in the lift car. 'I assume you have a key?' He undraped the handbag from his arm.

'Bastard!' Samantha repeated, and having been released, slowly slipped down the wall to squat on her haunches; her skirt rode up to her thighs. John pressed the ascent button. 'Rosalind,' Samantha moaned.

'Would saying I'm terribly sorry do any good?' John asked.

Samantha raised a tear-stained face to stare at him. The lift stopped, and the doors opened. 'Will you walk?' John asked.

Slowly Samantha pushed herself to her feet, absently straightened her dress. John waited for her to emerge into the empty corridor, then handed her the bag. 'I'm hoping your key is in there.'

She opened the bag, took out the key, and gave it to him, without speaking. Two hundred and seventeen was obliquely opposite the lift, on the other side of the corridor. He unlocked it, switched on the light. Samantha brushed against him as he entered. He closed the door. 'Can I get you something?'

Samantha walked across the room and opened the top drawer of the bureau, took out a half full bottle of Scotch. 'You can pour.'

He went into the bathroom, found a tooth mug. This he half filled. 'Water?'

'No.'

He returned to the bedroom. Samantha was sitting on the bed, hands dangling between her knees; she had pulled up her skirt again. 'You have one too,' she said, as he gave her the mug.

'Only one mug,' he explained. 'We'll share this one.' He sat beside her.

She drank, deeply, handed him the mug. 'How did she go?'

'Margo told you: she drowned.'

'How come she drowned and you didn't?'

He took a sip of whisky. 'We went over together. We jumped. We were holding hands. But when we hit the water we were separated. Then the ship went down and there was an undertow, and a lot of oil. I think it was the oil. Her face was covered in it. I reached her when we both surfaced, pulled her to the life raft, but she was dead.'

'You tried to take care of her,' Samantha said, starting to weep again, and reaching out for the mug. He let her have it, and she again drank deeply. 'But you say you didn't have her.'

'I didn't. I had ideas. I think maybe she had ideas first. But we never had the time.'

'Bastard,' she growled, and lay back on the bed, the glass held between her hands and resting between her breasts. 'We were close. You know that?'

'I didn't know that. But I would expect sisters to be close.'

'Do you have a brother?'

'I'm an only child.'

'Bastard.' She sat up, drained the mug. 'I'll have another of those.'

John considered. But he thought for her to pass out might be the best thing. He got up and poured another half mug. 'Listen,' she said. 'Fuck me.' She had kicked off her knickers.

He gave her the glass. 'I don't think that would be a good idea.'

'Why not? You did, once before.'

'That was a long time ago.'

'Three years? What are three years. Tell me why not? You still carrying a grudge because I told you I was just trying you for size?'

'I don't think so,' he lied as he sat beside her. 'Since we last saw each other, I have got married.'

'Shit,' she commented.

'That's one good reason. Another is that you are really in no state to know whether you want it or not. And a third is that it would be in the worst possible taste, right this minute.'

'Jesus. You are a creep. I'll tell you why you won't fuck me. Margo! She's got her teeth in you. God, I hate that woman. Hate her! Hate her! Hate her.' She drank some more whisky and her eyes rolled.

'I work for her,' John said. 'Not my decision. And she doesn't sleep with the staff.'

'Poor you. Oh, Johnnie...' She leaned against him, eyes half shut. 'If you won't fuck me, just hold me. I feel so ... so lonely.'

He put his arm round her shoulders and gave her a hug. 'Things will get better,' he promised her. 'They always do.'

'Better,' she muttered. 'Better.' The glass slipped from her fingers. John caught it before it hit the floor, but the remaining whisky was spilt. Samantha gave a little snore.

John lifted her onto the bed, took off her shoes. The dress was sufficiently low cut to suggest it did not need loosening, and he decided against any attempt to replace her knickers. He arranged her on her back, with two pillows under her head, arms folded on her breast and legs extended straight. Rather than attempt to insert her beneath the sheets he took a blanket from the cupboard and draped this over her as far as her neck. He stood by the bed and looked down at her. She was, with her eyes shut and sleeping, a most attractive woman. But because, he supposed, of her somewhat abrasive personality and her inordinate ambition, she was doomed never to create any worthwhile relationships ... except perhaps with her sister.

He wondered if he would ever see her again?

When he got downstairs, Margo was sitting with the colonel. 'Well?' she enquired. 'Have you had an enjoyable half-hour?'

'She got drunk, which I thought was an excellent idea, medicinally, and I put her to bed,' John said. 'I'm sorry about the scene, sir. I'm John Warrey.'

'Harrumph,' the colonel commented. 'Name's Ashbee. Sixteenth Dragoons. I'll have to report what happened, you understand. Senior officer present, what?'

'I understand that, sir. But I hope you'll be as lenient as possible. She and her sister were very close.'

'Harrumph. Close friend, are you?'

'They trained together,' Margo said.

'Yes, well, I'll see what I can do. Major Cartwright tells me you're off into the desert tomorrow.'

John raised his eyebrows. Top secret? 'If that's what she says, sir, then that is what we shall do.'

It was Ashbee's turn to raise his eyebrows. 'So I think we should have dinner and turn in,' Margo said, rising. 'You'll excuse us, Colonel.'

'Oh, quite. Absolutely.' Ashbee struggled to his feet, and Margo put on her cap and saluted. John wasn't sure where his cap was, so he merely stood to attention.

They had a table in the corner, sufficiently removed from the other diners. 'Aren't you being a bit careless?' John asked.

'What, with Ashbee? He's all right. Never remembers anything for more than half an hour. Now tell me what really happened upstairs.'

'I told you.'

'I'm sure you left a few things out.'

'Ah...' John drank his soup. 'Yes, I did. Sam called you a bitch, more than once. And remarked that she hated you.'

'I hope you paddled her ass.'

'I didn't, as a matter of fact. Because I happen to agree with her.'

They stared at each other over their

spoons. 'You mean that you hate me,' Margo said.

'Sometimes. I meant that you are a bitch. It was quite unnecessary to break the news about Rosalind's death quite so brutally. You said you weren't going to tell her at all.'

'Am I really supposed to be an agony aunt to all of your mistresses, whether or not they have been discarded.'

'Now you are being more of a bitch than ever.'

She delved into her main course. 'I would like an apology,' she said, with her mouth full.

'Sorry. Not tonight.'

She swallowed, and drank some wine. 'As your commanding officer, I demand an apology.'

'And I repeat, you're not going to get it.' He smiled at her. 'What are you going to do, have me placed under arrest? And then go off into the desert tomorrow all on your lonesome?'

'One of these days–' she said.

'You are going to break *my* neck. We should have a lot of fun.'

'Look,' she said, 'just finish your dinner and get lost, will you?'

What a way to start an expedition which might involve both their lives, John thought. But theirs had been a fairly acrid relationship ever since he had first found out that

94

she had been using him, and others, in the course of her intelligence work, long before a shot had been fired in anger. Nor, when he remembered the way they had fought their way across the desert the previous year, could her courage and determination, and ability, be questioned.

He reflected that it takes all sorts to win a war.

Next morning she was as spruce as ever, if distinctly cool towards him. 'How's your friend?' she asked as they got into the jeep to be driven to the airport.

'Still sleeping it off, I imagine.'

'And when she finally wakes up, you'll be gone. Poor thing.'

John didn't think it was worthwhile again trying to correct her impression of his relationship with Samantha.

'Gear check,' she said, and they went through the various items they would need.

'You said something about Arab clothes,' John reminded her.

'Sheikh Halim will provide them for us when we land.'

It was still dark when they reached the airfield, where the reconnaissance machine was waiting for them. 'Tony Bingham.' Their pilot, a flying officer, shook hands. He was a bluff, red-faced young man.

'You've flown before?'

'Once or twice,' John said.

'Once,' Margo told him.

'Ah, well, nothing to it. Just strap yourselves in and leave the rest to me.'

The Lysander didn't have much space inside. John and Margo sat side by side, while their gear was piled into the back. Bingham sat by himself at the controls. 'Supposing we can find this landing strip,' he said, 'we should take a couple of hours.' He spoke into his mike, and the engine was started. Then there was some more chat, and he taxied to the end of the runway.

'Scared?' John asked.

'I wish he had two engines,' Margo said.

The aircraft roared down the runway and was airborne almost immediately. Below them there was little to be seen, as the airport was blacked out, but once they were a couple of hundred feet up they could see the great glow of the coming dawn. 'Weather's fine,' Bingham shouted over his shoulder. 'Piece of cake.'

The sky lightened very rapidly now, and soon they were looking down at the unending desert, a mosaic of browns and yellows and whites. What memories that brought back. Far to their left the river wound its way through the landscape like a huge snake. 'Frightening, what?' Bingham called. 'But I'm told you people know it well.'

'I wish we were down there now,' Margo said. She was looking distinctly green.

'You're better off up here,' Bingham said. 'Safer, what?' The Lysander banked steeply as he took up a new compass course. 'Had to come this far south,' he explained, 'to make sure we didn't run into any flak. Difficult to say where those buggers have got to. Plain sailing now. Piece of cake.'

'If he says that once again I am going to wring his neck,' Margo muttered.

'I'd keep it till we're down,' John suggested. He looked at his watch. They'd been flying just on an hour. Halfway, then, if they were going the right way.

The engine coughed. 'Damn,' Bingham remarked.

The engine coughed again. 'Damn and blast,' Bingham said.

John's stomach told him they were descending, even if he couldn't see the altimeter. 'What's happening?' Margo asked, her voice suddenly high.

'We seem to have a spot of bother,' Bingham said. 'I'm going to have to put down and have a look.'

'Shit,' Margo said. 'Shouldn't we jump out?'

'And lose the machine? That wouldn't be too sensible. Anyway, we haven't any chutes. We'll be all right. Probably just some sand in the fuel line. This blasted climate.'

'God,' Margo said. 'God, God, God!'

John squeezed her hand. 'My fault.'

'Eh?'

'Well, when I try to travel by sea the ship gets torpedoed, and when I try to travel by air the plane develops engine trouble. I'm a jinx.'

'Thanks for telling me,' she said.

Bingham was speaking into his mike. 'Just giving my coordinates,' he explained.

'You mean you know where we are?'

'Well, within a few miles, I reckon. If I've got it right.' The engine was now spluttering. 'Fuel starvation,' Bingham remarked. 'Just as I thought. I say, old man, do these colours mean anything?'

They were now down to about five hundred feet. 'I'd say the white is soft sand,' John said, peering down. 'The yellow is firm sand, and the brown is probably indentations. You do realise the desert isn't as flat as it looks?'

'Well, we need a flat bit. You reckon aim for the yellow?'

'That's probably our best best.'

'I am going to be sick,' Margo announced. 'I know I am going to be sick.' All the colour had faded from her face.

'Hold it until we land,' John again suggested.

'Bastard,' she muttered.

'How about there?' Bingham asked.

John peered ahead. 'Can we have a closer look?'

'Not now,' Bingham said, as the engine faded altogether. 'Hold on.'

Margo held on to John's arm. John himself hunched his shoulders, and kept staring ahead, as the Lysander now began to come down very fast. Christ Almighty, he thought. I've survived bombardment, bullets, imprisonment and a torpedo, to end up dead in an aeroplane? It didn't make sense. Perhaps he had chanced his arm just too often.

'May be a bit of a bump,' Bingham told them, wrestling with the wheel in an attempt to get the plane's nose up. He had some success, but a moment later there was a considerable bump, and the wheels hit the sand. The machine went up again, leaving all their stomachs behind, then came down again. 'Wheee!' Bingham shouted. 'Neat!'

But they were still rushing forward, and John could only stare in horror at the wadi cutting across the improvised landing strip. 'Brake it!' he bawled.

Presumably Bingham, from his movements, tried to do so. But the wadi was already too close, and a moment later the wheels were over the edge. Immediately they caught in the soft sand of the dried river bed, and the nose went down. The propeller churned into the sand, and for a moment it seemed as if the machine was going right over. Then it settled with its nose firmly down, and its tail pointing skywards.

John had a distinct impression of being cut in two by his seat belt. Beside him Margo was screaming. Bingham was slumped over the wheel. And now there was a strong smell of petrol. 'Out!' he gasped. 'We must get out!'

Desperately he released his belt, and fell onto the back of the front seats. He ignored Bingham for the moment, to turn and reach up to release Margo's belt in turn. She collapsed into his arms, and he hit the side door with his shoulder, bursting it open and throwing the woman through the aperture. She landed on her hands and knees with another shriek, and then collapsed onto her face. 'Get up!' John shouted. 'Run. Take shelter.'

He reached over the pilot's seat and released Bingham's belt. Bingham was definitely unconscious and there was a bloody bruise on his forehead. He was also sitting awkwardly, as if he had injured himself further down. But John had no time to investigate that. He grasped Bingham's shoulders and dragged him up, then threw him as well through the opened doorway, jumping behind him, seizing the unconscious man again and rolling with him over and over down the wadi, while behind him there came a tremendous whoosh and a surge of the greatest heat he had ever known. They came to rest some twelve feet from the aircraft; the heat if anything had increased as the flames shot skywards. He realised that he was in severe pain.

He saw Margo crawling towards them, hatless, her hair coming down from its military bun in an auburn glow, face twisting. 'You're on fire!' she shrieked.

John released Bingham to go rolling into the sand. Margo reached him and poured sand over him. 'Bingham,' he gasped. 'Get Bingham.'

Luckily the pilot, while still unconscious, had not caught fire – John had been between him and the explosion. And the flames that had destroyed John's tunic were now out, but the pain was if anything greater. 'God,' Margo commented, kneeling between the two men. 'God! Don't die, Johnnie. For Christ's sake, don't die.'

The whole scene was spinning about him as John sat up and tried to gain control of his mind, which was whirling around in circles. He gazed at the burning plane, then looked down at himself. The tunic, shirt and vest had all been on fire at some stage, and were hanging in rags. The pain remained considerable. He had to concentrate. 'How is Bingham?' he asked through gritted teeth.

'He seems to be coming round. But I think he's broken his leg or something. He's lying very awkwardly.'

'He's alive,' John pointed out. 'Now come and have a look at me.'

She crawled to him, peered at his back. 'Ugh!'

'I think it needs covering up.'

'Yes, it does. But-'

'Do it,' he said.

She took off her tunic, which was itself somewhat the worse for wear, and laid it across his back. He bit back a moan of pain, as it seemed to glue itself to his flame-tortured skin. What it was going to feel like when someone took it off... She tied the arms together across his chest to keep the tunic in place. 'Thank you,' he said. 'I don't suppose we have any water?'

'We don't have anything,' she pointed out. 'What a shitting mess.'

'Margo,' he said severely. 'You and I have crossed the desert half a dozen times with very little.'

'When you were a whole man,' she remarked.

'You say the nicest things. I have hopes of recovering. Let's see to Bingham.'

The pilot was regaining consciousness, and doing some moaning of his own. With an enormous effort, John made himself move and crawled across the wadi to where Bingham lay. His left leg was certainly folded awkwardly beneath him. 'It's broken,' he said.

'That's what I thought.'

'So I think we need to set it, before he fully comes to. Otherwise he may not be able to stand the pain.'

He tore Bingham's pants open, gazed in consternation at the twisted limb, the shattered bone. 'Christ,' Margo said. 'I'm starting to feel sick again.'

'Do it someplace else,' John said brutally. 'Now, I am going to straighten that leg. Once I do it, I am going to need a splint.'

'Well, don't look at me,' she said.

'I am looking at you. I am also going to need something to bind it in place. Let's have your belt off, to start with with.'

Margo took off her Sam Browne.

'And your stockings.'

'Oh, really, John—'

'Just do it.'

She turned her back on him, and sat down to hitch up her skirt and release her suspender belt before rolling down her torn stockings, while he concentrated on Bingham. Whose eyes were opening. 'Hell,' Bingham said. 'That wadi ... what happened?'

'I'll tell you later,' John said. 'Would you

103

mind closing your mouth. Tight.' He wrapped his right hand in the remnants of his shirt.

'I'm in agony,' Bingham groaned. 'My leg–'

'Your mouth,' John said. 'Tight.'

Bingham gazed at him, then closed his mouth. Before he could have any time to reflect, John hit him as hard as he could. His fist, wrapped in the burned cloth, seemed about to disintegrate with the material, but Bingham gave a little gasp and collapsed. Instantly John seized the leg and pulled it straight. It was going to be a botched job, and he knew it would have to be rebroken and reset by experts ... whenever they could get to any experts. But for the moment it was straight. 'Belt,' he snapped.

Margo put the thick waist belt in his hand, and he laid it across the stricken, bleeding limb. 'Ties.'

He twined the first stocking round and round the shattered limb and the belt, drawing it as tight as he could. Then he used the second one, got it as tight as possible. By then Bingham was awake again, moaning and turning. 'I'm sorry, old man,' John said. 'We have nothing to give you.'

He and Margo looked at each other. He was struck with how white her legs were, lacking stockings; she hadn't bothered to replace her shoes. She made a face. 'You

104

look worse. Shit, what does it matter? How long do we have?'

It was now well into the morning, and although the sun had not gained its full power, it was high in a cloudless sky. He looked at the aircraft. The flames were beginning to die down, but there was nothing left save twisted metal. They had no food, no water, no shelter, no armaments ... and only half the clothes they had started out in. Together with two seriously injured men. 'Twenty-four hours?' he suggested.

'Shit,' she remarked again.

'The sun is there,' he said, pointing. 'Let's get into the shelter of the wadi. At least until noon.'

They dragged Bingham against the eastern wall of the dry river bed. He gritted his teeth in an attempt to stop moaning, not entirely successfully. But then, John was in agony himself, and gritting his own teeth, While he had been moving around, attending to Bingham, the pain had been there, but not overwhelming. Once he sat down, leaning his shoulder against the bank of the wadi – he dared not let his back come into contact with the earth – the pain seemed to rise in waves, out of his back, through his stomach, into his lungs, making it difficult to breath.

Margo knelt beside him, 'Don't die, Johnnie,' she said. 'For God's sake don't die.' She held his hand, and he saw her face wince as his grip inadvertently tightened.

'Seems to me we've been here before,' he muttered.

'More than once,' she reminded him. 'And we survived.'

But, as she had reminded him, on all the previous occasions he hadn't been hurt.

'Christ, Christ, *Christ!*' Bingham moaned. 'I can't stand it.'

'What are we to do?' Margo asked. 'Should you hit him again?'

'No,' John said. 'I don't think my fist would stand it. Not to mention his jaw.'

She sat beside him, still holding his hand. 'Do you think I should dig for water? Remember how Soroya showed us to survive?'

'Where there are desert flowers. You see any?'

She made a face, and stared at the plane; the flames were starting to die down. 'When it stops burning, I may be able to find something.'

'Chance would be a fine thing.'

He closed his eyes, but then the pain seemed worse. Margo moved, restlessly, ineffectually. Bingham moaned. John had no idea of how long they lay in the wadi, having the last moisture sucked from their bodies as the sun moved to the west and shone full upon them.

They were waiting to die, and he did not suppose it would take very long. But when next he opened his eyes he looked at a camel, and a man. Several camels, and several men.

Four

The Senussi

John blinked, assuming it had to be a mirage. But when he opened them again, the men and the camels were still there, only they were dismounting and coming into the wadi themselves.

Margo had apparently had her eyes shut as well, because now she gave a little shriek. 'Oh, my God! Johnnie!'

'You will be Miss Cartwright,' said the first man, allowing his burnous to drift away from his face to reveal the huge beak of a nose which almost met the prominent chin. Shades of Ali ben Fuad.

'You'll be Sheikh Halim,' John said. 'Please, old man, do you have any water?'

The water tasted like nectar, even through the pain. But that was already being relieved, as John was stretched on his face, Margo's blood-coated tunic gently removed while he attempted not to scream in agony, and an ointment applied to soothe the skin. Following which he was given something to drink that was certainly not water, and sent his brain drifting away through time and space.

Bingham had already been sedated.

When he came to it was because he was jerked into wakefulness. He was in a litter, lying on his face, which was suspended between two camels, and their movements were not co-ordinated. As soon as he stirred, suddenly once again aware of the pain in his back, one of the drivers called out, and a moment later Halim was walking by his head. 'You are fortunate to have survived the crash,' Halim said.

'How did you know where to find us?'

'We heard your position on the wireless. And then, one of my scouts saw the plane fall from the sky, and then the fire.'

'You mean we were that close?'

'We will be at my encampment in another half an hour.'

John sighed with relief, and then raised his head again. 'Miss Cartwright–?'

'Is right over there. I will tell her you've awakened.'

He was replaced by Margo. 'How many lives do you think we have left?' he asked.

She made a moue. 'Friends?'

He managed a grin. 'Friends. Partners, anyway.'

'We were always partners,' she reminded him.

It was dusk when they finally reached the encampment, situated in a small oasis, well down in southern Cyrenaica. It occurred to John that he, Margo and her expedition must have passed quite close to this oasis during their trans-Saharan journey in the spring of 1939, and that indeed the Senussi tribesmen who had attacked them could well have been Sheikh Halim's people – but that was before they had discovered they had a common enemy. Now they were greeted as friends and allies. People swarmed about them, and John was carried, with the utmost tenderness, into a cool house where he was laid as usual on his face and more ointment was applied to his back. He was also given water to drink and fed couscous by a woman who knelt by his head. He had little idea what she looked like, because she was entirely concealed beneath her haik and yashmak, but her hands indicated that she could not be very old, and the fingers gently inserting the food into his mouth were most acceptable.

Margo was eating a few feet away, from time to time staring at him with those deep green eyes. She had had a bath and been given clean clothing to wear, Arab clothing, lacking only the yashmak to conceal her face; the rest of her was wrapped up in a haik.

She was an odd woman, he thought, not for the first time in their stormy acquaintanceship. At the crash site she had sounded almost as if he was important to her. Well, he supposed he was, as he had just saved her life, and in the context of this assignment – but there had seemed more to it than that. And now she was clearly setting up to be hostile again – out of jealousy?

He gathered Bingham was in such pain that he was being kept under sedation; the Bedouin had no medical skills sufficient to reset the broken leg.

Halim also sat with them, together with three of his principal men – but no other women, apart from the girl acting as John's nurse. 'My father spoke often of you,' he told John. 'He had a high regard for you.'

'I sometimes feel I was responsible for his death,' John confessed.

'You fought shoulder to shoulder,' Halim said. 'And my father was killed. It is the Italians, the Germans, who are responsible for his death.'

'Rommel,' John ventured, although Sheikh Ali had been killed by the Italians long before any Germans had come to North Africa.

'Amongst others,' Halim agreed. 'Now you have come to lead us against the infidels. We must make you well, and strong, as quickly as possible.'

John glanced at Margo, who waggled her eyebrows. 'You know the situation?' he asked.

'We know that the Germans have gained a great many victories,' Halim said. 'We do not understand how this can be. Is not Great Britain the strongest nation in the world?'

'Ah ... not quite,' John said. 'She was once, perhaps. However, we shall beat the Germans, do not fear.'

'I have heard it said that this man Rommel will soon be in Cairo,' Halim remarked.

'Well, he will be, if he is not stopped,' John said. 'Our armies will do the best they can, but it would be better if he was not there at all.' Halim considered this. 'There can be no doubt that it was Rommel who was responsible for the death of your father,' John went on, hating himself for the lie he was telling. But he had been given an assignment, and he would carry it out.

'I know this,' Halim agreed. 'He would have given the orders. I understand. It is my duty to avenge my father's death. I know this.'

'Ah,' John said. The girl fed him some more water.

'You know where this man is now?' Halim asked.

'He will not be difficult to find,' John said. 'He will be with his army, before Mersa Matruh.'

'I see. Yes, I will speak with my people.'

'Sheikh Halim,' John said. 'You understand this will be a very dangerous mission.'

'It will be a suicide mission,' Halim said. 'That is the only way it can be done.'

'Yes,' John said. 'Will your people understand this?'

'My people will understand this. They will understand more if your government will give us rifles and machine-guns to fight the Italians. And the Germans.'

'Right now, my government has none of these things to spare,' John said. 'But when Rommel is defeated–'

'Or killed.'

'Of course.'

'I will speak with my people. You wish this woman to stay with you?' He was referring to Margo.

'Yes,' John said. 'I would like her to stay.'

Halim clapped his hands, and the remains of the meal were carried out, followed by the young woman and the three men. Halim bowed to them, and they were alone. 'What gets me,' Margo said, 'is the way these people always assume you're in command.'

'They prefer dealing with men,' John pointed out.

'Ha! Don't you think you went at that rather like a bull in a china shop?'

'I don't think we have the time to make any other approach. With the best will in the world, it's going to take a couple of days to get from here up to the coast. Then his assassin has to get to Rommel–'

'And die.'

'Don't remind me. This is a bloody dirty business. I suppose you'll be getting back?' he asked.

'Whenever it can be arranged. But I'm not leaving you or Bingham here.'

'Have you been in touch?'

'No. There have been rather a lot of radio calls to and from here. The enemy will be tracking them as well as they can. I think it would be better to leave it for a while. You're in no fit state to travel, anyway.'

'Bingham's leg needs resetting.'

'He'll have to live with it for a few more days.'

She had always been good at making decisions where other people were concerned, John thought.

Sleeping was not easy, as he tended to want to turn over whenever he got off, and was thus brought back to reality by the sharp pains in his back. But he did manage to doze off just before dawn, to awaken to find Sheikh Halim kneeling beside him. 'I have come to say goodbye,' the Sheikh said.

'Eh? Where are you going?'

'To find Rommel.'

John looked past him to where Margo was

sitting, drinking coffee. As usual, she waggled her eyebrows. 'You mean you're going yourself, with your assassin?' he asked. 'Is that necessary?'

Hamil's teeth gleamed as he smiled. 'I am going myself, to perform the execution.'

John tried to sit up, and collapsed with the pain. 'You? But you cannot do that, Sheikh Hamil.'

'I must do it,' Hamil insisted. 'It is my father we are going to avenge. I cannot delegate the duty to anyone else.'

'But ... your people? Who will lead them?'

Halim snapped his fingers, and a very young man came into the tent and knelt beside him. John didn't estimate he was much over sixteen years old, but his resemblance to the Sheikh was unmistakable. 'This is my son. He is named Ali, after my father,' Halim explained. 'He is the next leader of my people.'

Ali ibn Halim bowed his head. 'I am honoured to make your acquaintance, Captain Warrey.'

'As am I, to make yours,' John said. 'But Halim—'

'It is decided,' Halim said. 'I will take one woman with me. She will be, how do you say, cover? How may a man travel, without a woman for comfort? I shall say I have information regarding the British in the desert, information that must be given to

116

General Rommel himself. Once I am in his presence, I will stab him. But the woman is also good with a knife, and will act as my back-up, eh? In case I fail.' He grinned, to indicate that he did not expect to fail.

And the woman will die with you, John thought. What had he set in motion?

'Does she know she will not return?'

'She understands. So, I will not see you again, Captain Warrey.'

'Look ... I didn't come here to have you sacrifice yourself, Halim.'

'Our fate is written,' Halim said. 'I have been neglectful of my duty, in not avenging my father. I did not do this, because I did not know who was my enemy. Now you have pointed me in the right direction. I cannot wait any longer. And besides, is there not a great victory to be won?' He held out his hand, and John clasped it. 'Be sure it is won,' he said.

The boy Ali followed his father out of the tent.

'I feel like absolute shit,' John said. 'I should be going on that mission.'

'That was never intended,' Margo said.

'Damn, what a filthy mess. And the woman he is taking ... do we know her?'

'You do,' Margo said. 'It was the one feeding you last night. Her name is Uluma. Would you like some coffee?'

He wasn't sure he could stomach it.

117

The Senussi warriors saw their sheikh off with a great firing of rifles, but when Halim and his companion had disappeared over the sand dunes, the oasis sank into a kind of somnolence, in which the men sat around and muttered at each other, and the women did all the work. 'Primitive societies are indicative of how things are meant to be,' John remarked. Margo merely snorted.

He spent much of the day lying beside Bingham, having been carried into the tent where the pilot was situated. Bingham's pain had by now worn off to some extent, although he was in no doubt that in the long run he had serious problems. 'Any idea when we can get out of here?' he asked.

'Not for a day or two,' John said. 'We have to give Sheikh Halim a fair crack of the whip.' He presumed there was no breach of security now in telling the pilot the object of their exercise.

By next morning his own pain had dwindled into mere discomfort. As usual he was stretched on his face in his tent while the Arab women coated him with ointment. And as usual Margo sat beside him, looking sceptical. 'Odd to think that in different circumstances they would have you stretched on your back while they hacked away at your genitals,' she remarked.

'I'm all in favour of things the way they are,' he told her. 'Or are you feeling like having a go?'

'At something,' she said darkly. 'I feel so useless, sitting here while so much is going on. And having sent the Sheikh to his death.'

'And his woman.'

'Bugger his woman,' she growled.

Later John was carried into the radio tent, but there was a good deal of static, and what English was being spoken was interrupted and overlaid by Italian. 'There is a battle,' Ali said.

'When do you expect your father to reach the coast?' John asked.

'Tomorrow,' Ali said, simply.

Of course he knew his father was going to his death, but what a tragedy it would be were Halim to reach Rommel after the British had already been defeated beyond repair. Could that possibly happen?

Next day they learned that the British had definitely evacuated Mersa Matruh, and were in full retreat. Rommel was apparently pausing to regroup before launching his final assault. 'Where are the British now?' John asked.

'They have taken up a line at a place called Alamein,' Ali said.

119

Auchinleck's last line of defence, John thought. 'I think we really need to get back,' he told Margo. His back was now quite bearable, although the flesh remained fried and putting on even a haik required some gritting of the teeth; his principal problem was exhaustion – the trauma of the crash coming on top of the trauma of the torpedoed cruiser was taking its toll. 'We're doing no good here, and all hell is breaking loose there.'

'And Halim's mission?'

'If Rommel is dead, I have an idea we'll learn about it. At the moment, it doesn't look like it. But we may certainly assume that Halim is dead.'

'And his woman,' she remarked.

'If he is, we should hope she is too. Or the Gestapo will have her. Will you call?'

She went off to use the radio, and returned half an hour later. 'The RAF will attempt to get a plane down in a day or two. As they point out, there's a bit of a flap on up north.'

'I can imagine.'

Now that he was almost fit again, at least physically, Ali fitted him out with some clothes, an undershirt and a jibbah; he retained his relatively undamaged trousers and boots. Feeling almost civilised, he went to see Bingham. 'Sorry about all this, old man,' he said. 'But the end is in sight.'

'I'm the lucky one,' Bingham pointed out.
'Back home, eh? Desk job. Brrr.'

'You'll enjoy it when you get there,' John assured him, and went back to the radio tent. There was nothing new there, save that it seemed obvious that Rommel was preparing to attack El Alamein.

'If he gets through there,' Margo said, 'there's nothing for us to go back for.'

'You'd settle for the rest of your life in the desert?'

'There are worse places.' It was again dark, and they had strolled away from the oasis, up a low dune, boots sinking into the soft sand. Above them the moon was just a hint on the horizon, but the stars were very bright. And it was utterly quiet. 'I love the desert,' she said, and sat down.

He sat beside her. 'Despite the memories?'

'One learns to live with memories,' Margo said. 'One has to, or one would go mad.' She considered for a few moments, and John decided against interrupting her train of thought.

'When I was raped by those soldiers,' she said, 'I thought I *would* go mad. But then, afterwards, when it was just you and me and the desert, day after day after day, it all seemed so irrelevant. Would you believe that my only fear was that I might be pregnant?'

Again, there didn't seem a lot to say. He had saved her life on that occasion too, but

121

he had never been sure if she appreciated that or was the slightest bit grateful for it; she had never referred to it before. The question that interested him was, supposing she was grateful but was too inhibited to reveal it – which was not Margo – had she felt life was simply not worth living after the rape, which was understandable and acceptable, or had she felt he had just been doing his duty in any event, as her aide ... which was not the least acceptable?

'I suppose you feel I have let you down,' she remarked. 'Time and again.'

'Circumstances,' he said.

'After that experience,' she went on as if he had not spoken, 'I really did not wish ever to have any relations with any man ever again. And I thought you felt the same, in reverse.'

'I did,' John agreed.

'Because of Soroya.'

'Yes.'

'Yours lasted longer than mine,' she said, no doubt remembering that disastrous night in Benghazi.

'I'm afraid so.'

I loved that girl, Arsinoe had said. Everyone had loved Soroya – he suspected even Margo had had a soft spot there – save for the man who had riddled her naked body with bullets.

'But we can't escape each other, can we?' Margo asked. 'We're yoked together, time and again. Because we're partners, right?'

'Right,' he said.

'I'm sorry I'm such an abrasive person.' Margo, apologising? 'It's just that I'm so ... so...'

'Frustrated?' he suggested.

She shot him a quick glance. Then her mouth twisted. 'Yes, I'm frustrated. Life is a long series of frustrations. I'm not talking about sex. Although I've never had a good one. But the job... I set things up, on orders from London, or Cairo, or whatever, and I never know the outcome. Like right now. I'll never know how close Halim got. Oh, as you say, if he succeeds we'll probably find out about it, but we still won't know how *he* died, quickly and cleanly, shot by a guard, or tortured to death by the Gestapo. As for the woman—'

He squeezed her hand. 'I have an idea neither of us are really cut out to be soldiers. But as we are...'

Her face was very close, and he had an idea that she was about to kiss him, then she suddenly frowned. As did he. Sound was creeping across the desert. Very distant, at the moment, but sufficiently close to break the silence. It was a sound they had both heard before, often enough, a grinding noise. 'Shit!' Margo snapped, and scrambled to her feet.

The oasis was awakening as well, people

shouting, dogs barking. 'Let's get down there,' John said, and ran in front of her.

Two men on camels had ridden into the village, and were surrounded by anxious men and women, and children and dogs. They were speaking Arabic, in which language John was still hesitant. But Ali saw them and came across to them. 'There is an armoured column approaching,' he said. 'A squadron of tanks, with support. My scouts have seen this.'

'Those radio messages,' Margo said.

'Or someone confessed where she had come from, and why.'

'I will take out her eyes,' Ali growled.

'Yes, well, I think we need to worry about her later,' John said. 'What will you do?'

'What would you have me do?'

A squadron of tanks, John thought. When confronted with a similar situation, two years ago, he had recommended surrender to this boy's grandfather. And watched an entire village wiped out. 'We will fight them,' Ali declared.

The situation had hardly changed. Should the tribe abandon its oasis and attempt to flee into the desert, it would easily be hunted down by the Axis aircraft and shot to pieces. But to remain here, under the fire of tanks, would equally mean being shot to pieces. The desert promised more, for at least a few survivors. 'When will the tanks reach here?' he asked.

'In a few hours,' Ali said. 'But I do not think they will attack before dawn.'

'Then you must evacuate the village, and retire into the desert,' John said.

'Leave the village? The enemy will burn it down.'

'Ali, they are going to burn it down anyway. You cannot fight tanks with rifles. Would it not be better to have them burn the houses while they are empty, than while they are full of your people?'

Ali stroked his chin as if he wished to pull his beard, but he did not yet have one.

'But in the desert,' Margo said, 'once it is daylight, these people will be exposed to air attack.'

'They will equally be exposed to air attack here in the oasis,' John pointed out. 'And more vulnerable, because they will be concentrated. How many people do you have, Ali?'

Ali was still stroking his chin. 'There are seventy-one men, ninety-two women, forty-seven children.'

'And assorted dogs and goats. Right, two hundred and ten people. Divide them into bands of twenty-five, each led by a reliable man, have them leave the village and retire into the sand sea. The enemy tanks cannot follow them there.'

'The planes can.'

'The planes will seek you out, yes. You must expect heavy casualties. But if your eight groups are widely separated, some at least will survive. The enemy have no time to stay down here. They wish to destroy you and return to the main battle as quickly as possible. So your people will survive. And the oasis will survive.'

Ali continued to consider for another few seconds. It was, John understood, an enormous decision, an enormous responsibility, for a boy who had only a few days previously been informed he was about to succeed to the leadership of the tribe. But then he nodded. 'We will do as you say. You will come with us?'

'We certainly are not going to stay here,' Margo said.

'We must make all possible haste,' John said. 'But the evacuation must be carried out as quietly as possible. If the enemy discover what we are doing, they may risk a night assault. Now listen; you must carry your animals with you, and a supply of water, for at least two days. And you must make sure they understand. No matter what happens, they most continue into the desert for twenty-four hours. That is, until this time tomorrow morning. Only then can they return to the village.'

'I understand,' Ali said. 'Because by then the enemy will have gone again.'

'I believe so, yes,' John said. 'Wrap the radio set up in sufficient cloth to prevent sand getting in, and then bury it. It is far too big and cumbersome to take with us. And then we will know it is here when we come back. Do not forget to fold up the aerial and bury that as well.'

Ali nodded again, and hurried off to alert his people. Margo held John's arm. 'You're sure we're doing the right thing?'

'I don't think there is any alternative. Rommel didn't send a squadron of tanks all the way down here to take prisoners.'

'I'm surprised he felt he could spare any,' she said. 'What about Bingham?'

'He's our responsibility, I would say.'

'Ever ridden a camel?' John asked Bingham, as he assisted the pilot out of his tent.

'No,' Bingham said, regarding the waiting beast with distaste. His leg was tightly bound up and he was clearly in considerable discomfort.

'Well, just sit tight,' John recommended. 'You'll get the hang of it.'

When Bingham was seated, the camel lurched to its feet, promptly turning round several times as his grip on the rein tightened. 'Relax,' Margo advised. 'He knows what he's doing. All you have to do is stay up there.'

She and John mounted as well. Theirs was

127

the easy part. Around them was an incoherent mass of people, with their animals and various bundles, into which Ali and his elders were attempting to induce some aspect of order. Camels grunted and snapped, dogs barked, goats bleated ... John estimated they would be lucky to have even got out of the village by daybreak.

But gradually order was produced, and Ali gave the command to move. The eight groups radiated away from the oasis like the spokes of a wheel. Ali was the centre spoke. With him rode the three Britishers. There were eight other men, each with a woman mounted behind him, and a dozen women riding by themselves, with children mounted behind them; each camel carried a water skin as well as various bundles of belongings. Three more men were on foot, herding goats. Dogs ran to and fro, barking. And a baby kept wailing. 'A moving nation,' Margo said.

John looked at his watch. It was a quarter to three, and the moon was now full, bathing the desert. He wondered if the enemy could see them. If they could, they gave no sign, and the tanks themselves were invisible beyond the dunes. But they had stopped moving. Suppose it was all a false alarm, he wondered, and there is nobody there?

Dawn came suddenly, fingers of light streaming across the dunes well before the sun actually rose. 'We stop now,' Ali said.

'How far do you think we've come?' Margo asked.

'I think, fifteen miles.'

'Not far enough.'

'We stop now,' Ali said again.

There could be no argument, as it was time for prayer. The Arabs spread their mats and knelt towards Mecca, while John checked Bingham, and gave him water to drink. 'I'm not sure how much of this I'm going to be able to stand,' the pilot said. 'I can feel those bones grating.'

'Just hold on, old man,' John told him. For how long? he wondered.

Prayers completed, the Arabs breakfasted. John climbed up a nearby dune. He checked around him first, and was happy to see that the other seven groups had disappeared. Then he looked north, back towards the oasis, and could see smoke. The Italians had wasted no time. But the Arabs were already in soft sand, and if progress was slow, it would be quite impossible for tanks. He studied the sky, but it remained clear and blue. 'So far, so good,' he told Margo.

It was ten in the morning, and he reckoned they might have made another ten miles, before the first plane appeared. It was high

129

at first, but it soon came lower, and some distance to their right. It had spotted another of the groups. But John reckoned they would all be easily visible. 'We must expect an attack,' he said. 'Now, when it comes, we spread out, dig ourselves into the sand, and sit it out. The animals will need to be tended. Remember, survival is what matters. In this instance, survival of the individual, because the individuals who survive will reconstitute the tribe.' He felt like a Biblical prophet.

An hour later one of the Arabs shouted the alarm, and they looked back at six aircraft, flying quite low. 'Right,' John said. 'Scatter.'

This did not really conceal their position, because of the animals, which scattered even further. John concentrated on Margo and Bingham, getting Bingham out of the saddle, and digging a slit trench for him to lie in; Margo did the same for him while he hobbled the three camels. Then he discovered Margo had only dug one additional trench, so he slid in beside her. 'Cosy,' she said. 'How long do we stay here?'

'Until those bastards go away again.'

They listened to the *crump-crump* of bombs being dropped, and some of the women began to wail, but it was another group being attacked. There was in fact something uncanny in lying in the sand, listening, knowing that only a couple of miles away flesh and blood was being blown apart, and being perfectly peaceful themselves. It was even more evocative to have Margo lying beside him, touching him – wearing Arab clothing she was somehow far more of a woman than when in uniform or her preferred jodhpurs – or even on the rare occasions she wore a dress. He wondered if she felt the same. If she did, she didn't show it.

Then they saw the planes coming their way. Their markings were Italian; the Germans had none to spare for punitive expeditions. Ali's men started firing their rifles. John again did not suppose they were revealing their position – the animals did that. And there was always the chance they might hit something.

But only a very slim chance. The planes wheeled over the group and the bombs came down. Sand exploded skywards in huge plumes. Goats burst their lines and raced to and fro. Dogs barked furiously. Camels groaned. Women screamed. Men fired their rifles. It seemed as if the whole world had cut loose in a cataclysmic surge of noise. Then it was done, as the planes turned away. The attack had lasted only a few seconds.

John climbed out of his foxhole, looked around himself. The goats had scattered; several had been hit and lay in grotesque, ugly heaps. One of the camels had also been hit, but none of the dogs, who were looking thoroughly scared, and yelping rather than barking. More to the point, none of the humans had been hit.

Ali harangued his people, as they anxiously gathered round and gave him a hearty cheer. 'What have you told them?' John asked.

'That you are a great man and a great prophet, who will lead us always.'

'Well,' John said, 'for the next couple of days, at any rate.'

In accordance with his original plan, he made them continue into the desert for another twenty-four hours. He had no idea if the other groups were obeying the plan. He could only hope they were. The planes returned that afternoon, but did not attack Ali's group, although they could see them wheeling and diving several miles in the distance. 'How many do you think will survive?' Margo asked.

'Judging by us, most, I would hope.'

'Are we going back with them?'

'We have to, Margo. That's where the RAF plane will come looking for us.'

'If it's coming,' she said gloomily.

That night, having seen no more aircraft, they felt bold enough to light a fire and have a hot meal. But by then Bingham was running a high temperature and was from time to time delirious. 'Have you any more of that sedative drink?' John asked Ali.

'There is nothing. We left it in the village.'

'Then there'll be none there by now,' John mused. 'I don't suppose you have a shot of whisky, either?'

Ali shook his head, gravely.

'What are we going to do?' Margo asked.

'Sit it out. Or rather, he will have to sit it out. And pray that plane comes.'

'Shit,' she commented.

They commenced their return journey just before dawn. The Arabs were in a high good humour, laughing and cackling as they rode or marched along; their goats had been regathered into a flock, their dogs barked, their camels bellowed, their children shouted and their babies wailed. John could only hope they would be as happy when they regained whatever was left of their homes.

Once again, at dawn, while they were at their prayers, John surveyed the horizon and the sky. It was all clear. There was no sign of any of the other groups, but by now they would have become widely separated, he knew – although they should all be on their way back. He had a sense of foreboding, although he knew there was no alternative to what they were doing. And surely the Italians would suppose they had completely scattered the tribe, and prevented it from being a nuisance at least until the final victory was won.

At El Alamein! How he wished he could be there, for the Eighth Army's last stand.

His immediate problem was Bingham. The pilot was now tied to his camel, and alternated between periods of wakefulness, when his groans and occasional shouts of pain were all but unbearable to hear, and longer periods of blessed unconsciousness. That he was going to die unless help was very rapidly forthcoming seemed obvious. John could only pray that the radio had not been discovered, and was still usable. And that the RAF would have a plane to spare, and would still send it.

Margo rode beside Bingham, and occasionally touched his hand. She was revealing depths of feeling, of introspection, that he had never previously suspected her to possess.

They resumed their journey into the morning. 'I think we need a scout or two,' John told Ali.

'For what reason?' the new Sheikh, for such he now had to be considered, asked.

'We cannot survive in the desert for more than another day. If the Italians are still there, then we are going to die anyway.'

'If they are there,' John said. 'There won't be many of them. I think it makes sound military sense to find out.' He grinned. 'We may be able to get some of our own back.'

Ali considered, then nodded. 'You are right. I will come with you.'

'Your business is to be here, with your people.'

Once again Ali considered. Then he nodded again. 'You are right, as always. I have much to learn. But you will teach me, Warrey Pasha.'

John grinned. 'That sounds rather good. I'll teach you as long as I'm here, Sheikh Ali. Now find me a good man to ride with me.'

Margo would have gone with him, but he persuaded her to stay with Bingham; if there was any shooting he didn't want her around.

His guide was named Hashim, a large man with a ready smile. They equipped themselves with rifles; John also had his revolver and Hashim his sword, a wicked-looking curved blade. 'Do not move until one of us comes back for you,' John told Ali.

'And if neither of you comes back?'

John shrugged. 'Then you must do as you think best.'

'We will wait until nightfall,' Ali said. 'Then we will advance on the village.' His turn to shrug. 'We cannot stay out here, and die of thirst.'

135

'Make sure you do come back,' Margo told him. 'I am speaking as your senior officer.'

John grinned. 'When you speak like that you make me wish I could kiss you. I'll be back.'

They approached the village cautiously, much of the time walking beside their camels; whenever they neared a rise, one remained with the animals while the other climbed to the top and surveyed the situation. John would have given a lot for the binoculars lost in the plane crash, but at last he saw the oasis beneath him. It still smoked, and even the palm trees seemed scorched. Once again he cursed his lack of glasses, but so far as he could make out with the naked eye, the oasis was deserted. He studied the surrounding hills. The Italians could still be hiding behind there; he had no way of telling, save by exposing himself. 'We'll go down,' he told Hashim.

They mounted, as if they had to leave in a hurry they would need all the speed they could manage. For the time being they walked their camels down the slope. John felt terribly exposed, expecting at any moment to hear the crack of a rifle. He reminded himself that one never heard the shot that killed you, but it was not a lot of consolation. They approached to within a hundred yards of the trees, gazed at the rubbled houses, some still smoking.

'Will they have poisoned the water, effendi?'

'It's our business to find out.'

John slid from the saddle, gave the reins to Hashim, and went towards the oasis on foot. He unslung his rifle and carried it in both hands, although if there were Italian soldiers waiting for him he didn't suppose the weapon was going to do him much good. But the oasis remained silent; he was reminded of the famous opening scene from *Beau Geste,* where the French column from Tokotu had approached the silent Fort Zinderneuf – garrisoned by dead men!

His boots crunched on the sand and then on the village street. There were no corpses here, and apart from the somewhat sickening smell of burned stone and wood, the air was clear. Hashim now followed him into the village. 'They have gone away,' he said.

'If they were ever here,' John said. Because there were also several bomb craters, deep holes in the streets and around the shattered houses. 'Perhaps they let their planes do the fighting for them.' He went to where they had buried the radio set; here the ground was unbroken. 'There's a stroke of luck.'

'It is the water that matters, effendi,' Hashim said.

John nodded, and went to where the spring bubbled out of the earth. This too was untouched. Cautiously he tasted it. Pure nectar. 'We have indeed been fortunate,' he said. 'Return to Sheikh Ali, Hashim, and tell him he may bring his people back.'

Hashim saluted and mounted. John tethered his own camel, and continued his exploration. Something salvaged, anyway, he thought. Ali's people would rebuild their village, replant their crops – these indeed had hardly been touched – and resume their lives. Until the British needed them for another sacrifice!

But if Rommel had survived the assassination attempt, and did batter his way through the line at El Alamein, perhaps the British would not have need of them again. He sat down, with his back against a palm tree, looking at the water. He felt suddenly very tired, with good reason, he supposed, for he was still recovering from the wound he had received last December, from the experience of being torpedoed and from the burn to his back when the plane had gone up.

He needed another spell in hospital. Instead of which, the plane would no doubt come and take him and Margo to safety, and poor Bingham to a hospital to have his leg rebroken and reset, and hopefully, his fever brought down. And then?

Everything would depend upon what was happening at El Alamein. He yawned, and dozed, and awoke, sharply, to the sound of a click, close by his head. 'You see,' someone said in Italian. 'I knew one of them would come back.'

PART TWO

The Enemy

'I am afeard there are few die well that die in battle; for how can they charitably dispose of anything when blood is their argument?'

William Shakespeare

Five

The Escape

John leapt to his feet, but as he did so the rifle was wrenched from his hands, and instead he faced other rifles levelled at him. And... 'Umberto?' he asked incredulously.

The Italian officer was as dapper and handsome and flawlessly dressed as ever he remembered him. He had also accumulated several more medal ribbons. 'John Warrey,' Colonel Umberto said. 'You are a remarkable fellow, Glovanni. Did I not once describe you as a bad penny? Now I would have to say a bad sovereign.'

'You know this man?' asked the officer standing beside the colonel. John did not like the look of him at all. He wore a black uniform, there was a death's head insignia on his cap badge and an iron cross at his neck, and he spoke Italian with a pronounced accent.

'We are old friends,' Umberto said.

'He is English,' the SS officer announced.

'Absolutely. Captain Warrey, allow me to present Major Fritz Buelow, of the *Schutzstaffel*.' He changed to English. 'Our allies have this habit of putting one of their secret police into all our operations. Just to see that we behave properly, eh?'

'I won't say it's a pleasure,' John remarked.

'He is English,' Buelow said again, 'and wearing Arab clothes. He will be shot. Immediately.'

'Permit me to remind you, Major, that I am in command here,' Umberto said. 'I am sure that Captain Warrey has a lot to tell us.'

'Ah,' Buelow said. 'Yes. That is an excellent idea. Listen, *Englander,* you will answer our questions, or we will fill your mouth with sand, eh?'

John looked at Umberto.

'He is a tiresome fellow,' Umberto said, again using his perfect English. 'But a dangerous one. Now tell me what you are doing here.'

'What are you saying?' Buelow demanded.

'I am asking the necessary questions,' Umberto said.

John was looking around him. The oasis was suddenly filled with Italian soldiers, and he could see tanks on the hill beyond. They had, after all, been waiting. And he had walked into their trap. But only him, so far.

'You came here to mobilise the Senussi, once again,' Umberto said. 'This is a serious business, you know. And this attempt on Field Marshal Rommel's life–'

'Did you say "field marshal"?'

'Oh, yes. He has been promoted since his recent great victories. Did you send the assassin?'

John's brain whirred. Umberto did not know who the assassin had been – Halim must have been killed outright. But the woman... 'Please, Giovanni,' Umberto said. 'You and I are old friends. I do not wish to have to hurt you, much less have you shot. You must answer my questions.'

'Does this Jerry know you once helped me to escape?' John asked.

Umberto smiled. 'Are you going to tell him? My dear Giovanni, nobody knows anything about that incident save you, me, and the delectable Miss Cartwright. How is she, by the way?'

He didn't know about Margo, either. 'As far as I know, she is very well,' John said. 'You're forgetting Roberto Quesmi.'

'But he is not here,' Umberto pointed out. 'All anyone knows is that you escaped from my custody, and that I was found bound and gagged after you had gone. Killing your old friend Renaldo in the process.'

'He had it coming,' John said. 'Okay, I came here to activate the Senussi. When your people turned up, I had to make a decision. The last time I recommended surrender because they were outgunned. And your people massacred the entire tribe. So this time I recommended fading into the desert.'

Umberto nodded. 'Our planes saw them.'

'And strafed them,' John said.

'As I seem to have to remind you every time we meet,' Umberto said, 'we are fighting a war. These people are our enemies. Encouraged by you. Do you know what they do to Italian soldiers they capture?'

'As someone should keep reminding *you*, Umberto, they regard you as intruders into their country. As you are.'

'Much no doubt as the Egyptians regard you across the border. So we strafed your allies, and drove them into the desert. But you have come back, with a companion. You sent the companion off again.' Umberto grinned. 'Major Buelow would have had him too, but I decided to let him go. Because I knew the one who stayed behind would tell us what instructions had been given. Of course, I did not then know that the one who stayed behind would be you ... but I still have to know what message you sent off, and how far away are the Arabs. Now, answer me in Italian, so that the major may understand you.'

'They will not be returning here, if that's what's bothering you,' John said, praying that Ali would, despite the message, put out scouts and see the Italians before they saw him.

'How do you know this? You came back?'

146

'I came back just to see if it was worth-while returning. I sent my messenger back to say no. Ali and his people will seek a new home, deeper in the desert.'

'But you stayed, why?'

'I stayed to find out if you people were still about.' He grinned. 'As I did.'

'You went about it in a very strange way,' Umberto suggested. 'Sitting under a palm tree.'

'You showed yourself,' John pointed out.

Umberto regarded him for some seconds. 'He is lying,' Buelow said. 'Ask him about the radio.'

'What radio?' John countered.

'We traced radio signals coming from this area,' Umberto said. 'Presumably that was you?'

'I wish it were,' John said. 'Or I wouldn't be here now. My plane crashed, and I lost all my equipment. You can find the wreck if you really want to; it's not far from here.'

'Give him to me for half an hour,' Buelow said. 'I will get the truth.'

'I hope that will not be necessary,' Umberto said, and looked up as one of his men saluted smartly.

'A radio message, Colonel.' Umberto went off to the truck containing the radio equipment.

John grinned at Buelow. 'Foiled again, Herr Major.' Buelow glared at him. But

147

John knew his position was serious enough. Once again he had been captured, and once again, while not actually wearing British uniform. Umberto might be in command here, but once they rejoined the army...

Umberto hurried back. The trucks were already starting their engines. 'We must get back,' he said. 'Orders from the Commanding General.'

'Do I gather things aren't going quite according to plan?' John asked.

Umberto remained relaxed. 'Things are going even better than we could have hoped,' he said. 'Field Marshal Rommel has taken Mersa Matruh, with six thousand British prisoners. Your army is in full flight. We will be in Alexandria within a week. But he anticipates that resistance will stiffen as we move further into Egypt, and thus requires all his forces concentrated on the coast. As you admit, we have completed our task here. The Senussi are scattered, a spent force. Time enough to deal with them, once and for all, when the real war is won. Besides...' he gave one of his grins. 'The Field Marshal is interested to meet the famous Captain Warrey. You were on your way to meet him last year, you remember. When you escaped.'

'Famous? Me?'

'Your exploits are well documented, Giovanni. Let's move.'

148

At least John was spared the company of Major Buelow, who travelled in a separate truck. John was required to sit between Umberto and a military police sergeant, just behind the driver, as the column moved north, leaving a huge plume of sand and dust behind it; apparently Umberto intended to drive through the night. They dined off bocadilloes and red wine as the evening closed around them; each truck had two drivers, who took it in turns at the wheel for four hours each. 'I have arranged for the bombers to return tomorrow morning,' Umberto said, chattily. 'And if they see any signs of life, to blast the oasis one more time.'

'I know I owe you my life, old chum,' John said. 'But there are times you really make me wish to strangle you.'

'War,' Umberto said. 'It is a terrible thing. You know, I come from the north. It is beautiful country. The people, and the lakes ... there is no finer place to be than Tuscany. And I am stuck out here in this miserable desert, killing people. That is no business for a civilised man.'

'Amen,' John agreed. 'But you do it, quite happily.'

'I do it, because it is my duty, as do you do it because it is your duty. I would wager that you, personally, have killed more Italians

149

than I, personally, have killed Englishmen. As a matter of fact, I have never, personally, killed anyone. Whereas you, a mass destructor—'

'It wasn't something I planned, believe me,' John said. 'I was a little upset because one of the bastards ... I beg your pardon ... had just shot Soroya.'

'Sad,' Umberto sighed. 'Sad. Such a splendid woman. What will you do when the War is over? You understand that it will first be necessary to spend some time in a prison camp. But that will be in Italy. You should hope it is in the north, in Tuscany. But afterwards, when Britain surrenders...?'

'I shall return home to my wife. But if I have to wait until Britain surrenders, I shall be a very old man.'

'Always the jokes,' Umberto said. 'But ... your wife? I did not know you were married.'

'When last we met, I wasn't.'

'Ah, a rushed, wartime romance. That is very romantic.'

'Actually,' John said. 'We were engaged to be married even before the War started. Things just got held up for a while.'

'And all the while you were carrying on with Soroya, and Miss Cartwright? You are a devil.'

John didn't waste his time correcting his impression of Margo. He felt the Italian rather admired his amatory prowess, as much as his ability to kill. All without meaning to.

Somewhat to his surprise, John slept, and awoke at dawn as the column rumbled into another oasis, this one apparently inhabited by friendly, or at least, subdued, Bedouins. Here they were able to wash and shave – Umberto insisted that his men remain at all times smart enough to go on parade – and have a comfortable breakfast. 'We will be at the coast road by this evening,' Umberto said.

'Any news from up there?'

'We will be recommencing our advance in a day or so, once the area around Mersa Matruh has been entirely pacified. You will be in at the death, Giovanni. The death of British Imperialism in North Africa.'

It was a difficult point to counter, and became more so as they reached the coast, as promised, that afternoon. They first of all passed through what had clearly been a recent battlefield. Burned out tanks were scattered in every direction. Some few were still being repaired by engineers and mechanics. 'Our eighty-eights did that,' Buelow said proudly, having joined them for the day's drive. 'Anti-aircraft guns, eh? But the most potent anti-tank weapon in existence.'

Once again, not a point John felt he could dispute; he had seen those 88s at work during Rommel's first counter-attack, the previous year. Then they reached the road, and could look at the Mediterranean, breaking in gentle surf on the beach. John reckoned they were only a few miles east of Tobruk, a part of Cyrenaica he knew very well.

Here there was a faint glimmer of hope, for the road was almost entirely occupied by a line of petrol bowsers, driving east. 'There is the great problem with war in the desert,' Umberto remarked. 'Supply.'

If the RAF could appear now, and drop just a couple of bombs on that lot, John thought. But the skies were clear. Still, they were worth counting – if he was ever going to get the opportunity to use that information. And immediately he had to face another fact – a long line of British infantry, walking the other way, guarded by half a dozen Italian soldiers. They looked as dejected as only prisoners of war can, and there were far too many of them. 'You will soon join them,' Buelow said. Another presumably incontrovertible point.

The column now broke up, the military policemen going into Tobruk to resume their duties, the tanks making off to rejoin their brigade. Umberto transferred to an open command car, together with John.

Disagreeably, Buelow transferred with them, and they were driven along the coast road, behind a blaring horn, as they threaded their way in and out of the supply column. 'Where does this stuff originate?' John asked.

'Mostly from Tripoli,' Umberto told him. 'That is a very long way, eh? We are trying to repair the facilities in Benghazi and Tobruk, but your people did a good job of demolishing them and it will take time.'

They stopped for the night in Sollum, where the evidence of recent battle was again all around them; John had by then counted over a hundred supply vehicles, although now they seemed to have outreached them. But the Italians holding the position were jubilant, and John had several glasses of rather vinegary red wine forced upon him. At dawn they were on their way again, now definitely moving into a battle zone. Here again there were the wrecks of British tanks, wherever possible being repaired, but John was interested to note that there were also quite a number of German and Italian tanks, also under repair. 'Engines do not get on well with the sand, eh?' Umberto commented.

'How many vehicles do you have serviceable?'

Umberto grinned. 'Enough. You have suffered even greater losses.'

'The difference is that we have a lot more coming. Do you?'

'Of course.' But Umberto had stopped smiling.

'I thought all your material was earmarked for the Russian front.'

'I have told you, we have sufficient to finish the job here in Africa. As for your reinforcements, it will do you no good as when we have completed the conquest of Egypt they will have nowhere to land, eh?'

They were stopped at a command post, and then waved through, to arrive a few minutes later at Mersa Matruh. The village was almost as destroyed as Ali's oasis had been, but was crawling with German troops, and a villa had hastily been repaired sufficiently to act as a headquarters; radio aerials sprouted like hair, guards stood to attention, and officers in high-peaked caps hurried to and fro. 'The Field Marshal is expecting you,' said an aide, and led them up a flight of stairs, lacking bannisters which had been blown away, but otherwise intact. As was the gallery above, although there were a few ominous creaks as the aide opened the door and stamped to attention.

'Colonel Umberto, Major Buelow, and the Captain Warrey, Herr Field Marshal.'

The three men entered the room and stood to attention. John had seen Rommel before, when he had been taken prisoner during the withdrawal from Benghazi the previous year, although they had not actually met. He had been struck then by the way what were essentially soft features came together to make a granite-hard face, only relieved when the field marshal smiled. Now he was struck at how much the man seemed to have aged in the past year, at the way his complexion was mottled, clearly visible even beneath the heavy suntan.

An ill field marshal, he thought. But still apparently well enough to beat the British! He was equally interested in the huge wall map, dotted with pins and flags. If he could get close enough for a look at that ... which again supposed he would ever have the opportunity of using the information.

'Sit down, gentlemen,' Rommel invited, speaking Italian, and his aides brought chairs to place them before his desk. 'Oh, you too, Captain Warrey. I have heard a lot about you.'

'As I have heard a lot about you, sir,' John said, sitting between Umberto and Buelow.

He and Rommel gazed at each other for several seconds, then the field marshal smiled. 'I would hope every British soldier in North Africa has heard a lot about me, Captain. Why are you not in uniform? Do you not know that you are contravening military law?'

'I was involved in a plane crash, sir, and my tunic and shirt were burned, as well as my cap. The Arabs gave me this gear and the burnous.' He raised the jibbah. 'These are British army trousers, and boots.'

Rommel gazed at him for a few seconds, as if uncertain whether or not he was having his leg pulled. Then he looked at Umberto. 'Report!'

'We attacked the Senussi oasis, Herr Field Marshal, inflicted heavy casualties, scattered them, and drove them into the desert. They will not again constitute a threat for a considerable time.'

'By which time, hopefully, they will be entirely your responsibility, Colonel. And where did you capture Captain Warrey?'

'He was with the Senussi, Herr Field Marshal.'

'Ah. Leading them?' He looked at John.

'Advising them, sir.'

'In which capacity, did you advise them to send the assassin who attempted to take my life?'

John reckoned there was no point in lying. 'I'm afraid I did, sir.'

Rommel again regarded him for several seconds, surprised by his honesty. 'No doubt on orders from Whitehall,' he remarked at last.

'I do not know where the orders originated, sir.'

156

'But you were given them, and you carried them out. Do you regard assassination as an honourable way to fight a war?'

'No, sir. But I am a soldier, and my business is obeying orders.'

'I understand that. But *you* understand that as a self-confessed accessory before the fact, you can be condemned for attempted murder?'

'Yes, sir.'

Rommel's face slightly relaxed. 'However, the attempt failed. As did that other attempt, by your commandos. I am not that easy to kill.'

'May I ask what happened to the agent, sir?' There was no necessity to let the field marshal know Halim's identity.

But Rommel already knew. 'You mean Sheikh Halim? He was shot. In attempting to reach me.'

'And the woman?'

'She is in custody.' He glanced at Buelow, who nodded. 'It was she who gave us the information we needed, both as to the sheikh's identity, and where he originated. But I had you brought here for a different reason. I am told you are a man who knows the desert, especially the Egyptian and Cyrenaican deserts. Is this true?'

'I have spent some time in them, sir,' John said cautiously, trying to look Rommel in the eye and at the same time scan the desk.

There was an open diary by the field marshal's left hand, and on it, a date was circled. If he could just make out the date...

'You have crossed the Calanscio Sand Sea, and also the Great Sand Sea, I understand,' Rommel said.

'Yes, sir.'

'And also the Qattara Depression?'

'Yes, sir.'

'Is it, in your opinion, usable by armoured vehicles?'

'No, sir.'

'Not even tanks?'

'Possibly by tanks, but slowly and with great difficulty. There would be no chance of any supply truck accompanying them. It is actually a vast salt marsh.'

'But that would be the opinion you would give, would it not, if you supposed I was hoping to attack through there?'

'It is my opinion, sir, no matter what you propose to do.'

Another several seconds of study. Then Rommel gestured at the map on the wall. 'Do you know where your Eighth Army is now?' A brief smile. 'What is left of it.'

'No, sir.'

Rommel got up and went to the map. John hastily did likewise, before he could be stopped. Pins, flags ... several clustered around the frontier post of Al-Jaghbub, another place he knew well, both from

158

before the War and his first sortie after it had begun. Al-Jaghbub was close to the Egyptian border, about level with the southern end of the Depression. It was, of course, a garrisoned position. But he would swear one of those flags represented a tank squadron. 'I will tell you,' Rommel was saying, pointing. 'It has withdrawn, in some panic I may say, to a position about eighty miles from here. Its right wing rests on the village of El Alamein, and its left on the edge of this Qattara Depression. That is a front of only about forty miles, and I assume Auchinleck feels he has sufficient forces to hold such a short line. He also assumes, I presume, that his desert flank cannot be turned, because of this depression. Would that be your view?'

'Yes, sir.'

'Isn't there a way round this Depression? Did you not lead a squadron of tanks round it, two years ago, in a successful raid on the Italian lines of communication?'

'I did, sir. A squadron of tanks. And it took us several days. On the way we lost our supply trucks. We were fortunate to be able to fuel in Al-Jaghbub. I do not think an army could do it. Certainly without the man-oeuvre being discovered.'

'But it is possible. Were it accomplished, the war in North Africa would be won. We could be in Cairo before Auchinleck could withdraw to Alexandria.'

'Yes, sir. You would need a vast back-up, sir, and complete control of the air.'

Rommel's smile was acid. 'And neither of those, as I am sure you are aware, Captain Warrey, do I possess. But, at the moment, Auchinleck is scarcely better off. And I do possess one enormous asset, Captain: morale. My men are used to winning. Your Eighth Army is rapidly becoming used only to losing. So, we have but to win once again. Just once more, I think, will complete the business. Now I must do a very distasteful thing. I am going to ask something of you, Captain. But I wish you to understand that your answer will in no way affect your status as an officer and a prisoner of war.'

'Yes, sir.' John braced himself, he had a pretty good idea of what he was going to be asked.

'Accepting that we are going to win this battle in any event,' Rommel said, 'and that if it comes down to a slogging match a large number of your comrades will be killed, and accepting also that if your friends the Senussi attempt to take any part in the battle they will be wiped out, would you be prepared to guide a squadron of tanks round the bottom end of the Qattara Depression, by the shortest and quickest possible route, to cause a diversion in the British rear?'

'You mean to attack Cairo, sir?'

'I assume that would cause a diversion,' Rommel said, drily.

'You know I cannot do that, sir.'

'Of course. And I hope you know that I had to ask; it is a commanding general's duty to win a battle by any means that comes to hand, certainly where casualties may be avoided.'

'I understand that, sir.'

Rommel nodded, and returned to stand before his desk. John hastily followed, to stand on the other side, between Umberto and Buelow. 'Well, then,' the field marshal said, 'you will have to go to a cell until shipment can be arranged to Italy. I will not see you again, Captain Warrey. But I will wish you good fortune.'

'May I reciprocate, sir?'

Rommel raised his eyebrows. 'Do you think I will need fortune, Captain?'

'Every general needs fortune in battle, sir.'

1 July. The circled date was 1 July. And today was... John realised he had no idea; he had quite lost track of time since the plane crash.

Rommel smiled. 'A good general, that is, a general who wins, should make his own fortune, Captain.'

Both Umberto and Buelow were standing, and John did also, saluting, before the three of them left the room. 'He likes you,'

Umberto remarked.

'Well I liked him.'

'Which is not to say you would not kill each other if you met on the battlefield,' Umberto said. 'I find this very sad. Ah, well, I will take you into Tobruk for tonight. Tomorrow you will go to Tripoli for shipment to Italy.'

'I will take the prisoner, Colonel,' Buelow said.

They had reached the head of the stairs. Both Umberto and John checked to look at the SS major. 'He is my responsibility,' Umberto asserted.

'After he has been released by us,' Buelow said. 'I am sure you are aware, Colonel, that all prisoners taken in this campaign are considered in the first instance to be the responsibility of the German Army. That it is convenient to hand them over to you in most instances does not alter that fact.'

'And what reason can you have for holding Captain Warrey?'

'There are a few points regarding what he has told us, and more importantly, what he has *not* told us, which need clarification,' Buelow said.

'Field Marshal Rommel gave no orders about this.'

'Field Marshal Rommel is preoccupied with the coming offensive, Colonel. But he will be grateful for any further information

162

we may be able to obtain. You will come with me, Captain Warrey.'

John looked at Umberto, who glared at Buelow. 'I will also come with you,' he said.

'And I do not think that is at all necessary, Colonel,' Buelow said. 'I am beginning to find your interest in this prisoner, the fact that you are old ... acquaintances, somewhat odd. Perhaps worthy of investigation.'

Umberto hesitated – he could be putting his career on the line.

'I shall be all right, Umberto,' John said. 'I am sure that Major Buelow will remember that the Field Marshal said I was to be treated as an officer.'

'Well...' Umberto held out his hand, 'I will wish you good fortune, Giovanni. Perhaps, when this is all over, you will come to visit me in Tuscany. With your wife, of course.'

'I think that might be rather fun,' John agreed.

Umberto gave Buelow a long stare, then went down the stairs. Buelow gestured, and John followed, more slowly. For all the confidence he had suggested to Umberto, he was feeling a little apprehensive. He had never actually come into very close contact with the Germans – when he had been taken prisoner the previous year it had been strictly an Italian affair – but he did know that some of their methods of waging war, certainly in Russia, were barbaric. On the other hand, he reminded himself, Rommel was clearly a gentleman of the old professional school.

When they reached the courtyard, Umberto's car was just driving out. Another car waited for them, and this was driven by an SS chauffeur, with another SS officer sitting in the front. Buelow gestured John to sit in the back, and sat beside him. They followed Umberto along the road to Tobruk. 'You are in British Intelligence,' Buelow remarked.

'That is correct.'

'Your business being to stir up trouble behind our lines here in Cyrenaica.'

'My business is to act as a political agent for His Majesty's Government with the Senussi, who are our allies.'

'They are in rebellion against the Italian Government.'

'Who are our enemies,' John said equably.

Buelow glanced at him; they stared at the road. 'I will be interested to learn more of your dealings with the Senussi,' he said.

'Do you suppose I am going to tell you of them?' John asked.

Buelow smiled. 'Yes,' he said.

He didn't speak much more until they reached Tobruk, while John was left to some very unpleasant reflections. He even contemplated jumping out of the car, but he didn't think that would do him much good as it was travelling at some speed, and even if the Germans didn't shoot him he'd probably break something. He had to be patient. And he was interested to see Tobruk again after nearly a year. It was even more bomb and bullet shattered than he remembered, although this time there had apparently not been a great deal of fighting before the surrender.

And even amidst the rubble there was a good deal of activity; it was dark before they entered the town, but no one appeared to be paying much attention to blackout regulations; the surviving inhabitants of the town had got used to the changing fortunes of war, and obviously they had to be happier under nominal Italian rule than under British.

Horn blaring, the car swung down a side street and past an armed black-uniformed sentry into a small courtyard. 'What we call home,' Buelow said chattily. 'It is small, and a bit broken in places, but it is the best we can do at the moment. Captain?'

John stepped down, observing that there were two other cars in the yard, but no drivers visible. He walked past another sentry into an outer lobby, where there were several clerks, half of them women, he was surprised to see, very trim in their white shirts and black skirts, with little black ties.

Buelow gestured at an inner door, and he entered an empty office, although it contained a paper-laden desk and was clearly Buelow's own, for the major sat behind the desk, at the same time ringing a little bell. 'Sit down, Captain,' he invited. 'Let us keep this as civilised as possible, eh?'

'I'm all in favour of that,' John agreed.

The door opened and one of the woman secretaries came in, with her notebook and pencil. She sat in the remaining chair, against the wall, crossed her knees, produced a notebook, and looked terribly efficient. Which wasn't difficult as she wore horn-rimmed spectacles. The rest of her – yellow hair drawn up in a tight bun, shirt-front effectively strained, features regular if not beautiful – was quite attractive. 'Freda will take down whatever you say,' Buelow said.

'If I say anything,' John remarked.

Buelow's smile was cold. 'I am sure you will think of something, Captain. Colonel Umberto is an old friend, is he not?'

'In a manner of speaking. We knew each other before the War. He happened to save my life. Since then, we have obviously found ourselves on opposite sides. But we endeavour to be, as you say, civilised about it.'

Freda wrote vigorously.

'Quite. He took you prisoner during the retreat from Benghazi, last year, did he not?'

166

'I was taken prisoner, certainly, Herr Major. And Colonel Umberto, as Chief of Police, was my overall custodian, yes.'

'But you managed to escape. While in his custody. Was that not rather fortuitous?'

'I suppose it was. I managed to turn the tables on him while we were alone, bound and gagged him, and got away.'

'Is that not rather too Boy's Own Paperish to be true, Captain? Come now, Colonel Umberto let you go, did he not? After arranging it to look as if you had, as you say, managed to turn the tables on him.'

'That is nonsense,' John lied.

Buelow considered him for several seconds, then opened a box on his desk and took a cigarette. 'Have one.'

'I don't smoke.'

'Ah.' Buelow's expression suggested that John might soon wish he had. He lit his cigarette, drew smoke into his lungs. 'Very well. Now let us talk about the Senussi. Umberto accepted everything you had to say, although he must have known it was all a pack of lies.' He waited.

'I really don't know what you're talking about,' John said.

'My dear Captain, the Colonel is supposed to know all about the desert tribes. I would not claim to have his years of experience, but I have studied the matter. The Senussi live in the desert. That it is convenient for them from time to time to inhabit an oasis, and even build a village there, is not an important fact of life. The Italians have driven them out of God alone knows how many villages over the past fifteen years, and they have simply regrouped out in the desert, and made themselves a new home. Is this not true?'

'You obviously know more about them than I do, Herr Major.'

'So, you will say that this tribe which the Colonel so efficiently scattered, is not already regrouped somewhere else, ready to resume its activities?'

'That is my opinion, yes.'

Buelow leaned forward, a sudden movement. 'You think you can play games with me, Captain Warrey? You think I do not know how to make men talk?'

'Uh-uh.' John held up his finger. 'Officer, etcetera. I refer you to Field Marshal Rommel.'

Buelow stared at him for several seconds. 'You persist in treating this as a game, eh? We know all about you British, You will come with me.'

He stood up, as did Freda. John did likewise. He decided against trying to anticipate what might be going to happen next. He had to prepared for some discomfort, he reckoned, but also to be alert; Buelow, and indeed his staff, it seemed, were totally confident. Too much so. Apart from the man outside the front door, and the one on the gate, there did not appear to be any security; he did not think that either Freda or any of her friends in the outer office would be of any great value in a fight.

Freda opened the door for him, and he stepped into the passage. An armed guard clicked to attention. Three! Freda said something to him in German, and he stood at ease. Clearly, even if she was only a secretary, she was an important secretary.

She led him to the stairs, took the ones leading down. This didn't look so good. Buelow was immediately behind him, having closed the door at the head of the stairs. They came to a corridor, along which Freda again led them; it was lit by a succession of naked bulbs suspended from the low ceiling, clearly a recent and makeshift wiring job. At the end of the corridor there was a door, and another armed guard, who once again came to attention, and was stood at ease by Freda. Four! This guard had a bunch of keys hanging from his belt, and he unlocked the cell door for them. This door, John noted, had a Judas window, which was presently closed. He reckoned that might be his greatest danger, for by now he had worked out just what he intended to do. There might be four guards, but they were very widely separated, and by closed doors. And Freda clearly was Buelow's personal secretary, and therefore a woman to be obeyed.

Freda entered the cell and held the door for him. He had to duck his head to follow her, as the lintel was low, but there was sufficient headroom beyond. Here again there was a single electric light bulb, glowing where it hung from the ceiling. The room was large, and remained gloomy, but he immediately made out the naked figure of a woman strapped to the opposite wall by thongs at her wrists, which suspended her arms over her head. Her head was drooping, and concealed by the mass of black hair, but she looked up when she heard the door. Uluma!

He recognised her instantly, even if he had never expected to see her like this, small, dark, surprisingly voluptuous ... and defiled. Buelow also came into the room and closed the door. John heard the key turning in the lock behind them.

By now his eyes were becoming accustomed to the gloom, as he looked around the cell. There was a single chair, in the very centre of the floor, and two tables. One was against the far wall; on it was a large gramophone. The other was closer to the prisoner. On it was the contraption that

170

resembled a portable telephone – save that there was no speaker or receiver. John had become familiar with this instrument of torture during his training – but suddenly that seemed a very long time ago. Not for Uluma. At the sight of Buelow she began to shiver. 'Please,' she said in Italian. 'I have told you everything–'

She frowned, as she in turn focused on the rest of the room, and recognised John. He looked more closely at her. There were marks on her body, but he reckoned they were mainly from being manhandled rather than any beatings. No doubt the electricity had proved sufficient.

'You know this man,' Buelow said. It was not a question.

Uluma licked her lips. 'Water,' she muttered. 'Can I have water.'

Buelow nodded to Freda, who went to a barrel on the far side of the room, dipped a tin cup, and held it to Uluma's lips; the Arab woman drank greedily. 'When we first brought her down here,' Buelow said, 'and she asked for water, she spat it out, over Freda. That made Freda very angry. Tell the Captain what you did to our little friend, Freda.'

It was Freda's turn to lick her lips. 'Freda can be a tigress when aroused,' Buelow confided. 'And she is always aroused. You know this man,' he said again.

Uluma's head flopped up and down. 'He is the one of which you spoke,' Buelow suggested. Again Uluma nodded. 'There, you see,' Buelow said to John. 'Electricity. One of the marvels of the modern age. When you think that before electricity we would have had to pull out her fingernails, perhaps burn her with an open flame, all very unpleasant. Electricity is much cleaner, don't you think? And now, you see, it is useless for you to attempt to refuse to answer my questions. Uluma has told us all about you, about why you were sent to the Senussi, and about Major Cartwright. Now she is someone I would like to lay my hands on.'

'I'm not sure you'd enjoy that,' John said. 'So what happens now?'

'Now, you will be sent to a prison camp in Germany, where they know how to deal with people like you.'

'And the woman?'

'Oh, she I think I will give to my men for a while. Then they can throw her out. She is of no more use to us. But first, I think we will play with her a little more. Freda.' Freda switched on the radio, and turned up the volume. 'Her screams would otherwise disturb the neighbourhood,' Buelow shouted.

'Please!' Uluma begged. 'Please?'

Buelow went to the table and took the

alligator clips from their rest. John reckoned he would never have a better opportunity than this, both because of the noise and because Buelow for the moment was totally occupied. He stepped up to the officer, and swung his hand in the karate chop he had been taught at training school. It wasn't a clean hit, but Buelow grunted and sagged. Before he could recover, John had whipped the Luger from his belt holster and hit him again, with all the strength he could summon. Buelow collapsed on the floor.

It had happened so quickly Freda had had time to do nothing more than scream, but the noise was drowned by the radio. Then she ran for the door, but John got there first, catching her shoulder and spinning her round so that she thudded against the wall. Her glasses came off and she blinked at him myopically. He grasped her neck with his left hand, put his face beside hers, while he jammed the muzzle of the Luger into her stomach. 'Listen very carefully,' he said. 'You, me, and Uluma are going to walk out of here. If you do not help us, I am going to shoot away your spine. Understand?'

He slightly relaxed his grip, and her head moved, up and down. 'Right. First thing, release Uluma.'

He gave a quick glance at the judas window, but it remained closed; if the guard had heard even a trace of the scream over the music, he would assume it had been the Arab woman. Freda hesitated, biting her lip, then went to the Arab woman and released the ropes holding her wrists. Uluma sank down the wall, closing her arms over her breasts, still shivering.

'Why don't you tie him up?' John invited. 'Good and tight.'

Uluma stared at her tormentor, then moved forward, hands turned into claws. 'After he's tied up,' John told her. 'And gagged. Take off his tunic, first.'

Uluma crouched over Buelow like a bird of prey, taking off his belts, then his tunic, boots and socks. His socks she stuffed into his mouth, secured them there with the handkerchief she took from his pocket. Then using his belts she trussed him, ankles and wrists behind his back, and the whole drawn tight. Freda watched her with wide, terrified eyes.

By now Buelow was himself regaining consciousness, blinking, trying to move; blood stained his fair hair from where John had hit him. Still Uluma crouched over him, and now her hands moved to unfasten his britches.

'You'll have to dream about that, for the time being,' John told her. 'Not that I don't believe he has it coming, whatever you had in mind. But our first business is to get out of here.'

'You'll never make it,' Freda said, some of her courage returning as she picked up her glasses, made sure they were not broken.

'You'd better hope we do,' John told her, 'because you're in the firing line. Where are Uluma's clothes?'

Freda pointed with her chin at a pile of cloth in the corner. Uluma was already there, sorting out her various garments. Buelow moaned and writhed. Toin stood over him. 'As you say,' he said, 'real *Boy's Own Paper* stuff. The beauty of it is that no one expects it to work. You need to compare notes with Umberto.'

Uluma was dressed. 'Now, then,' John said. 'Switch off the radio.'

Freda obeyed. Her shirt front was rising and falling briskly, and she kept putting up her hand to make sure her glasses were still on her nose. Her brain was clearly working overtime, but she had been impressed by the way he had dealt with Buelow, and then herself, she could have no doubt that he would use the gun if he had to. 'The guard will ask questions,' she said.

'No he won't, if you do everything right. Call on him to open the door. And Freda, I may not be able to speak much German, but I shall kill you if I have the slightest doubt about anything.'

Freda took several deep breaths, then spoke through the door to the guard. A moment later the door opened, and John presented the pistol. 'Inside.'

Presumably the guard did not speak English, but he could understand both the situation and that his life was on the line. John closed the door on him. 'Do your stuff,' he told Uluma. 'Tell him to lie down,' he commanded Freda.

Freda did as she was told, and the guard did as he was told. Uluma got to work, and a minute later he was bound and gagged alongside Buelow, who looked as if he might have a stroke at any moment. 'Well done,' John said. 'Now, Freda, I am going to put the gun in my pocket, but it will still be pointing at you. All you have to do is lead us out of here, answering any questions in a convincing fashion, and direct us to some transport, and you may well live to a ripe old age.'

'They will not let us through, like this,' Freda objected.

'I've been thinking about that,' John agreed. 'Uluma, take the guard's pistol and remove the magazine.'

Uluma obeyed. 'Now give the gun to Freda.'

Uluma hesitated, then handed Freda the empty pistol.

John looked longingly at the tommy-gun the guard had also carried, but he couldn't risk it. Instead he put the discarded pistol magazine into his pocket, then gave Uluma Buelow's cap. 'Put that and the tunic under your haik,' he told her.

'Now, Freda,' he said. 'Take the guard's handcuffs, and cuff Uluma. With her hands in front.' Uluma gave him a quick glance, and he winked. 'We're on the same side, remember?'

She held out her wrists, and Freda cuffed her. 'Give me the key,' John commanded. She obeyed. 'Right. Now here's how we go. You first, Uluma. You next, Freda. With your gun on Uluma. I will be right beside you, with my gun on you.'

'You are not handcuffed,' Freda said. 'They will suspect.'

'I wasn't handcuffed when I came in,' John reminded her. 'So it's a risk. What we need to do is move very smartly, very confidently, and very quickly. With you saying all the right things. Okay?' He smiled at her. 'I'm trying to save your life.'

She hesitated, then went to the door. Behind them, Buelow drummed his heels on the floor.

Six

The Rescue

Somewhat to John's surprise, his ploy worked. It was now close to dusk, and the various clerks and officials were thinking of calling it a day, while the sentries were less keen than earlier. They all knew Freda, while few of them could actually identify either Uluma or John. Freda seemed totally in command of the situation, urged along her captives with snapped commands and prods of her pistol, and within a few minutes of leaving the cell they were in the open air. She marched them towards the row of parked command cars. 'That one,' she said, gesturing John to take the wheel and Uluma into the back.

'You too,' John said in a low voice.

'You promised—'

'You have to see us out of town, sweetheart,' he told her. 'And how can I be nice to you if you're not there?' He passed his weapon back to Uluma, between the seats. 'Just blow her open if she doesn't behave.' Uluma grunted.

Freda sat beside him, pistol now held

against him. The key was in the ignition, and a moment later they were driving out of the gate and on to the street. John didn't know if there was a curfew or not, but it obviously wouldn't apply to German command cars. He drove slowly; in the dark it was impossible for anyone to tell that he was not a German officer. 'We need food,' he said. 'Have you money?'

'No,' Freda said.

'Ah. Well, then, we'll have to see what we can do. Uluma?' He pulled the car into the gloom beneath an overhanging wall. The building behind was in darkness. 'Let's try the tunic.'

It was a rather loose fit, even when crumpled from being rolled up beneath Uluma's haik; it carried her scent, which was vaguely pleasant. The cap was also a shade too large, but it sat easily enough. 'Now, Uluma,' he said. 'Food and money. Can you do it?'

Uluma placed the pistol in his hand, and faded into the darkness. 'It's her trade,' John explained. 'One of them.'

'When will you let me go?' Freda asked.

'Don't be impatient.' Very lightly he ran the gun muzzle up the front of her shirt. She gave a little gasp. 'We have a lot of unfinished business. And I imagine that, even with Uluma's skill, we have some time to kill.'

'They will shoot me.'

'Of course they won't. You were abducted at gunpoint, and then you were raped. It will be rape, won't it?'

She gave another little gasp, but did not attempt to withdraw.

They heard the tramp of booted feet. 'They will certainly shoot *you*,' she said.

'Then we'll go together.' He put his arm round her waist, brought her body against his, the pistol pressed against her stomach. 'Take off your glasses,' he whispered.

She obeyed and he kissed her mouth, then let his free hand wander over her shirt front. Very hard nipples, he thought. The feet were very close, and suddenly a flashlight beam cut through the darkness. The man holding the flashlight gave a startled exclamation, and the light went off. Then he said something, and the feet moved away. Slowly John released her, kissing her nose instead.

'Why did he not challenge you?' Freda asked.

'Because he saw my cap and my tunic, and it never occurred to him that anyone wearing a German officer's uniform would not be a German officer,' John explained. 'People are inclined to see only what they expect to see.'

'You are a very bold and ruthless man,' she said.

'You say the sweetest things.' He did some

more gentle massaging of her breasts. 'Do tell me you're having a good time.' She was back to her gasping. 'If you wish me, take me now,' she said.

'It will have to be a little later, darling,' John told her. 'When we have less distracting surroundings. But we can canoodle a bit. I can do that while concentrating.' It had occurred to him that the German patrol might still be about.

She came to him willingly enough. He wondered if she was somehow hoping to get the gun off him. She would of course really be chancing her arm, as he kept the pistol muzzle resting against her hip, and he very rapidly deduced that she was not truly a woman of action, but no more that what she appeared – a secretary whose sole aim was the preservation of her life. She was also very responsive, and after his recent experiences he was also in the mood.

Because the future looked bleak. He had no doubt that he and Uluma could escape into the desert; they both knew this particular piece of desert very well. But he had quite failed in his objective. Therefore was it not his duty to attempt to regain Rommel's presence, and kill the man? But that was almost certain to fail. Rommel was just too alert, and too well guarded, as had now been proved on two occasions. He would merely be going to his death to no purpose.

While on the other hand, he had first-hand knowledge of what the field marshal intended, knowledge that would be invaluable to Auchinleck, if he could be told in time. That was surely his prime objective, now.

'We go now,' Uluma said. Both their heads turned to gaze at the Arab woman, who was carrying a bag. 'We must hurry,' she said.

They could hear shouting behind her. John hastily pushed Freda off his lap and started the engine. Uluma took the pistol from his hand and got into the back seat, leaning forward. John gunned the engine and they drove to the outskirts of the town. 'Do your stuff,' John said, and handed her Buelow's identification card.

Freda had been drawing deep breaths and straightening her uniform. Now she fumbled in her breast pocket and took out her own card as well, presented them both to the sentry who stood beside the car as it drew to a halt. He inspected them by the light of his torch. This was the most critical moment, as everything depended on whether or not Buelow had as yet got himself free and to a telephone. But the sentry only looked up once, and then into the back, where Uluma smiled at him, her gun hidden under the flap of her haik. 'We are on our way to the Field Marshal,' Freda explained.

The sentry stood to attention, and the

barrier was raised. A moment later they were through.

The road running along the coast was as ever crowded with men and materiel as Rommel built up to what he intended to be the final campaign of the North African war. No one took the least notice of the command car, except to wave it impatiently on whenever it threatened to slow the traffic. John remembered the road well from his earlier adventures, and he knew just where to swing off and drive down a subsidiary track leading south. Here there was less traffic.

Neither woman had spoken while he was weaving in and out of trucks and tanks and weapons carriers, but Uluma had clearly been thinking. 'You have had sex with this woman?' she enquired.

'Only to pass the time,' John assured her. Freda snorted.

'Now you give her to me,' Uluma suggested. Freda gave a startled sound.

'I didn't know you were that way inclined,' John said, trying to concentrate on the road.

'They tortured me,' Uluma said. 'Shall I tell you what they did to me?'

'I'd rather you didn't,' John requested.

'She was there,' Uluma said. 'She tortured me with the others.'

'Hm,' John commented, and glanced at a

plainly terrified Freda. 'Did you really?'

Freda licked her lips. 'I had to. Buelow made me.'

'That's what they all say. I'd say you're lucky you're not a man, otherwise Uluma might have a go at your more important private parts.'

'I am going to cut off her breasts,' Uluma said. 'Afterwards.'

'After what?' John asked.

Freda clutched his arm. 'It is not a joke. This woman is serious. She is a savage. You do not know.'

'I do know,' John said, freeing himself. 'But from all accounts you have been the savage, up to now.'

'I will take her now,' Uluma decided, knocking off Freda's cap and twining her fingers in her hair, pulling the bun loose.

'Please!' Freda screamed.

'You'll have to be patient,' John said. 'You wouldn't enjoy it in a moving car.'

'When do we stop?' Uluma asked. She seemed to have a one-track mind. Not that John could blame her, after what she had experienced. How the hell was he going to stop her at least killing the German woman?

'Soon,' he said, and stared into the darkness; the headlamps were blacked out for the upper two-thirds, which meant there was just a dull glow on the surface in front of them. This became more rutted and uncertain as they drove south. 'Halt!'

John instinctively pressed the brake, and the command car scraped to a halt in a flurry of dust which made the night even darker than it was. He had not spotted the command post, which had shown no light up to this moment. Now he gazed at a torch, and ... he could not decide how many men.

But the man had spoken Italian, not German. That was a relief. 'We are on a mission into the desert,' he said.

'Identification, please, Captain.'

John handed over his card, and the sentry inspected it, then turned to an officer who had appeared at his side. 'You are under arrest,' he said.

'Me?' Freda demanded, her voice a quite real mixture of fear and indignation.

'You are Freda Shultz,' the officer said. 'We have received a radio message of how you help the Englander escape. This is he.' He did not appear to notice Uluma, making herself as small as possible in the back. 'Raise your hands in the air and step down,' the officer commanded. Whereupon Uluma shot him in the chest.

He gave a gasp, and half turned with the impact of the bullet at such close range, then dropped to his knees before slumping to the ground. 'Oh, my God,' Freda shouted.

John shot the sentry before he could level his tommy-gun, at the same time grasping the man's belts. 'Oh, my *God!*' Freda screamed.

The sentry was subsiding down the side of the car. John grabbed his tommy-gun before letting go of him. In the back seat, Uluma was firing again and again, into the now visible camp fire, which was beside the road and beyond two tents from which men were emerging. John now sprayed them with fire, and they went to ground. 'Here!' he tossed Uluma the tommy-gun, and started the engine again.

Men were screaming and shouting to either side, and one tried to get in front of the car. John drove straight at him, and the impact hurled him to one side. Then they were through the barrier, which shattered as the car struck it, and on to the open road, racing south.

'Oh, my God,' Freda kept saying, over and over again. 'You killed them.'

'I think we probably did,' John agreed. 'Some of them. Are they following, Uluma?' He had seen a truck parked beyond the tents.

'I do not see them,' Uluma said, caressing the tommy-gun as if it might have been her baby.

'They will be calling for assistance,' Freda said; the thought was apparently restoring some of her confidence. 'At daybreak they will find us.'

'You could be right.' John checked the fuel gauge; it was a quarter full. 'How many men would compose a post like that?'

Freda shrugged. 'Six, maybe eight, with a lieutenant and a sergeant.'

'We know the lieutenant is dead, and at least three others, I would say,' John said, and slowed the car. 'And I don't think they will be expecting us to come back.'

'Are you mad?' Freda enquired.

'Just desperate. There's not too much difference.' He turned the car. By his kilometre meter he reckoned the post was about two miles back. 'We'll walk it,' he told Uluma, reloading both the pistols, and checking the tommy-gun. There were enough rounds left in the drum to fire two bursts.

'You'll be killed,' Freda protested.

'You had better hope we're not, otherwise it's going to be a long hot day,' John told her. 'Take off your stockings.'

She glared at him but then raised her skirt and obeyed. John tied her ankles together and then her wrists. 'Fill her mouth with sand,' Uluma suggested, having watched with interest.

'I don't think that's really necessary,' John said. 'No one is going to hear her out here. See you tomorrow, darling,' he told Freda.

'Bastard!' she shouted. 'I will die of thirst.'

'Not if I come back.'

They laid her on the back seat, but just in case she managed to get free, John took the keys out of the ignition. 'Before you die,' Uluma said with great satisfaction, 'the crows will come and peck out your eyes.' Freda moaned.

'Let's go.' John set off into the darkness, the Arab woman at his heels.

'Why are we doing this?' Uluma asked.

'Because we need petrol. Gasoline.'

'But by the time we have killed the Italians, and got the gasoline, and filled up our car, it will be daylight, and they will have sent planes, and reinforcements.'

'Therefore it is our business to confuse them as much as possible. Without getting ourselves killed. Listen. I need to get back to Egypt very quickly. To do that, I will need a radio. They have a radio at that post.'

She said nothing for a few seconds, then gave one of her grunts. 'At least we will die killing Germans,' she said. 'And the crows *will* feed off of that woman's eyes. Maybe other parts as well.' She seemed an easy woman to satisfy.

It was past three by the time they came in sight of the post. The fire still glowed, and they could see the men; the dead bodies had been assembled and covered with a tarpaulin, and the living were huddled around the fire, drinking presumably coffee, although John suspected it might have been laced. He also suspected that these were not front-line troops, but reservists sent to man a position where there had not been anticipated there would be any fighting. In any event they had clearly determined to call it a night until the pursuit force arrived. It was going to be a massacre.

But he was fighting a war, and he had no alternative. He touched Uluma on the arm, and pointed. She understood immediately, and moved several feet to her right. John went to the left. He had both one of the pistols and the tommy-gun, but he reckoned the automatic weapon would do most of the trick. He looked at Uluma, who was looking at him. He reckoned she was as fine a fighting soldier as he would find anywhere in North Africa, and she was imbued with the desire for revenge. He almost felt sorry for their adversaries, who had had no part in her mistreatment.

He drew a long breath, stood up, and opened fire. The bullets chattered into the unsuspecting men, throwing them left and right. One or two reached for their weapons, but were cut down before they could properly determine where the shooting was coming from, as Uluma had also joined in the shooting from her position to the right.

It was all over in a matter of seconds, the six bodies sprawled in the sand. Only one was still alive, whimpering with pain. Uluma crouched beside him and rolled him onto his back, then began unbuckling his belt.

The Italian soldier screamed with a mixture of pain and terror. 'No,' John said. Uluma looked up, frowning. 'No cutting up,' John told her.

'It is the law,' she protested. And grinned at him. 'And it is much sport.' She squeezed the front of the soldier's britches. 'He is a big one.'

'I said no,' John repeated. 'You are fighting for me, now, so you do what I tell you.'

She pouted. 'He will die anyway.'

'Not necessarily.' John knelt beside her, examined the wound. It was in the man's side – he was actually hardly more than a boy – and John reckoned it had broken several ribs, but he did not think it was life threatening. 'Listen,' he said. 'I am going to bind you up as best I can. Then when your people come in the morning they will be able to help you.'

'Do not let the woman have me,' the soldier begged.

'I will not,' John promised.

'It is the law,' Uluma grumbled. 'These men–'

John had to make a hasty decision. He needed Uluma, and he needed her entirely

191

behind him for the foreseeable future. And the other Italians were all dead, anyway. 'All right,' he said. 'You may have them.'

'It is not as much sport, when they are dead,' she pointed out.

'But it is the law,' he reminded her.

She made one of her gurgling growls, and fell to work. John preferred not to look. He busied himself with binding up the soldier's wounds, obviously causing the boy considerable pain, but eventually stopping the bleeding. 'Water,' the boy whispered. 'Can I have water?'

John found a water bottle and gave it to him, then began hunting through the post and the truck. This was as much to keep himself occupied while Uluma did what she felt she had to do, but he did find a good long-range radio, and also a first-aid kit which contained some analgesics. He gave the soldier a couple of these and lifted him into one of the tents to shield him from the coming sun – by now the eastern horizon was showing a faint glow. 'We go now?' Uluma had found a haversack, in which she had placed her trophies; John could only hope there wasn't any food still in there which she might later produce for lunch.

'In a moment. Give me a hand.'

There were several spare jerrycans of petrol, and these they loaded into the back of the truck, together with the radio and the

192

batteries. John connected the aerial and tied it to the side of the truck. They also loaded it with what food and water they could find, enough for a couple of days, he reckoned, and with the discarded rifles and ammunition; then he got behind the wheel. Uluma sat beside him as they drove into the last of the night. 'You wish to fuck that woman?' she asked, leaning against him.

'Not really.' It was the safest reply he could think of at the moment.

'Then you want to fuck me,' she suggested.

Not while there's a knife within throwing distance, he thought. 'Would you believe that I actually don't want to fuck anybody right this minute?' he asked.

She considered this. 'I would like to fuck you,' she said.

'I'm sure you'd be terribly disappointed.'

'You are a great killer of men,' she pointed out. 'A mighty warrior. All the desert knows how you killed seven Italians, last year. And now—'

'I'm into double figures,' he agreed. Christ, what a crazy world.

'You take me back to my people?' she asked.

'I am hoping to get you back,' he said. 'But I must return to my people, as rapidly as possible.'

'It is many days, from here to Egypt,

193

across the desert,' she observed.

'Not by aircraft.'

'How you get aircraft?'

'By the radio.'

'But you not use the radio.'

'I will, but as far away as possible from where the enemy can trace it.'

She brooded on this. 'You leave the German woman?' she asked.

'I might. If you'll promise to behave. She is a prisoner of war.'

'I have been a prisoner of war,' Uluma said darkly.

'Not quite the same thing. You were a would-be assassin.'

'She tortured me.'

'Oh, don't let's start that again. Look. There is the command car.'

'But not the woman,' Uluma pointed out as they pulled in beside the abandoned vehicle.

'Shit,' John remarked.

Uluma had taken a quick look at the discarded stockings, which indicated that Freda had manage to free herself, and then at the tracks in the sand. 'We find her,' she said confidently.

'I don't think we'll bother to do that,' John said. He was just as happy to have Freda remove herself from Uluma's proximity; the German woman was no longer of any value, at least to him. But he didn't like the

194

thought of her dying of heat and thirst in the desert.

'She tortured me,' Uluma pointed out, yet again.

'And you'll be tortured some more if the Jerries get hold of you again. I think we should get as far as we can before dawn.'

Which was already rising up out of the eastern sky.

Uluma obeyed with some muttering. John abandoned the command car and drove the truck into the desert. When it was full daylight, he braked, and tried the radio, using the call sign that had been agreed. To his delight, and relief, he raised an Eighth Army operator almost immediately. 'Position? We need a map co-ordinate.'

'My problem is that I don't have a map,' John said.

'Well where are you?'

'I would say sixty or seventy miles south-south-east of Tobruk.'

There was a brief silence while obviously maps were being consulted. 'Then you are about eighty miles north-west of Al-Jaghbub,' the voice said.

'Could be. But I can't go there. It's an Italian frontier fortress.'

'You are also about eighty miles north of the Calanscio Sand Sea.' The voice ignored his protest.

'That sounds about right.'

'Can you make that?'

'I doubt it. The Jerries are going to be up looking for me at any moment.'

'It's your best bet. We will have people waiting for you. You say you have vital information?'

'Yes,' John said, suspecting that if he did not, they might not after all have people looking for him.

'Then we will find you,' the voice said, confirming his suspicions. 'Can you keep in touch?'

'Probably not,' John said. 'This is a battery-operated set. Over and out.'

'They come?' Uluma asked as he closed down the radio.

'Not exactly. We go.'

That seemed to please her, and he headed south, over a continuing rough track which he remembered from some years ago when he had crossed it with Margo as part of an, ostensibly, photographic expedition. He found that he could maintain a steady twenty miles an hour, if they could put up with the continuous jolting, but that was still four hours travelling ... with only the sand sea at the end of it.

Uluma produced food, bocadilloes and cups of thermos coffee. 'Just where have you been keeping those?' John asked, suspiciously.

'In my bag, here.'

'Which bag?'

She chuckled. 'You British are so fastidious. Do they not taste good?' He had to admit they tasted very good.

Uluma munched, contentedly. 'We are going back to my people.'

'Could be.'

'When we go back to my people, I shall be your woman.'

'I think we need to consider that, very carefully.'

'You have the woman, Cartwright, already?'

'Ah ... no.'

'There is no need to lie to me,' she pointed out.

'I am not lying. Major Cartwright is my boss. My leader. My sheikh.'

'How can a woman be a sheikh?'

'We do things differently.'

'Well, then, there is no problem, eh?'

'Well, there is. I have a woman.'

'One woman?'

'That's all I need.'

Which was a lie, he knew.

'This woman is English?'

'As a matter of fact, yes.'

'You have her in Cairo?'

'No. She's in England.'

Uluma considered this for some time. Then she remarked, 'England is a long way away. You need a woman here.'

'I need a lot of things,' John told her. 'A woman is low on the list.'

That at least shut her up for a while, as she no doubt considered the various interpretations of his remark. Meanwhile he drove south as fast as he could over the rough track. By ten o'clock he had covered some hundred kilometres, and they were surrounded by empty desert. And, so far, an empty sky. Uluma gave him some water to drink and they shared some more of the food. 'Where this airplane?' she enquired.

'I have no idea.'

'I have never flown in an airplane,' she confided.

'Well, you're not going to this time either. You're going back to your people, right?'

'I will come with you to Cairo,' she said, generously.

'Why?'

'I wish to sleep with you. Do you know what the Germans did to me?'

'You weren't going to tell me.'

'They pushed things up my ass,' she said. 'And into my sex. Then they caused me great pain. That woman was there when they did it. She laughed when she saw what they were doing.'

John was more than ever glad that he had let Freda get away – even if she probably deserved whatever had been coming to her. 'What did you do?'

'I screamed. What would you have done.'

'Probably the same.'

'Then they fingered me, all over,' Uluma said. 'The woman too. While they laughed.'

'I am sorry, Uluma.'

'When they did that, I did not know if I would ever be able to have sex again,' Uluma said.

'I can understand that.'

'So, now, I wish to find out. I would like to find out with you.'

'Well, obviously I would like to help you in any way possible—'

'You sent Sheikh Halim and I to do this thing,' Uluma said.

'Yes,' John said. 'I did. Well ... shit—' He braked and the truck slewed sideways. He had seen the tents just appearing over a low rise. But of course the Italians *would* have a post on the edge of the sand sea.

And almost certainly the post would have been informed that there was a runaway and murderous English officer in their vicinity. Uluma took out her pistol. 'We fight?'

'I don't think we have too much choice.'

Carefully she checked the magazine, then checked her spare. Then she grasped one of the rifles. John checked his tommygun and the pistol he also carried. 'How we do this?' Uluma asked.

'I think our best bet is to drive in at full speed, firing at anything we see. There can't be more than half a dozen of them, and if we take them by surprise we may just get them all.'

'You are a great fighting man,' Uluma said, admiringly. 'We will kill them all. And I will have more trophies to show my people.'

'Sounds like a good idea. You ready?'

She nodded, thrusting the rifle forward, and placing another beside her; the pistol was on her lap. John backed the truck onto the road, staring at the tents, the tops of which were just visible, although there did not seem to be any sentries on the rise, as he would have expected. But he did not have the time to work out how the Italians were thinking. 'Geronimo,' he muttered, and pressed the accelerator to the floor.

The truck bounded forward, sliding and slithering, as the track was now almost disintegrated in loose sand. It roared up the rise and down the other side. Uluma started shooting, while John concentrated on keeping the vehicle straight, then braked again immediately in front of the tents and leapt out, tommy-gun thrust forward, to check in horrified consternation. There were three men in front of the tents, sprawled on the ground, dead; their throats had been cut and at the arrival of the truck a buzz of angrily disturbed insects rose from their bodies. 'Shit,' Uluma commented. She had also jumped down and was looking into the first tent. 'They are all dead.'

John scratched his head. 'Then let's get out of here.'

'We must see–' She stood above the dead men, muttering to herself; their pants had been torn off and they had already been castrated. John felt distinctly sick. 'There must be food,' Uluma said, and went into the larger tent.

John retreated to the truck to wipe his brow, and looked at the sky. This was warfare at a level even he had not encountered before. Then he saw the plane, coming low over the sandhills to either side of the track. 'Take cover!' he bellowed, and ran away from the tents and the truck.

Uluma emerged from the tent, her bag again full, saw the plane, and also ran. The aircraft swept low, wings spitting red. Uluma gave a little shriek and threw herself to one side, disappearing into a hollow. John was sprawled on the sand, all manner of emotions flitting through his mind. Uluma was an absolute savage, but the thought of her being torn up by bullets after what had already happened to her...

The plane was circling for another run. John got up, ran to a hollow of his own, lay on his stomach, the tommy-gun cradled against his shoulder. The plane swooped lower yet, not firing now, but searching; he could see the leather helmets in the cockpit, peering down, one man pointing.

He opened fire, and the wings waggled as the startled pilot took evasive action. The plane had shot past and now it was turning again. But as it did so, there was another burst of firing from a new direction. This time the plane was hit, and there was a little puff of smoke from the engine. Again the wings waggled as the machine sought to gain some height. John stood up to obtain a better aim and fired again, but missed, or the bullets fell short. The plane straightened, gained some height, and then suddenly dived, hitting the ground with an enormous whumpff. There was an immediate explosion, and a pillar of smoke and flame shot skywards.

John sank to his knees in a mixture of relief and exhaustion. Then he looked over his shoulder at the line of men coming over the ridge behind him. With them was a woman: Margo.

Seven

The Counter-Stroke

Ali was at her side, as were several of his tribesmen; the machine-gun remained where they had been firing it, in the dip beyond. John could not believe his eyes.

'We listened on the radio,' Margo explained. 'To both sides. About how you have been committing mass murder again.'

'It was them or me.'

'It always is,' she agreed. 'Now let's get the hell out of here. That pilot may have had time to radio. And we have a plane coming for us tomorrow morning.'

'Uluma!' he said.

'We heard about her too. Where is she?'

John ran back to where Uluma had disappeared, gasped in relief as he saw her sitting up, spitting sand, but also cleaning sand from her pistol. 'Are you all right?' he asked.

'Shit,' she growled, then saw Ali standing above her. 'My lord!'

'I am glad you survived,' Ali said.

'She's had a hard time,' John said.

'She can tell us about it as we go,' Margo suggested.

There were camels waiting for them, as well the machine-gun, all in the next hollow; had the aircraft been less intent on strafing the truck it would surely have seen them, only a hundred yards further on. 'You took a hell of a risk,' John pointed out, as they loaded the machine-gun and mounted up.

'That is war,' Ali said. 'But you were taken by the enemy and escaped ... that is a great feat of arms.'

'I had Uluma.'

'I know. A splendid woman. She was with my father when he died. She has told me this. And that they treated her very badly. But she has survived. I would take her as my wife.'

'Ah ... would? Is there a reason why you cannot? I think it is the reward she deserves.'

'She has been had by other men,' Ali pointed out.

'I assure you–'

'Oh, not you, Warrey effendi. But the Germans, and the Italians ... they are terrible people.' He gazed at the desert over which their camels were hurrying. 'There is another reason.'

'Oh, yes?' John asked, with a sinking heart.

'She wishes to be *your* wife.'

'Ah. That's not possible.'

'Because she has been had by other men.

But I have been told this is not the same in your world.'

'Ah, yes. But, you see. I am already married. And we British—'

'Are only allowed one wife. Major Cartwright has explained this to me. It is barbaric.'

'Absolutely. Major Cartwright...' he frowned. 'Discussed marriage with you?'

'I asked her to become my wife.'

John scratched his head. 'You do realise that she is old enough to be your mother?'

'Is that a problem?'

'And that she, too, has been had by other men?' He felt it was caddish to mention the matter, but he also felt it had to be done.

'But it is different in the West,' Ali said again. 'She is a lot of woman. Are you saying that she not a virgin?'

'You mean you didn't ask her?'

'I did not think it would be proper.'

'Well I can assure you she's not. She also was a prisoner of the Italians for a while.'

It was Ali's turn to say, 'Ah. Anyway, she refused me, because she said she could never be a wife. She could only be *the* wife.'

'I can believe that. And you weren't prepared to give up your other wives.'

'What was I to do with them?'

Quite a dilemma for a sixteen-year-old boy, John reckoned.

It was mid-morning before another aircraft appeared, high in the sky. The Bedouin went to ground as John had taught them, spreading well out, nestling in hastily dug foxholes. But the plane's search was cursory, and it did not find them. 'That was a spot of luck,' Margo said, as they gulped a hasty meal of dates and water before resuming their journey. 'Seems they've lost interest in you.'

'That's because they have more important things on their minds. What day is it?'

'Wednesday the twenty-ninth of June.'

'Shit! When is that plane coming?'

'Dawn tomorrow morning, if we get to the landing strip in time. What's the hurry?'

'Rommel launches his attack on El Alamein the day after tomorrow morning.'

She turned her head, sharply. 'How do you know?'

'It's my, our, business to find these things out, right? I also happen to know he's meaning to turn the Qattara Depression.'

'That would be a hell of a risk.'

'He's a man who takes risks. And if it came off, it would guarantee him victory. He'd be in Cairo before Auchinleck could get back to Alexandria.'

'Jesus,' she muttered. 'Can't we radio that information?'

'With the Axis listening in?'

'Um. We'll pray for the plane.'

They rode into the afternoon, exhausted

and suffering from the heat, but Ali understood the seriousness of the situation and made his people keep going, foregoing their usual siesta when the sun was at its hottest. 'Just like old times,' John remarked, riding beside Margo.

'You can say that again. I see you have even accumulated a new woman.'

'In a manner of speaking. And you're a fine one to talk, as you've been having nooky with the sheikh.'

'He has not laid a finger on me,' she said. 'He's a perfect gentleman.'

'I was thinking of mental nooky. You should've gone for it. Weren't you saying only the other day that you'd like to spend the rest of your life out here? And with a sixteen-year-old boy. Never a dull moment.'

'I'm still considering it,' she said. 'Maybe after the War is over.'

'I won't hold my breath.'

They kept going all night, half asleep in their saddles.

'I think we're riding your camels to death,' John said.

Ali shrugged. 'They will survive.'

'What is the situation in the village?'

'It is destroyed. But we will rebuild it. Will the Italians come back again?'

'If they win the battle they're about to fight, yes.'

'Can you stop them doing this?'
'I can try. If I get back to Egypt in time.'
He nodded. 'The plane will come.'

At dawn they reached the flattened sand which was the airstrip. Here they found some more of the tribe, and Bingham. He looked terrible, and John realised he was still in considerable pain. 'Is the plane coming?' he asked.

'We believe it is,' John told him.

The Bedouin were saying their prayers, as the sun rose out of the east. 30 June. John could imagine the seething activity up north, with the British still unaware exactly when the storm was going to break, or how. He stood up, scanned the horizon.

Uluma stood beside him. 'You take me with you?'

'I don't think I can this time,' he said. 'The plane will only take three besides the pilot.'

'I can sit on your knee,' she suggested.

'It's a matter of weight, and trim ... look, I will come back.' Now, why had he said that? Just to keep her happy? Or simply because he could not say no to a woman?

'When?'

'As soon as I can. There is to be a great battle. I will come back when it is over.'

'I will wait,' she said, apparently content.

'The plane!' Margo pointed.

208

Bingham was loaded into the back, Margo and John sat immediately behind the pilot. 'You go to victory,' Ali assured them.

'That's the idea.' John looked into the crowd for Uluma, but she was not to be seen. She was genuinely grief-stricken.

'It utterly defeats me, the effect you seem to have on women,' Margo remarked as they took off. 'Some women.'

'Aren't you lucky you're not some women,' he countered.

To avoid any risk of encountering enemy aircraft they flew directly east and landed at Cairo. Here an ambulance was waiting for Bingham. John shook the pilot's hand. 'You'll make it,' he said. 'When next I go into the desert, I want you as my pilot.'

'Don't make it too soon,' Bingham said, managing a smile.

Another plane was standing by, their pilot having radioed ahead, and John hastily transferred.

'Aren't you even going to change your clothes?' Margo enquired.

'Later.'

An hour later he had landed in Alexandria and was being driven to Eighth Army command headquarters, some distance east of Alamein. He had not liked what he saw in Alexandria, where there was the usual evidence of a complete breakdown in control, with long queues outside the banks and streams of vehicles leaving the city to drive south, and now he liked even less of what he saw of morale as he was driven out to Alamein. But at Army Headquarters there was an air of calm, although he could tell at a glance that here too morale was low.

John was shown immediately in to the commanding general. 'Warrey! You've been having an adventurous time, I understand. Doing one of your Houdini acts on the Germans.'

'I was lucky, sir.'

'So you said the last time. But you weren't lucky enough to do Rommel.'

'No, sir, I was not.'

'Well...' Auchinleck studied the map on his desk. 'All we can do is wait, now. We're as prepared as we ever will be. We've done our boxes. And every day he delays, our reinforcements get closer. American tanks, Warrey. Grants. That's what we've been promised. So—'

'The Afrika Korps will attack at dawn tomorrow, sir.'

Auchinleck raised his head, sharply. 'You're not claiming Rommel told you his plans?'

'No, sir. But he was unwise enough to interview me in his office.'

'And you kept your eyes open. Well done. Anything else?'

210

'Yes, sir. He's not as strong as you think. I don't think he has more than a couple of hundred tanks fit for service, and half of those are Italian.'

Auchinleck stroked his chin. 'Are you sure of this?'

'Again, sir, I was taken up virtually to their front line. There is only one road.'

And with that small force he thinks he can break through our lines? Mind you, we'll still be outnumbered as regards tanks.'

'He does intend a frontal attack, sir. But only as a holding operation. He plans to win by a flank attack.'

'That's not possible.' Auchinleck pointed. 'You told me that wasn't possible, Warrey.'

'I said he could not pass through the Qattara Depression, sir. He knows that. He means to go south of it.'

Auchinleck frowned as he studied the map. 'Damned risky.'

'Yes, sir. But he's prepared to take that risk.'

'If he commits the majority of his tanks to that route, he's exposing himself to a counter-attack up here.'

'I don't think he is contemplating taking *such* a risk, sir. But he knows you are expecting large reinforcements, a lot more than he is likely to get with the Germans so heavily committed in Russia. So he knows he has to win now. Even a limited column,

211

if it gets round behind the Depression, could tear Cairo apart.'

Auchinleck continued to study the map. 'And if I take you at your word, Warrey, and start moving troops south of the Depression, and his aircraft spot the movement, he will then launch a frontal attack upon our weakened position. And I would almost certainly get the chop.'

'Yes, sir. But with respect, sir, he is going to launch that frontal attack in any event. And in his position, the flanking movement will have to be of a limited size.'

'How limited?'

I would have thought not more than a squadron of tanks.'

'Who, if they can get round the Depression, could still, as you say, cause havoc. You used that southern route with a squadron of the Seventh Armoured Brigade, back in 1940, didn't you?'

I did, sir,' John said, heart pounding.

'So you probably know it as well as anyone in the Army,' Auchinleck mused. 'I could just about spare you one squadron of tanks. Do you know a fellow called Blanchard?'

This time John's heart leapt. 'I do, sir. He was my CO on that raid. I didn't know he was still about.'

'Well, he is. He's a colonel now. But as you say, he knows you, and he knows the desert almost as well as you do. What will Rommel do, exactly?' He gestured John to come round and look at the map himself.

'Well sir, it is my estimation that he already has his flanking force in position at Al-Jaghbub. From Al-Jaghbub, and swinging south of the Depression, it is approximately four hundred miles to Cairo. I assume he has made adequate fuelling arrangements, so that with dedicated men he can reach Cairo in two days.'

'Surely we will be able to pick him up from the air, and bomb the hell out of him.'

'Yes, sir. So he will have to travel by night, which will double the time. But he will wish to make all possible speed, thus my guess is that he will head for Bahariya Oasis, from where there is a good road, well, relatively speaking, north-west to Cairo.' John jabbed the map. 'It's also a well-used road by the locals. My guess is that if he can reach the road he will chance his arm in daylight against the RAF, on the basis that they'll have a problem trying to bomb him without hitting civilians. Civilians who are officially on our side.'

Auchinleck continued to stroke his chin. 'He will have to be stopped by ground forces. By you and Blanchard. Can you get there in time?'

'From our position here it is two hundred miles to Bahariya. Provided we can be fuelled, a squadron of tanks could get there in nine hours.'

'So we can get there before him, unless he has already started moving.' Auchinleck picked up his phone. 'Rogers? I wish a concentrated air reconnaissance patrol put out over Al-Jaghbub. Yes, I know they will probably be shot at. But I need to know if there are any troop movements in that position. Now, man, now.' He thumbed the phone again. 'Metson? I want a squadron of bombers standing by to attack in the south. Yes, the south. I'll tell you where and when.' Another thumbing of the phone. 'Smith? Locate Colonel Blanchard and have him report to my caravan. Now.'

He hung up. 'Hopefully the reconnaissance aircraft will locate those tanks, and then the air force should be able to deal with it. Just in case they can't, I'll send Blanchard's squadron to Bahariya. You will accompany him as guide. I don't want a single one of those Panzers to get through, Warrey.'

'Yes, sir.'

Blanchard arrived in half an hour, looking as always massively calm, but clearly delighted to see John. 'I heard a rumour you were back,' he said. The two men clasped hands.

Auchinleck had waited with his usual patience. Now he outlined the situation.

214

'Understood, sir,' Blanchard said. 'I will need logistical back-up.'

'Arrange whatever you require,' Auchinleck said. 'And keep in touch. Now move it.'

'How many of the old squadron are left?' John asked as they hurried to the squadron laager.

'We lost Layton,' Blanchard said. 'And too many of the others. That was during that fight a month ago. The bastards came at us from every direction. Bigger, faster, and still using those eighty-eight anti-aircraft guns as anti-tank weapons. It was grim.'

'I can imagine,' John said, recalling the first German counter-attack in the spring of the previous year when he had first been taken prisoner, having watched the British tanks being shot to pieces.

'They keep promising us bigger and better machines,' Blanchard said. 'American jobs. Grants and perhaps even Shermans. But they haven't got here yet. What I'm saying is, if the RAF don't stop this lot, we may have a problem. This box idea is a waste of time. They may be unassailable themselves, but they are too widely spread out. They can't provide local support, with the result that the Axis tanks just run riot over the rest of the field. And once the fellows in the boxes get the idea that the enemy is behind them, morale goes down the drain. However...' he held out a tank regiment beret. 'Welcome back. I bet you lost the last one I gave you.'

The first face John saw at the depot was Harry Plassey, with whom he had also fought the previous year. 'Johnnie!' They shook hands. 'What's up?'

'We're moving out,' Blanchard said.

'The whole squadron?' Plassey looked west; the British Army was dug in, with various boxes, or strongpoints, utilising hillocks where possible. So skilful was the camouflage it was difficult to tell they were in the middle of an army at all. Equally, beyond them, the desert looked empty. 'Not another withdrawal? The boss said we were going to fight here.'

'We are,' Blanchard said. 'Ours is a special mission. Hopefully we'll be back for the main event. Now,' he told his assembled officers. 'Speed is of the essence. We will be followed by our support group, including tankers, but we can't wait for them. They will be there to refuel us after the battle, if there is one.'

'But we cannot carry sufficient fuel to reach Bahariya Oasis, find an enemy, and fight him,' someone objected.

'Exactly. So we are going to rendezvous with bowsers at Birket Qarun. That is on the Cairo-Bahariya road. Once we're topped up we're good for the next twenty-four hours. Right? So move it. Johnnie, you're coming with me.'

It was now past noon, and the tank crews snatched a hasty early lunch while their vehicles were being checked out. By two o'clock they were on the road, watched by amazed spectators from other units. 'Running away, are we?' a shirtless soldier shouted.

Blanchard, sharing his cupola with John, gave him two fingers. 'This really is like old times,' he said. 'Now tell me what you've been doing for the past six months? I heard a rumour you got married.'

'I did.'

'Congratulations. Someone you knew, or just a passing fancy?'

'A childhood sweetheart.'

'Hm. I'm not sure that's to be recommended. And since returning here?'

John told him about being captured, briefly. He did not mention either Margo or Uluma, or the mission to assassinate Rommel, giving the impression that he had just been trying to stir up the Senussi. 'You live too exciting a life,' Blanchard remarked.

They reached Birket Qarun at dusk, and as arranged the bowsers were waiting to top them up. So was a crowd of interested Egyptians. 'I wonder how many of these are German agents?' Plassey muttered.

'They'll need radios to do us any harm,'

217

John pointed out.

Blanchard was on *his* radio. 'Air reconnaissance has found nothing,' he said, peering at John over the top of the set.

'Odd,' John remarked. 'Did they look at Al-Jaghbub?'

'They did, and were chased off by anti-aircraft fire.'

'So the tanks could still be in the town, concealed.'

'Well, if they are, they're leaving it a bit late,' Blanchard said. 'You couldn't have made a mistake, by any chance, old man?'

John studied the map. 'They looked at Siwa Oasis, too?'

'They did. Nothing there either, and no sign of any recent activity.'

'They spoke to the garrison down there?'

'There isn't a garrison down there any more, John. They were withdrawn to hold Alamein.'

John chewed his lip. 'You mean they didn't see *anything*?'

'Nothing worth reporting, apparently. A few tracks.'

'Where? East of Al-Jaghbub?'

'East of Siwa. But that doesn't mean a lot. There's been quite a lot of action down there. Beginning with us, remember?'

'Get them again,' John said. Blanchard raised his eyebrows. 'What they consider not worth reporting and what we might consider worth knowing are not necessarily the same things,' John pointed out.

Blanchard nodded to his operator. 'They'll sweep again at dawn, sir,' the radio operator said, after calling.

'By which time the enemy tanks could have advanced a hundred and fifty miles,' John grumbled.

'Can't be helped. They won't see anything at night.'

'I really would appreciate a further report, on what they saw today,' John said. 'Everything, however unimportant.'

Blanchard nodded. 'Raise that, Wilkins,' he told his radio operator. 'Let's you and me have a drink,' he suggested to John, and the officers left the tank, now surrounded by even more spectators, as it was dusk and the shops and bazaars were emptying.

'You go fight?' enquired one Egyptian lad.

'We fight for Egypt,' Blanchard told him.

The boy preferred not to offer an opinion on that. 'You go Bahariya?'

'Where we go is our business,' Blanchard snapped. 'Piss off.' The boy rejoined his fellows at a respectful distance, and Blanchard poured John, himself and Plassey each a shot of whisky. 'If you're right, Johnnie,' he said. 'Will they be in Bahariya before us?'

'I'll tell you that when I get the report,' John said.

The squadron sergeant major saluted. 'Refuelling complete, sir.

'Have the men had a meal?'

'Not all of them, sir.'

'See that they do, and prepare to move out in one hour. And, Sergeant Major, see if you can keep these damned people away from the tanks.'

'Yes, sir.' The sergeant major saluted, and a few minutes later they could hear him bellowing in the distance. The officers' batmen prepared a meal for the tank commanders – strictly bully beef and beans and coffee. John did not have a batman, but Blanchard's man did for them both.

They had not finished eating when the radio operator, Wilkins arrived with a sheet of paper. 'They weren't too happy, sir,' he confided.

'I can imagine,' Blanchard said. 'This what you wanted?'

John chewed slowly as he scanned the paper. 'Heavy track marks north of Al-Jaghbub. That's reasonable. No evidence of armour in Jaghbub; heavy anti-aircraft fire. As if they had something to hide. Some tracks evident east of Jaghbub. No sign of armour in Siwa. Some tracks evident east of Siwa. Arab encampment twelve miles south-east of Siwa. No evidence of armour. No tracks east of Arab encampment... Holy shit!'

'Found something?'

'Arab encampment twelve miles south-east of Siwa? The only Senussi in that vicinity are the chaps I went to see, and they were a good deal west of that. What is more, there is no way they were going to move east, into Egyptian territory, no matter whose side they're on.'

'So who are this lot?'

'That lot, concealed by the tents, are a squadron of German tanks.'

Blanchard frowned. 'How can you be sure? These could be another lot of Arabs.'

'Two reasons, William. Firstly, Arabs camp where there is water. There is no water twelve miles south-east of Siwa. Secondly, there are no tracks east of the so-called Arab encampment.'

Blanchard gave a low whistle, and studied the map. 'If they are there...' he made a mark at the position south-east of Siwa, 'they are a hundred and seventy miles from Bahariya. We are a hundred and forty. We can still be there ahead of them.'

'Except that the word is 'was',' John said. 'My bet is that they left their encampment a couple of hours ago, as soon as their commander felt the RAF were done for the day. They'll have been listening to our radio.'

'Shit,' Blanchard commented. 'Then we'd better get a move on. Gentlemen!' The commanders hurried for their tanks, and the squadron roared off into the night, cheered by the Egyptians.

Now at last the road was empty, and they could make good time. The moon had risen, and the desert was bathed in sharp light, and equally sharp shadow. Yet it was one of the longest nights of John's life, especially as no one had any idea what was happening to the north. Auchinleck's position was a strong one, but then Tobruk had always been considered unassailable. Yet Rommel had taken it by assault so quickly no one had had a chance to react. Until it was too late.

The man was certainly a genius at tactical warfare. But he was not a god, John kept telling himself. His victories were gained by imaginative strokes such as turning the Qattara Depression. If that could be checked...

'Squadron halt!' Blanchard said into his VHF mike. Ahead of them were the lights of Bahariya.

'Talk about blackout,' Blanchard remarked. 'Think they're there already?'

'No,' John said, praying he was right. 'There hasn't been sufficient time, and if they were there, there'd be no lights. They can't know we're coming.'

They peered into the darkness with their binoculars; it was just coming up to three, and the desert night was cold and still; there was hardly any breeze. But what there was came from the west. 'We should hear them long before we see them,' John said.

'Time for a cup of tea,' Blanchard said. 'Pass the word back, Sergeant Major. But no lights.'

The men brewed the tea in the shadow of their tanks, strung out along the road, while John grew more and more anxious as no sound came from the expected direction or any other direction. 'Raise HQ, Corporal Wilkins,' he said, 'and tell them that we need that reconnaissance down here at first light.'

Wilkins obliged, and held the earphones away from his head. 'All hell is breaking loose up there, sir. Rommel is attacking. HQ says it has no planes to spare at the moment.'

'Shit,' John commented.

'It was what you said would happen,' Blanchard pointed out.

John looked at his watch. Four. There had been eight hours of darkness. In eight hours the Germans could have covered a hundred and fifty miles or more. They had to be within earshot. 'Shall we advance?' Blanchard asked.

John took off his beret and looked into it, seeking inspiration. Then he snapped his fingers. 'We, I, have been assuming that they'd stick to the tracks and then the road, for greater speed.'

'Seems sensible.'

'Suppose they didn't?'

'Why shouldn't they? You yourself said they can't know we're here.'

'I could have been wrong. Maybe one of those gyppoes did have a radio. Or more likely, the Jerries have cracked our code and have been reading our signals.'

'So you reckon they could have turned back.'

'I don't think they'll have turned back. I reckon they may have left the track and cut across the desert. They'd be clear of the Depression by now.'

'Using the desert would cut their speed in half,' Blanchard objected.

'True. But it would also cut thirty or forty miles off the distance they have to cover, and if they moved early enough, they could be almost behind us already.'

'Shit, Johnnie, you sure know how to cheer a fellow up,' Blanchard grumbled. 'So what do we do? Pull back to cover Cairo?'

'I think we need to find and destroy those Jerry tanks. If we leave them alone, there's no saying where they'll go. They could even swing up behind Auchinleck, and cause all manner of problems.'

'But if we don't know where they are–'

'We have to find out. Look, you hold the

road with the main body, just in case they're still coming by the obvious route and maybe have been delayed. Give me Plassey and a troop of tanks, and I'll cut across the desert for a while and see what I can find. If they do come up the road, engage them and shout for us.'

'And if you run into the lot of them with just one troop of tanks?'

John grinned. 'We'll scream rape and you can come and get us.'

John and Plassey had been out on their own before, back in that famous raid in 1940. Now they shared the cupola on Plassey's tank, bodies pressed against each other, as the tank troop left the road and began crossing the desert as fast as they dared. 'I seem to remember that the last time we did this together one of my tanks lost a track,' Plassey said. 'And that was in daylight.'

'Keep your fingers crossed,' John said. 'It's the same for both sides.'

They drove due west for an hour, then stopped engines and listened. 'Not a damn thing,' Plassey said.

John supposed that tank commanders were not the most reliable people at hearing things, locked up as they were for so much of their time in a confined space with an engine roaring just beneath them. But he could not hear anything either. 'So we keep going,' he said.

Plassey flashed his torch at his commanders – they were maintaining radio silence – and the tanks were about to start out again when the sergeant in command of the rearmost vehicle called out, 'I hear engines, sir.'

'Where?'

'Bearing two-seven-eight, sir.'

'Shit! They're in front of us,' Plassey complained.

'Full speed,' John suggested.

Plassey signalled, and the tanks moved forward as fast as they dared, bouncing and rattling over the uneven ground, risking imminent damage to the tracks but getting away with it. Half an hour later Plassey again brought them to a halt. Now they could all hear the growl of engines in front of them. 'We're catching them up,' John said,

'How many, do you reckon?'

John listened, and tried to calculate. But to the east the sky was now lightening; it was five o'clock. 'Let's find the tracks,' he said.

Once again they advanced, relying on the fact that as the Germans were moving they would not hear the British engines. Fifteen minutes later they crossed the tracks. 'At least a dozen,' Plassey said.

'Then I would say this is their main body,' John said.

'Right. We'll signal Blanchard to get this way as rapidly as possible.'

'The Germans will hear us,' John pointed out.

'Then we'll have to hold them up,' Plassey said with a grin. 'The troop will attack.'

The message was sent to Blanchard, and the tank troop rolled forward. John didn't really have the time to reflect that this had to be a suicide mission; he had virtually created the scenario himself. They topped the next rise, and looked down ... on fifteen German tanks which had just turned and were coming towards them. Their message had certainly been heard and understood.

'Here we go!' Plassey said into his radio. 'Cut through them, then turn and head back for the road. Hopefully we'll meet the Colonel coming this way.' But Blanchard had to be at least two hours away.

John dropped down from the cupola, and Plassey followed, banging the hatch shut and then taking his place before the range-finder. 'Traverse right,' he told the gunner. 'Up two degrees. Range: six hundred yards. Fire.'

The gun exploded and the interior of the tank became filled with acrid smoke. 'Missed the bastard,' Plassey growled. 'Fuck it. Traverse left, down three. Fire.'

Once again the tank bucked with the recoil of the gun. 'What the hell is the matter with that thing?' Plassey demanded.

'They're travelling at some speed, sir,' the gunner pointed out.

'Clarke has bought it, skipper,' the sergeant said, peering through the slit above the wheel.

'Shit!' Plassey growled. 'Right! Right, swing right! Traverse!'

John was aware of a huge bang which left him too dazed to understand what had happened for a moment. 'Out!' Plassey bawled. 'Get out!'

John could hardly hear him, but now he smelt smoke and scorching heat. The gunner was already up the short ladder, throwing open the hatch. He scrambled out, gave a shriek, and turned half round before collapsing, his legs still dangling against the ladder. 'Move him!' Plassey commanded. 'Johnnie! Up you go.'

John hesitated. 'So you may get hit,' Plassey said. 'Stay here and you'll cook.'

John grasped the gunner's legs and heaved the body up and out. The gunner rolled across the front apron and hit the ground beyond. But that saved John's life. Again there was a burst of firing, but directed against the already dead body. John, following, also rolled across the apron and hit the ground beside the gunner's bullet-riddled body, but now with the tank between him and the enemy. The heat was intense, exactly as it had been next to the burning aircraft – was it only a week ago? He knew he had to get away before the tank exploded, but he was thinking of Plassey.

He pushed himself up, saw the driver emerge from the cupola and roll down the side; he had been hit in the explosion and was a bloodstained mess – when he hit the ground he did not move. Plassey was last. At least the firing at their tank was over, the Germans having recognised that it was out of action. But Plassey was caught in the explosion as the tank went up. The force of the blast threw John backwards and he hit the ground with a thump that knocked all the breath from his body. He rolled, gasping, regained his knees, saw nothing but flame in front of him. Somewhere in that holocaust was Plassey and his crew.

He tried to go forward, was driven back by the heat, and fell down again. He listened to the sound of firing from all around him; his ears seemed to have returned to normal. In fact, apart from a few singes and several bruises, he seemed to be unhurt.

And now there was noise close at hand. He realised he was lying down again, and raised his head to watch tanks rolling out of the desert behind him – British tanks.

Eight

The Patient

John stood to attention beside his bed, and the general came in, followed by a staff officer, and of course, by Sister. He still swayed slightly. Although he had been allowed to exercise, indeed made to do so, regularly for the past week, he was still weak at the knees. 'Well, Warrey,' Auchinleck remarked. 'Nine lives, is it?'

'A few less by now, sir. But I can't imagine why they have kept me here for four weeks.' He gave Sister a censorious glance.

'Yes.' Auchinleck glanced down the list. 'There's quite a lot here. In one fortnight you managed to survive being torpedoed and left adrift for several days, a plane crash, being taken prisoner by the enemy, and a brew-up. The principal problem seems to be extreme exhaustion. I'm not surprised. I think you'll have to go home for a spell of R and R.'

'Please, sir,' John said. 'That isn't necessary.'

Auchinleck raised his eyebrows. It was very rare for any soldier not to welcome a return to England – and he knew that this officer had only recently been married. 'There is also the matter of these recommendations,' he went on, looking at another list given him by the staff officer. 'For distinguished conduct, by Colonel Blanchard, in that you led a vastly inferior number of tanks to attack the enemy in your determination to prevent his flanking movement–'

'With respect, sir,' John protested. 'It was Captain Plassey's decision to attack without waiting for the rest of the squadron.'

'Modesty is unbecoming in these circumstances, Warrey,' the general admonished. 'I am reading your commanding officer's report. Then there is one for distinguished conduct, by Sheikh Ali ben Halim al-Fuad, for saving his people from destruction at the hands of the Italians.'

'You mean they actually survived?' John asked.

Auchinleck gave him an old-fashioned look. 'And then there is a recommendation for bravery in pulling a wounded officer from a burning wreck, while severely injured yourself.'

'But sir, I didn't. They were all dead, anyway.'

'This recommendation was made by Major Cartwright. It refers to your saving the life of Flying Officer Bingham.'

'Good God!' He had forgotten all about that.

'Major Cartwright has recommended you for the Victoria Cross.' John sat down without thinking, or asking permission. 'And lastly, of course, there is my own recommendation for your escape from German hands, and the information you managed to bring us, without which we might not have won the Battle of El Alamein.'

John raised his head. 'You mean we won that battle, sir?'

'Well, let me put it this way: we didn't lose it. But we might have done had those Jerry tanks got round our rear. As it is, Rommel has withdrawn to lick his wounds. So, all round you are to be congratulated, Warrey. You will certainly get promotion, although I am doubtful that you will get the Victoria Cross. I agree that you should have it, but you weren't actually engaged with the enemy at the time you saved Bingham's life, eh? We'll see what can be done. I am sure your new commanding general will do his best for you.'

John stood up again. 'Are you leaving, sir?'

A shadow crossed Auchinleck's face. 'I may have stopped Rommel getting to Alexandria and Cairo, Warrey. But I didn't actually beat the bugger. Winston himself is coming out for a chat. He's due tomorrow, but I think I have the message. Yes, I am leaving. Your new commanding general will be General Alexander.'

'And the Eighth Army, sir?' He knew that Auchinleck had sacked General Ritchie, after the fall of Tobruk.

'General Gott will take over there.'

'General Gott,' John said, thoughtfully.

'Have you met him?'

'Yes, sir. I shared a plane with him, a couple of weeks ago.'

'By Jove, so you did. Well, as soon as you are out of here I am sure he will find something for you to do. If you are determined to stay here. I'm told that in any event they mean to keep you in here for another month. Good luck, Warrey.'

John stood to attention. 'And to you, sir.'

The door closed. 'Now, Sister,' John said. 'What's all this nonsense about me staying here for another month? I'm as fit as a fiddle.'

'I'm afraid we don't agree with you, Captain,' Sister said. 'Have you looked at your back recently?'

'It doesn't hurt.'

'That's because a lot of the skin, and the nerve ends, are dead. You are very lucky you haven't got gangrene. Have you any idea what it was those fuzzy-wuzzies coated you with?'

'They were not fuzzy-wuzzies,' John pointed out. 'They practice a more honourable and religious way of life than we do. And no, I have no idea what they used. Some kind of ointment. But it did the trick.'

'In a manner of speaking,' she remarked, disdainfully. 'There are also various cuts and bruises not yet entirely healed. But the most important thing is general exhaustion. In the four weeks you have been here you've been sleeping twelve hours in every twenty-four.'

'Because you're sedating me.'

'Not that much. Would you mind getting back into bed? We are trying to make you fit enough to resume service, Captain Warrey. There is absolutely no point in your going back into the desert, or up to the front line, in your present condition. Another month will do wonders.'

He supposed she was right. 'And I am to spend the entire month in solitary confinement? I want to be moved into a ward. I'm sure you need this bed for more serious cases.'

'It is official policy that all intelligence officers should be kept in private wards,' she said. 'Suppose you started talking in your sleep?'

'I wonder what I'd say. So tell me,' he said, 'where is the front line? Still at El Alamein?'

'How should I know?' she asked. 'This is Cairo.'

'Well, can I write a letter?'

'Who to?' She was suspicious.

'I have a wife, who will be expecting to hear from me about now.'

'When did you last see her?'

'At the beginning of June.'

'And it is now the fourth of August. She will hardly expect to be hearing from you already. I'm afraid all Egypt is a top secret area, Captain. For the next couple of months, at any rate.'

'Do the Egyptians know this?' John asked, innocently.

Obviously they didn't. John spent another restless and irritable fortnight, fretting at the inactivity while understanding that he was gradually being returned to full health and strength, even more frustrated at being unable to communicate with Aileen – he received one letter from her but as she was blissfully unaware that anything had happened to him it was filled with sweet nothings – until at visiting hours one morning a large bunch of flowers arrived, behind which was Arsinoe. 'Good God!' he said. 'How did you get in here? This is a security wing.'

'I have a friend,' Arsinoe explained. 'He works in the morgue.'

'That figures. But how did you know I was here? Don't tell me, you have another friend.'

'No, no,' she said. 'It is the same friend. He knows things. I would have come sooner, but they told me you were all asleep, most of the time.'

'I haven't been very well,' John confessed.

'So they say.'

'That is what I am saying. Are you not glad to see me?'

Actually, he was. Whatever her innumerable faults, Arsinoe was like a beam of sunlight in a dark world. 'Yes,' he said.

'I pick these flowers myself,' she said, placing them on the table.

'I didn't know you had a garden.'

'I pick them in the park.'

'Arsinoe, that is stealing.'

'They do no good in the park,' she said, and leaned across him. She smelt of musk, and her black hair flopped over his face. 'Will you not kiss me?'

He had never actually kissed Arsinoe before. Her various advances when he had been her lodger had been far more practical, and he had managed to evade those too. Now ... her mouth closed on his. 'I have missed you so,' she said. 'You come, you go, and we never have a chance to get together.'

He could not stop himself putting his arms round her. Her blouse was thin and his first stroke established that she was not wearing a brassiere. This was confirmed as she rubbed her barely concealed breasts up

237

and down his face. 'But now,' she said. 'We get together, eh?'

'My dear girl, this is a hospital.'

'That is why there is a bed,' she explained.

'But I am sick.'

'You don't look sick to me,' Arsinoe pointed out, and whipped back the sheet. 'Aha, you are not sick at all. That is a big one. I want that one inside me. I wanted this from the first time I saw you, Warrey. I will just take off my clothes, eh, and lie with you.'

'Arsinoe,' John protested.

But she was away, kicking off her shoes and lifting her blouse over her head in the same movement, 'Soroya told me,' she said, her voice faintly muffled, 'how good you are in bed. You made Soroya very happy. Now you will make me happy too, eh?'

'Arsinoe–' how he wanted to make her happy too, he thought – because of the desert, and all those who had died in the desert, and Uluma, and Freda, and the men he had killed, all bubbling away inside himself, overshadowed by the tank battle and the death of Plassey, more memories to haunt him for the rest of his life, only to be lost in the comfort a woman's arms. That was what men had wives for, in reality. Arms in which to lose reality, and enter a world of pleasant dreams. But his wife was thousands of miles away.

'And I make you good too,' Arsinoe promised, allowing her skirt and knickers to join her blouse and shoes on the floor. She was a perfectly entrancing sight. 'So good.' She advanced to the bed, and he put his arms round her, squeezing her buttocks while she gave a little squeal of pleasure.

'Captain *Warrey!*' Sister stood in the doorway like an avenging angel. 'Who is this person?'

'Ah...' John hastily released Arsinoe and dragged the sheet over himself. 'My landlady.'

'Your *what?*'

'His landlady, asshole,' Arsinoe said. Sister goggled at her in consternation.

'Ah ... I think maybe you'd better get dressed,' John suggested.

'We no have sex yet.'

'Yes, well that is going to be difficult.' Quite apart from Sister's presence, he no longer had an erection.

'What is she doing here?' Sister demanded.

'Ah ... she came to enquire about my laundry. Whether I wanted her to keep it or send it here.'

'Your laundry?'

'His laundry, asshole,' Arsinoe agreed.

'Look, will you please get dressed,' John begged.

'You come, you go...' Arsinoe giggled.

'Then you no come.' But she picked up her clothes.

'But *how* did she get here?' Sister inquired.

'Ah ... she gets about,' John said.

'I have friends,' Arsinoe said darkly, settling her blouse and fluffing out her hair as she slid her feet into the high heels.

'Well all I can say–' Sister began.

'Please don't,' John said. 'Or there'll be a punch-up. Listen, Arsinoe, I'll come and see you when I get out. That's a promise.'

'You come, you go,' Arsinoe complained, and gave another giggle. 'This time you come good, eh? I will wait.' She gave Sister an imperious glance and stalked from the room.

'She should be arrested,' Sister said. 'I will have her arrested.'

'I should think that would be a waste of time,' John said. 'I am quite sure she has slept with half the Cairo police.'

'You mean she is a ... well–'

'Actually, she isn't,' John explained. 'She never charges. She just likes doing it.'

Sister gave up. 'I came in to see if you were decent,' she said. '*Are* you decent?'

'Absolutely,' John said. 'At this moment I couldn't be more decent.'

'You have a visitor. A proper visitor.'

'Don't tell me. Major Cartwright.'

'However did you know that?'

'I'm psychic,' John told her.

240

Sister propped him up in bed and made sure his pyjamas were in a proper state. Then she arranged the bedclothes neatly. 'Please try to behave yourself,' she recommended.

'My dear Sister, Major Cartwright is my superior officer.'

She sniffed, and opened the door. 'Captain Warrey can see you now, Major,' she said.

Margo was very trim in a freshly pressed uniform, complete with new belt and sidecap, all things he knew she had lost in the desert. It was amazing the way her complexion survived her various safaris, but then she more often than not wore a veil. 'Well,' she remarked, 'quite the hero.'

Sister left the room, discreetly closing the door behind herself.

'Various people seem to think so,' John agreed. 'Thanks.'

'For what?'

'Recommending me for the VC.'

'Well, I felt I had to recommend you for something, or I wouldn't have been doing my job. I'm told you won't get it. But you might get the George Cross.'

'Sounds great. I gather Ali is holding on.'

She nodded. 'Of course, if we don't win, he's on a hiding to nothing.'

'But we will win?'

'Oh, yes,' she said confidently. 'Stuff is just

pouring up the Suez Canal.'

'You don't suppose it's pouring into Tripoli as well?'

'They're having a more difficult time, as we still hold Malta, which is right across their supply route. And we've new generals.'

'I had a lot of time for Auchinleck,' John said. 'Is this new brass any better? From what I've read, Alexander is great at last ditch evacuations. Last man on the beach at Dunkirk, led the exodus from Burma a couple of months ago ... but has he ever actually won anything?'

'There's always a first time. And there's Gott to lead the Eighth Army–'

'I've met him. He looked, and sounded, good. But is he better than Rommel?'

'When you come down to it,' Margo said seriously, 'it's the equipment that counts, nowadays. Of course it has to be well used, but it's still the ultimate factor. Rommel gained his initial victories because of that eighty-eight anti-aircraft gun, which he discovered could destroy our tanks while our two-pounders were merely bouncing off his. That shattered more than our tanks: it did for our morale, as well. But now that the Yanks are supplying us with tanks off which the eighty-eights might bounce, it'll be a different matter.'

'I don't happen to agree with you,' John said. 'It's still the man that matters. And not only at the top. Men like Plassey, who went into battle against impossible odds, just to hold the enemy up. Now there is both heroism and leadership.'

She glared at him for a few moments, then smiled. 'We never did agree on anything, did we? How much longer are you staying in this dump?'

'They tell me a fortnight.'

She got up. 'Well ... we have a lot of unfinished business. I assume you will be returning to Shepheard's?'

'I shall be returning, or going, to wherever I am sent. They are even muttering about sending me home.'

'When?' She looked genuinely concerned.

'Not for a while, if I have anything to do with it. I want to see this business finished. I've caused too many deaths not to have that satisfaction.'

'Halim still on your mind? What about wifey?'

'Wifey will have to wait. She doesn't know anything about my sojourn in the desert, anyway. So she isn't losing any sleep.'

'As I've said before, anyone who gets too close to you needs their head examined. But get in touch with me the moment they let you out.'

'Do you mean you need your head examined?'

'I'm still your immediate CO,' she pointed

out. 'I have no doubt that in a fortnight's time I shall have something for you to do.' She went to the door, checked. 'By the way, who was that bint who came scuttling down the stairs while I was waiting? Had she anything to do with you?'

'She had just got out of this bed,' John said.

Margo stared at him for several seconds. Then she said, 'You ought to be seen to,' and banged the door behind her.

'You do seem to know how to upset people,' Sister said. 'Major Cartwright came down the stairs like a clap of thunder.'

'Her problem is that she doesn't know whether she is coming or going,' John said.

'Well, I hope that's the last of them. You're not supposed to entertain women in your room, anyway.'

'I have a suspicion,' John said, 'that there may be one to go.'

Samantha arrived the next week. 'Well, hi,' she said, somewhat apprehensively from the doorway. Sister was flitting in the background. Samantha closed the door on her. 'I saw Margo in the hotel last night,' she said. 'She told me where you were.'

'And you just came along.'

'Oh, I had to get a pass,' she explained. 'Doesn't everyone?'

244

'It all depends who you are,' John said.

She digested this, then sat in the chair by the bed. Like Margo, she was in uniform, which suited her even better. 'I think I owe you an apology.'

'What for?'

'Well, the way I behaved that night.'

'I think you had a reason.'

'Maybe. But I went OTT. And you didn't take advantage of me.'

'I had a lot on my mind.'

'Like going off into the desert and all but getting yourself killed. Now you're a hero.'

'I've been a hero before,' John said. 'It didn't get me very far.'

'Well ... how long are they keeping you in here?'

'Another week.'

'Gosh, that long? Margo said you've been in here six weeks already. Are you very badly wounded?'

'I'm not wounded at all. I was pretty badly burned, so now I'm under observation.'

'But in a week you'll be right as rain,' she said enthusiastically.

'I hope so.'

'Well, you know where to find me.' She leaned over the bed and gave him a long, slow kiss. 'I really would like to make it up to you,' she whispered.

'Well,' Sister remarked. 'She is the first

245

woman to leave this room looking pleased.'

'She's an old friend,' John said. 'Tell you what, Sister, I don't think another fortnight is going to be long enough for me to recuperate properly. I think I should stay here until I'm actually posted somewhere, preferably out of Cairo.'

'A fortnight,' she said.

But three days later he had another visitor, Commander Jones.

The commander looked, as always, somewhat like a ferret. But a fairly agitated ferret, today. 'How are you?' he enquired.

'There are differing opinions about that.'

'Well, I want you out of here. There is a bit of a flap on.'

'Don't tell me Rommel is back on the attack?'

'No. It's General Gott. He's dead.'

'What did you say?'

'Killed in an air crash,' Jones said. 'Actually, he was killed a couple of weeks ago, but it's been kept under wraps. Still is.'

'Good lord. So who'll command the Eighth Army now?'

'Well as you imagine, they're rushing around like a lot of chickens with their heads cut off. Now they've come up with a chap called Montgomery.'

'Never heard of him.'

'Well, neither have a lot of people. He saw some service as a divisional commander in

France a couple of years ago. Since then he's held a command in south-east England, waiting for the invasion.'

'Which never came. Does he know the desert?'

'I don't think so.'

'So, do the powers that be really think he's the man to beat Rommel?'

'They have to try something,' Jones said. 'The thing is, we desperately need information as to what Rommel is up to. We have a lot of material coming in, and our navy and the RAF out of Malta are doing their best to stop an equivalent amount reaching Rommel. But we don't *know*. You brought in that accurate estimate of his strength just before El Alamein. He suffered severe casualties in that dust-up. We need to get some idea of his replacements, and his fuel situation, before we can think of taking him on again.'

'That's a bit of a tall order, Commander,' John said. 'When I obtained that information I was a prisoner. If I'm taken prisoner again, after having killed quite a few of the enemy, I imagine they'll shoot me.'

'We've been in touch with Sheikh Ali. He's willing to help. Anxious, even.'

'He's a glutton for punishment,' John remarked.

'Well he has his dad to avenge. Not to

mention his grandfather.'

'This could go on forever. He should hang about until he has a son himself.'

'He's only sixteen,' Jones pointed out. 'But we have to use him. The point is, his people can wander about behind the German lines almost at will, as long as they pretend to be ordinary Arabs and not Senussi. There is no way the Germans, or the Italians, for that matter, can tell the difference. Thus they can spot things, and make up lists. But they won't know what is what. To them a tank is a tank. We need to know the make of tank, and how many of each. Just as we need to know what German infantry are available to Rommel, and how many Italian. Again, the Arabs can probably find out these things for us, but they're not too good at getting them down on paper. And as I said, we need to know how he is off for fuel. We need someone on the spot to interpret and correlate all the information they bring in.'

'And I'm the only one you have. What about Margo?'

'I think Margo has had the desert for the time being. She's actually on leave. Besides, Ali specifically asked for you. He thinks you're the bee's knees.'

'All because I contrived to get his father and several of his people killed,' John mused, 'It's a strange old world, isn't it, Commander?'

'You leave tomorrow morning at dawn,' Jones said. 'Have you ever used a parachute?'

'A parachute? Good lord, no, Don't tell me–'

'We cannot use Sheikh Ali's airstrip at the moment; the Italians have bombed it to hell. His people are working on a new one, but it will not be ready for another fortnight at the earliest,' Jones explained. 'You will have to jump. I'm sorry there is no time to practice, but the pilot will show you how it's done. It really is very simple.'

'Have you ever jumped, Commander?'

'Not my scene, I'm afraid. I leave that sort of thing to you field johnnies.'

John gulped. 'And how do I get back?'

'Ali still has his radio. You will call us on the frequency he knows and uses. Then we will send a plane which will use the strip; it should be repaired by then.'

'And if it isn't?'

'I think you had better make sure that it is, Captain. I think that is everything. A car will pick you up at four a.m. ... here?'

'I don't think so,' John said. 'This could be my last mission. Can you get me discharged now?'

'I can.'

'Then have the car pick me up at Shepheard's.'

Jones gave him an old-fashioned look.

'You do realise this is as top secret as you can get.'

'Yes, sir.'

'Nobody, but nobody must know of it.'

'Yes, sir.'

'But you wish to go out and get drunk.'

'No, sir. I wish to go out and get laid.'

Jones raised his eyebrows. 'Margo? I told you, she's been given short leave.'

'Definitely not Margo.'

'I see. Well ... I'll have you discharged. Let me down on this and I'll have you cashiered.' He stood up, a slight frown creasing his forehead. 'How you handle this is up to you. I'm not going to ask questions. Just get that information.'

'Yes, sir. How much time have I got?'

'There is time, providing Rommel isn't planning another attack with sufficient forces to be awkward. The new commanding general still has to get here and take stock of the situation. He'll almost certainly want our logistics to be topped up.'

'But you don't reckon there is time for me to wait until Ali's strip is ready?'

'No,' Jones said. 'The sooner we can obtain that information the better.'

Sister glared at him from the foot of the bed. 'You are discharged,' she said, her voice like a clap of thunder.

'Great. I told you I wasn't as sick as you thought.'

'Brass,' she commented darkly, and draped a new uniform, cleaned and pressed to perfection, over a chair. The shoes shone with brown brightness. The cap badge had been polished. 'Make yourself presentable, and then dress,' she commanded. His shaving gear was also laid out, and he hastily obeyed her. She departed, banging the door behind her.

Ten minutes later an orderly knocked and entered. 'Any gear, sir?'

'I'm afraid not,' John said. No one took any notice of him as he went down the stairs; Sister had disappeared and the nurse on the reception counter did not seem to notice him. He had officially disappeared, he realised.

A staff car was waiting for him, and drove him to the hotel. Cairo sweltered in the August heat; the river was low, and somehow that seemed to accentuate the temperature. And he in any event felt that he was not really a member of this crowded world any more. Because he had just been sent to his death? There was a strong possibility of that if he was going to find out what Jones, and presumably Jones's superiors, wanted. Jones had not spelt it out, but there was only one way he was going to get the information HQ wanted –

and it was not by sitting at a safe distance evaluating reports brought in by illiterate Arabs. Auchinleck, he thought, had at least given him his orders personally. So he was entitled to feel just a little bitter.

Had he meant what he had said to Jones, to the commander's obvious disapproval? He couldn't be sure. He definitely wanted to have sex, with someone; the last woman he had held naked in his arms had been Aileen ... Aileen! She knew nothing of the life he lived, supposed that intelligence was a matter of sitting in an office correlating reports. So what was the next thing she was likely to *know* about him? A simple note: I regret to inform you that your husband has been reported as missing, and must be presumed dead. Because they wouldn't *know* either.

Outside of that ... but at this moment, and for the foreseeable future, he was no longer her husband. He no longer existed, save as a machine carrying out a mission. A machine that needed servicing. Very badly. And Arsinoe was the woman to do it. They had been trying to get together for three years. Well, she had. He had always resisted it. But he no longer wanted to resist it, and she was the woman who had put him in this mood.

He went to Reception. 'Any mail for Warrey?'

The clerk checked. 'Yes, sir. This envelope.'

OHMS. Containing a pay cheque, no doubt. Nothing from Aileen, for the simple reason that she did not know where he was.

'We have kept your room for you, sir,' the clerk said, eagerly.

'Great. Is Major Cartwright still checked in?'

'She is not here at the moment, sir. I believe she's on leave.'

'When did she leave?'

'Yesterday, sir.'

And the moment she had departed, Jones had come to see him. Now there was something to think about. 'There's no need to tell anyone I'm here.'

'Of course, sir.'

He put the envelope in his pocket and walked across the lobby to the lifts.

'Captain Warrey?'

He turned, frowning, for a moment could not place the ATS officer. But she was familiar. 'McLean,' she explained.

'Good Lord!' He peered at her. Her face was a mask of tragedy, dominated by her eyes, large and dark and luminous. He thought they were rather beautiful eyes, was surprised he had not noticed that before. But when last he had seen her it had been in a darkened aircraft. Now they were slightly swollen. She had been weeping. That figured. 'I heard about the general,' he said, lamely.

'Yes.'

'And, well ... are you stationed here, now?'

'I'm on my way home, as soon as it can be arranged.'

'Ah. Well...' But she so obviously wanted someone to hold her hand, at least for a little while. 'Let me buy you a drink.'

'I don't. Drink alcohol, I mean.'

'You're not a Muslim?'

'Of course not. It's just that... I suppose I've never tried.'

'Then I think it's time you did.' He held her arm, escorted her into the bar, which at this hour of the morning was empty. 'Morning, Sharif,' he said. 'Two Bloody Marys.'

'Yes, sir, Mr Warrey.' Sharif busied himself.

'They seem to know you very well here,' McLean said.

'Well, I've been around a few years, on and off. Do you have a first name? Mine's John.'

'Lauren.'

'That's nice. Unusual.' He picked up their drinks and led her to a table in the far corner of the room.

Lauren McLean was wearing gloves which she now took off as she sat down – and he gazed at the wedding ring. 'Mud in your eye,' he said, sipping. Sharif made brilliant Bloody Marys.

Lauren sipped also, and gave a little shudder. 'Isn't that very strong?'

'It's what the doctor ordered. I didn't know they allowed married women to go overseas.'

'They don't. I happen to be divorced.'

'Ah.'

'Well...' She also glanced at her ring, and flushed. 'Separated, actually. And I desperately needed something to do. I mean, I was already in the ATS, but that seemed such a dead end. So ... the general is ... was, an old friend of my family.'

He studied her as she spoke. Her voice was low and composed, although she was clearly under strain. Her face was a trifle sharp, perhaps made more so by the tight bun in which her dark brown hair was confined. It was not an old face – he put her down as around thirty – nor was it at all ravaged by experience or exposure, but it bore a mark of infinite tragedy. She had good legs and there was nothing wrong with the way her tunic was filled. 'So he took you on and pulled strings.' he suggested.

'Yes.'

'And you were very fond of him.'

'Yes.' Another quick flush. 'It's nothing like what you think. He was like a father to me.'

'So you said on the plane,' he reminded her.

255

'Yes.' She drank deeply, apparently without thinking. 'Gosh. That stuff does grow on one.'

John signalled the barman, while as usual asking himself what he was doing. 'It's strange, us meeting against like this,' she said. 'And you're a hero. There's talk of medals.'

'Just talk,' he said.

'And you have one already.' She touched the MC ribbon.

Sharif placed two more Bloody Marys in front of them.

'Oh,' Lauren said. 'Do you think I should?'

'Have you somewhere to go?'

'Not really, until tomorrow morning.'

'Snap.'

She emptied her first glass.

'And when you go,' he said, 'what do you go to? Or is that a secret?'

'Not really. I go back to my original unit, in the first instance. Then it's arranging motor pools and that sort of thing.' She gave a shy smile. 'Not exactly heroine-type stuff. What about you? Are you really leaving tomorrow morning too?'

'Yes, I am.'

'But that *is* top secret.'

'Yes, it is.'

She began on her second drink. 'And very dangerous, I suppose.'

'You'll have to ask me that when I come back.'

She raised her head, and he was shrouded in those huge eyes. 'But you will come back?'

'I always have. I'm an optimist.'

'Yes. Well ... I'm sorry I was so stand-offish on the aircraft. I got the idea that ... well, you were on the make. So many men are.'

'Oh, I would have been,' he agreed. 'In any other circumstances. I wasn't exactly feeling on top of the world. But usually I'm the world's biggest cad.'

She darted a glance at him. 'I don't believe that.'

'You'd better. Most heroes are cads. What I mean is, if you have the sort of adrenalin that makes you a hero, which is usually the result of carelessness, or entirely losing your temper, or being so fed up you don't give a damn, then you also have the sort of adrenalin flow that makes you want more from life than perhaps the ordinary bloke. Are you with me?'

'Oh, yes. But I don't believe you. What about the type of adrenalin flow that makes you rescue wounded men while under fire?'

'That's different. That's loyalty to your comrades. It's not something I know anything about.'

'But you've done it twice,' she pointed out. 'The reports were sent to the general, and I read them.'

'Pure fiction.'

'All right,' she said. 'So you're a cad. Prove it.' Her little pointed chin jutted at him.

'I was going to ask you if you'd care to while away a hot afternoon showering in my room. But I've changed my mind.'

'Why? Did you suddenly remember that you have a wife?'

'That's a good point. I spend a lot of time remembering that I have a wife.'

'But she doesn't understand you.' Her lip was threatening to curl.

'I doubt it. We don't know each other well enough to understand anything. Like I said, I'm a cad. I'm also scared stiff. I am very likely going to be killed sometime in the next week or two, and it's not something I want to have happen. So ... one makes little grabs at life, the good things in life, while one can. Like the condemned man ordering a bottle of champagne for his last meal. Can you understand anything of that?'

'I can. I do.' She finished her drink, got up, swayed a bit, and then regained her balance. 'That was a near run thing. I think I'd like to share your shower, Captain Warrey.'

As John held Lauren's arm to escort her across the lobby to the lifts, Sharif gave him an encouraging smile. The door closed, and the lift moved upwards. 'Listen,' he said. 'I'm not sure you really want to do this.'

'Why not?'

'You're drunk.'

'On two Bloody Marys?'

'You're not used to them.'

'True. I'm squiffy, not drunk. I'm not going to pass out on you or anything. And isn't a cold shower the recommended treatment?'

'And when you wake up, and say to yourself, what in the name of God have I done?'

She pushed her finger into his chest. 'I am not going to do that, Captain. I think you need me, right this minute. I know I need you. We're two souls who are about to be cast adrift. Maybe we have already been cast adrift. You, some time ago. Me, recently. But the timing doesn't matter.'

'I think it does.' He unlocked the door of his room.

She looked up and down the corridor. 'Do they have house detectives in places like this?'

'I'm sure they do. This is a very respectable hotel. But there is a war on, and circumstances change. If anyone knocks on my door I'll tell him to go away.'

'And if he doesn't?' She went into the room and John closed the door.

'I suppose I'd have to hit him, or something.'

She turned to face him. 'I'd like you to

believe that I have never done anything like this before.'

'Snap.'

She cocked an eyebrow. 'Oh, really? You have quite a reputation in Cairo, I have gathered.'

'Because I had an Arab mistress. Most men do. But not in places like Shepheard's.'

Lauren sat on the bed. 'And when you got tired of her, you pushed her out into the desert.'

John sat beside her and took off her cap. 'Long before I got tired of her, someone put a bullet in her gut.'

She stared at him, then absently reached out and retrieved her hat. 'I'm sorry.'

'So am I. Saying that, I mean. It was both stupid and unnecessary.'

Lauren got up. 'I don't think so at all. How long ago did this happen?'

'About a year.'

'I think you loved her.'

'Yes, I do. I mean did.'

'You mean, do,' Lauren said, and went to the door.

'Now you're offended.'

'No,' she said. 'I'm not offended. I think it must be marvellous to be loved like that. And I know it must be hell to have lost her. Do you love your wife as much?'

'I wish I knew,' John said. 'No shower?'

'There's one in my room,' she said, and

closed the door behind herself.

How stupid can you be? he asked himself. But the fact was, Soroya was going to haunt him for the rest of his life unless he found a replacement. There never could be a replacement, of course. Not for the real Soroya, who had laughed, and sworn, and been both innocent and the most worldly of women, all at the same time. Soroya had *gurgled* her way through life with an ingenuous enjoyment at being alive. Up to the very moment of her death. He did not suppose he had ever really understood her, but they had shared in a way it is given to very few people to share. It was the sharing that mattered. He had not yet achieved that pinnacle with Aileen, and he did not know if he ever would. Soroya continued to lie between them, as she did between him and any other woman, even those who were just drifting through his life.

He should have gone to Arsinoe. Arsinoe, who lived all of her life on a single level, and a very shallow one at that, was the one woman with whom he thought he could have sex, and not think of Soroya. But today he could not even consider sex with Arsinoe.

PART THREE

The Arabs

'...little of this great world can I speak,
More than pertains to feats of broil and
  battle.'

William Shakespeare

Nine

The Spy

John spent the entire day in his room, eating room service food and drinking the better half of a bottle of whisky.

He had been given a mission such as this once before, when General O'Connor had wanted to find out just how many men and tanks the Germans were committing to North Africa. That had also been a suicide job, save that it wasn't – he had been going to wear uniform, and at that time he had only killed in open combat. Besides, he was dealing with Italians, who were far more inclined to obey the rules than the Germans. The worst he had expected, presuming he had not tried to resist arrest, would have been prison. In the event, he had never even got started, because Rommel had struck first – as he had a habit of doing. And he had still wound up a prisoner!

Things were different now. He was a wanted man, by both Italians and Germans, and he suspected it was the Germans who would be given first pick. Overlying all of that was the consideration that he must again involve Ali and his people in deadly danger. So Ali wanted it. He was a young man anxious to prove himself to his people, and his fellow sheikhs. He also had both a father and a grandfather to avenge. But the possible cost ... on the other hand, if the Germans and the Italians were really to be expelled from North Africa, the cost was going to be pretty high anyway.

He reported to the airfield just before dawn, and experienced a severe case of *déjà vu*. Not that his pilot looked the least like poor Bingham. 'Jonathan Light,' he said, shaking hands. 'Ever jumped?'

'I'm afraid not,' John confessed.

'Well, jumping is no problem. You just step out of the aircraft on my say so. Your cord will be attached to a hook in the cabin, and will open automatically at a count of about six seconds.'

'What happens if it doesn't?'

Light gave him an old-fashioned look. 'Then you have about ten seconds to make your last will and testament. But it will happen. I mean, your chute will work. It always does. Well, ninety-nine times out of a hundred.'

'Thanks a bunch,' John said, as the ground crew helped him into a leather flying suit over his uniform, complete with leather cap, and then into the various straps which were pulled tight. There was also a sergeant waiting to strap a haversack to his chest. 'Just for the jump, sir. You can wear it more properly on your back after you're down.'

It was as heavy as lead. John checked the contents. A revolver and a cartridge belt, filled to capacity; a first-aid box; various other pills and remedies; a book of maps and two notebooks; several bars of chocolate. 'Special stuff, sir,' the sergeant said. 'Slow to melt.'

'You mean I don't have to eat them all at once,' John suggested. There was also one of the very new radio transmitters, small and compact, carefully packed to resist impact. John added his cap before strapping the haversack shut.

Another parachute was attached to a large metal carrier.

'Am I taking my own food supply?' John asked.

'Gear for the Arabs, sir,' the sergeant explained. 'Tommyguns, cartridges, replacement batteries for their radio ... that sort of thing.'

'The problem is landing,' Light said. He had been waiting patiently for the fitting out to be completed. 'You will come down with approximately the same impact as jumping off a twenty-foot-high wall, or from a twenty-foot-high window. Have you ever done that?'

'From a window, no. My lady friends usually have doors available. From a wall ... no, I don't think I've done that either.'

'Can be tricky, without practice. Waste of time for me to take you out there and have you break a leg, what? Ever done any unarmed combat?'

'Yes.'

'Well, then, remember to roll with the impact. Relax all your muscles, and roll. You with me?'

'Absolutely.'

I have got to be out of my tiny mind, he thought, looking down on the largely blacked-out city as they took off. Presumably Margo and Lauren and Sammy were all in bed and fast asleep. Arsinoe, he imagined, would also be in bed although he couldn't be sure *she* was asleep. He wondered if Jones was asleep? Presumably, if one had Jones's job, one simply couldn't lie awake thinking about the men one had just sent to their deaths – that way lay the loony bin.

The dawn came up as splendidly as always, and they were, as the last time, flying south of west. 'Last time I was out here I crashed,' John shouted, chattily, leaning forward to Light's shoulder.

'Heard about that,' Light replied. 'Young Bingham, wasn't it? You saved his life.'

'I was saving my own as well.'

'That's not what I heard. You're to get a gong.'

John leaned back; it seemed everyone in Cairo, maybe in Egypt, knew his business. And had given him a quite spurious reputation as both a hero and a womaniser. 'Won't be long now,' Light shouted over his shoulder. 'We're looking for a harka.'

Hardly a harka, John thought; it was a word he associated with an Arab army, and Ali certainly did not possess that.

They flew lower now, over the desert, and the *déjà vu* returned. He had forgotten to ask Light if his various feed tubes had been cleaned recently. But the engine continued to growl reassuringly. There was a pair of binoculars hanging beside him, and he used these to scan the sandhills and wadis beneath him – and occasionally the sky to make sure there were no enemy planes out. Then... 'I see them,' he shouted.

'Clockwise?'

'Four.'

Light peered in the required direction. 'Certainly camels. They have to make the right signal.' The Lysander drifted lower, and the camel riders looked up. A moment later a bright light burst above them; someone had fired a Very pistol. 'You'd think they were shooting at us,' Light remarked. 'You happy?'

'No,' John confessed, 'but I reckon they're my friends.'

'Right. I'm going up to a thousand feet. Stand by.' The aircraft climbed steeply, and the Arabs became specks. Then Light banked sharply, and levelled off. 'We'll go back as close as we can,' he shouted. 'Would you like to open the door, old man?'

John drew a deep breath and released the door catch. It swung back against the fuselage with a bang, and to the noise of the engine was added the sound of the wind. 'How do you shut it again?' he bawled.

Light tapped an instrument at his side, and John saw that it was actually connected to the door by a length of rope. The instrument itself was a sort of crank, which would certainly be needed against the force of the wind. 'Well, the best of luck,' he shouted.

'And to you,' Light called. 'Drop the gear first. Attach the line.'

John obeyed, watched the chute open with a great sense of relief.

'Stand by,' Light shouted. 'Stand by ... Go!'

John was standing in the doorway, hanging on as the wind caught at him, telling himself not to look down. Now he stepped out, and was aware of a most peculiar feeling, so much so that he almost forgot to count. Then he did in a great hurry as he seemed to turn upside down. A moment later there was a jar at his shoulders, and he found himself floating. He twisted his head to and fro, and saw the Lysander still quite close; Light had reduced speed and was slowly winding in the door.

Now he had to look down; the sand was only a few hundred feet beneath him. He looked left and right, and could not for the moment see Ali's people. Suppose they were not, after all, Ali's people? But they had fired the signal pistol.

He peered at the uneven, vari-coloured surface beneath him. What he really wanted was soft sand, which should be white. But there weren't many patches of that – the majority were brown or slate coloured, suggesting rocks or at least a hard surface. Now he was not more than a hundred feet up. Relax, Light had said. Relax and breakfall and roll. Relax and breakfall and roll.

Fifty feet, then twenty, and he seemed to be travelling very fast, both downwards and sideways as there was a puff of wind. The temptation to draw up his feet was enormous, but he left them hanging, drawing great breaths. Then they touched, and he was whipped sideways. Desperately he tugged on the cords, but the wind had caught it and he was pulled off his feet and hit the ground with a thud. He was dragged for several feet before he could get the chute under control. Then he sat up, panting. He felt that he had been run over by a bus, but there was no sharp pain to suggest he might have broken anything. Amazingly, his flying gear was only torn in a few places.

He freed himself from the chute, pulled off the leathers and stood up feeling much cooler. But he also felt dizzy and dropped to his knees again for a few moments while his head cleared. Then he took off his flying helmet and replaced it with his cap, removed his haversack from his chest and slung it behind his back where it belonged, and finally checked the chambers in his revolver. Well, he thought, I've arrived. Where is the reception committee?

A moment later they came over the nearest rise – five men on camels, leading another camel. And a woman. 'Warrey!' Uluma shrieked, dismounting and running forward to throw herself into his arms. 'I knew you would come back.'

The Arab camp was some twenty miles away, and it was late afternoon before they got there. For all his aches and pains, John had never felt so good: his depression of the previous day had quite disappeared. This was the life he felt he had been born to live.

Ali was all smiles: the great Warrey was back, and all was going to be well. And the equipment he had brought was enough to gladden any guerilla's heart.

They ate mutton stew while Ali listened to what John had to say. Around them the desert was quiet. John gathered they were some miles from the oasis. 'Have the Italians never come back?' John asked.

'A plane flies over from time to time. But they are too busy farther north. Now you wish us to go up to the coast?'

'I wish to go up to the north.'

'Disguised as an Arab. You will be shot. You will need support. I will come with you.'

'You? Who will lead your tribe?'

'My Uncle Osman.' Ali grinned. 'He thinks he should be leading them anyway.'

'And you wish to be shot also.'

Ali shrugged. 'I wish to harm the Germans.'

'We need to work as quickly as we can,' John said. 'How long will it take us to get up to the coast?'

'Where on the coast?'

'I think Benghazi. I am too well known in Tobruk. My understanding is that the docks in Benghazi have been repaired and that it is a principal entry port for the Afrika Korps supplies.'

'Benghazi,' Ali said thoughtfully. 'A week,

if we travel light.'

'Right. Now, I need to keep in contact with Cairo. I have a radio, but it does not have the range. I must therefore use your radio here as a relay. Is yours still working?'

'Oh, yes. That is how we knew you were coming. But if we use it too much we must expect another attack from the Italians. They will trace your signals.'

'So your people will have to keep moving.'

'With the radio and the batteries?'

'I'm afraid so. And the movement must be towards us, not away into the desert.'

Ali did some more considering. 'This is a big operation.'

'It may win us the War.'

'It *will* win us the War,' the young sheikh said enthusiastically. 'Now tell me, is Miss Cartwright well?'

'She was when last I saw her,' John said.

'Good. Good. I am still hoping she will consent to be my wife.'

'Ah...' It would clearly be a mistake to dampen his enthusiasm. 'She is very fond of you,' he said.

'And you have Uluma,' Ali said. 'She is very much in love with you. And you saved her life. She has refused to go with any other man because she belongs to you. She is very anxious to become yours.'

John knew there was no way he could convey to Ali that he simply could not sleep with a woman after watching her castrating several men, even if the men had been dead. But there was no way of conveying that to Uluma either, without causing deep offence.

'I know this,' he said. 'But I have taken a vow...'

'A vow?' Uluma demanded. 'What is this vow?'

'It is a vow of chastity,' John explained. 'When I left you the last time, I was badly wounded, and spent many days in hospital. They thought I was going to die,' he went on, warming to his theme. 'I thought I was going to die. So I took a vow, that I would remain chaste until the War was won, if I could be allowed to live.'

He reflected that, quite inadvertently, he might almost be telling the truth.

'Until the War is won?' Uluma was horrified.

'It will not be long now,' John assured her.

Uluma put a brave face on it; she knew that vows, of chastity or anything else, were not to be broken. 'I will wait,' she said. 'I am your woman. I have known this from the beginning. I knew you would come back. I will wait until we have won the War.'

They returned to the oasis the next day, and for the next two days were hard at work preparing the expedition. Ali decided against going to any elaborate lengths to make John look like an Arab; he was in any event heavily sun-tanned, and he was allowing his beard to grow. But he did attempt to teach him some words of Arabic, and some Bedouin habits. And gave his habitual grin. 'You had better leave the talking to me,' he said. 'And keep in the background. With your wife, eh?'

'You mean I am to take Uluma?'

'As I must take a woman. I will take Halil. We are Bedouin going to market. How may a man travel without at least one wife? Besides, Uluma is useful if we run into trouble.'

'I've seen her at work,' John agreed, wondering how long his vow was going to work, if he was going to have to spend virtually his entire time in her company. 'Now – passes. We will need passes.'

'That is no problem,' Ali said. 'My uncle Mamun has passes. We will first of all go to his oasis. Then, I have uncles and cousins in both Benghazi and Tobruk as well. We will contact them, eh?'

John frowned. 'I think we need to keep this as secret as possible.' It seemed likely that, if Ali had his way, the entire province of Cyrenaica was going to be called upon for help – and possible betrayal.

'There is no need to tell them who you are

276

and what you are doing. I will contact them, so that they will know I may need their help.'

'To do what, exactly? It is not my intention to engage in any shoot-outs.'

Ali tapped his nose. 'Who knows what the future will bring? It is best to store all the ammunition possible, is it not?' John had to agree that made some sound sense.

The rest of the tribe would be left under the command of Ali's more immediate uncle, Osman. Their business was to complete the reconstitution of the airstrip, while attempting to make it look as if it had been untouched since the bombing. But a special group was chosen to handle the radio; they were to move out of the oasis if they had to use it more than once and for any length of time, and send a signal from some miles away in the hopes of confusing the Italians. The next day Ali, John and the two women left, mounted separately, leading two camels laden with dates, apparently for sale, but also carrying the small radio, as well as two tommy-guns carefully concealed beneath the fruit. John had discarded his uniform for haik and burnous, and he had not shaved since leaving Cairo; his beard was only a couple of days old, but it would grow quickly enough, he hoped. He was also concerned to discover that it was speckled with grey.

'This is because you are a man of experience,' Ali told him, somewhat enviously; he still had no more than a few stray hairs.

They crossed the Calanscio Sand Sea. John had done this before, with Soroya and Margo, and he remembered it as a most unpleasant place. Progress was very slow, even the camels finding the going difficult, and water was very strictly rationed. No one spoke much, not even Uluma. But in the sand sea they were safe from Italian patrols, and though they saw the occasional aircraft, four Arabs trekking across the desert were of no interest.

It took them a week, then they regained the stony desert, and made the oasis where Mamun was sheikh. He regarded them with some suspicion. 'I am at peace with the Italians,' he said. 'They are too close, we are too few.'

'But you would like to see the back of them, uncle,' Ali pointed out, hopefully.

'If it can be done without harm to my people,' Sheikh Mamun said. 'When they have won the War, they will come down here to make trouble again.'

'They are not going to win the War,' Ali said.

'What do you know, boy? Did you not know that this general, this Rommel, has attacked the British again?'

'What did you say?' John asked.

'I said that the Germans and the Italians have attacked the British again, at a place called Alam Halfa.'

'And they have won this battle?'

If they have done that, John thought, then what am I doing here? 'I do not know,' Mamun said. 'But they have always won before. Who is this man?' he asked Ali.

'He is a British officer, come to help us win the War,' Ali said.

'I am not at war,' Mamun insisted. 'What is that?'

'It is a radio, so that we can send messages.'

Mamun and his people peered at the set. John obligingly switched it on, and they jumped back at the crackling sound. But he needed to use it anyway, having been out of touch for nearly a fortnight. 'Desert Rat,' he said, having found the correct wavelength. 'Desert Rat in position.'

'I read you, Desert Rat,' came the answer. 'I have a message for you.'

'Send your message.'

'The message reads, support follows. Repeat, support follows. Maintain position until relief. Out.'

John gazed at Ali in consternation. 'What does that mean?' Ali asked.

'I have no idea. Support? There was no

talk of support. Relief? I am not due to be relieved yet.'

'Can you not call them back and ask what they mean?' Ali asked.

'I don't think that would be a good idea,' John said. 'Our objective must be to keep our signals to a minimum, or the Italians will be able to trace them. I think we'll just ignore that last one. Abdullah,' he said into the set 'Take down anything else that comes through, but do not reply until you are specifically requested to do so. You will not, in any circumstances, say anything about me or Sheikh Ali, or our whereabouts.'

'I understand,' Abdullah said earnestly.

John preferred not even to think about what sort of a muddle Cairo might have got into now. He was more concerned with making another effort to persuade Uluma to remain with Sheikh Mamun. But she refused. 'How may a man go about his business without a woman?' she asked, looking at Halil for support, and getting an appreciative nod.

'Listen,' John said. 'This is highly dangerous. If they catch us, they will use electricity on us again, and then they will hang us.'

'We will be together,' she said confidently.

John looked at Ali, who shrugged.

Mamun's people had obtained several

passes, mainly by theft, John suspected, and these were altered for them; fortunately, the Italians had not got around to requiring photographs of the desert people – who did not like being photographed in any event – and the thumbprints were easily replaced. Two days later they were ready to go, walking their camels up the track towards Benghazi.

Soon enough they encountered an Italian checkpoint, but Ali did the talking and showed the passes and the soldiers were content with leering at Uluma and Halil, who both inadvertently revealed a good deal of leg as they dismounted from their camels. John remained in the background, holding the animals, his burnous half across his face. 'That was easy,' Ali said, as they resumed their journey.

'Let's hope it stays that way,' John said. He still did not know the outcome of the Battle of Alam Halfa.

Two days later they were in Benghazi. John had been imprisoned there the previous year, but now his beard was coming along well, and with his tan much heavier than a year before, and his Arab clothes, he did not think he ran much risk of being recognised, even supposing any of his erstwhile captors were still about; he was assuming, and hoping, that Umberto was still in Tobruk.

They made their way to the house of ibn-Salud, Osman's nephew, where they were welcomed somewhat more warmly than in Mamun's oasis. 'The Italians,' Salud said. 'Pouf. But there are so many of them.'

'We're here to find out just how many,' John said. 'Tell me about the battle.'

Salud shrugged. 'I do not think the Germans won it. But I do not think they lost it, either.'

The next day they took their places in the market selling their dates, buying various garments from other hawkers – the women enjoying themselves immensely – while they watched and waited. The docks had been largely repaired and Benghazi was an entry port. It was also on the main road from Tripoli, many miles to the west. Thus everything destined for the front rolled along this road and there was a steady stream of tanks as well as trucks. More interested in the tanks in the first instance, John identified several Panzer Mark III specials, armed with the new long fifty-millimetre gun, and even one or two Mark IVs, with the seventy-five millimetre. These were formidable tanks, but he didn't reckon there were enough of them to make a difference, certainly if the Eighth Army was being equipped with Shermans.

And the main German armour remained the old Mark III with its short fifty millimetre. Save that they struck him as being slightly different. 'I have got to get a closer look at those tanks,' he told Ali, who was conducting more business.

Ali nodded, and waited until the next lot of tanks had temporarily been halted by a traffic jam, then jabbed one of the camels with his knife. Instantly there was pandemonium, the animal leaping and yowling and snapping and upsetting all those around him, together with the stalls and the vendors, sending Uluma and Halil shrieking for cover, and attracting the amused attention of the German soldiers. John left the market and slouched across the square to where the tanks were waiting, for the moment unchecked by anyone. Now he saw what was different – these tanks were more heavily armoured than any he had previously encountered.

Something to be noted; the English two-pounders had had a hard time knocking out even the old version – he suspected that their light shells would now merely bounce off this stuff. 'Hey, you!' a voice bellowed in Italian. 'Get away from there, scumbag.'

John looked round at the military police-man. He was between him and the market, so he ran round the tank, and found himself in the midst of several trucks. These were clearly heavily loaded, and the drivers were gathered beside them, chatting. John ran round these as well, paused in the shelter of the last truck. This was shrouded in canvas, but being for the moment alone, he flicked up the corner nearest to him, and peered inside, frowning at the row after row of neat round containers. Mines!

There were over a hundred of them in this truck alone, and there were a good dozen trucks. Anti-tank mines, he thought, defensive, not offensive weapons. If these trucks were bound for the Alamein position, as they had to be, and if they were only part of a much larger group – over the past couple of days he had seen a good number of similar vehicles – then Rommel was intending to use the Qattara Depression in reverse, as it were; far from intending to launch another attack on the Eighth Army, he was intending to stand fast and stop them attacking him – unless they were prepared to advance through minefields.

'Hey!' the MP was shouting again.

John ran off into the crowd.

Ali had regained control of his apparently errant camel and equally his excited women, and they met up at Salud's house that evening. 'I have a fair idea of Rommel's strategy,' John said. 'But not enough of his numbers. I think we have to go east for awhile.'

Ali stroked his chin. 'I do not know how

far they will allow us.'

'We must see what we can do.'

They left Benghazi the next morning, riding and driving their camels. There was quite a lot of local traffic on the road, certainly as far as Derna, and progress was very slow, as every so often they were forced off the road by German and Italian MPs, to allow convoys of tanks, men and trucks to pass. John was able to note the size and mark of tanks, as well as the regimental markings on the various soldiers. He was gradually accumulating a picture which he hoped would be of use to the new commander, Montgomery.

It took them several days to reach Derna. By then John was thoroughly at home in both his clothes and his situation; he was almost feeling like a Bedouin himself, enjoying the constant banter exchanged with other travellers, the bonhomie around the campfires at night and the great rushes to the side of the road whenever the RAF swooped overhead seeking to bomb the transports. 'These people are our friends?' Uluma complained.

She was managing, obviously with great difficulty, to keep her hands off him.

The next day they left the road and trekked into the desert. When they were sufficiently remote from all military activity, he called the oasis. 'Desert Rat,' he said.

'Desert Rat. Do you read?'

'Desert Rat,' replied an unmistakeable voice. 'I wish a rendezvous, Map G, section three, sub-section A. How soon can you make this?'

'What the devil are you doing there?' John demanded.

'I am taking charge of this operation,' Margo said. 'This area is my responsibility. Why have you not called in on schedule?'

Whatever had happened to Jones? John wondered. 'I was busy,' he said.

'Repeat, how soon can you make the rendezvous,' Margo said.

'Five days,' John replied.

'That is too long.'

'You'll have to be patient. I am still busy. Desert Rat out.'

'That was Margo!' Ali cried, delighted.

'Good news for some,' John remarked. 'She seems anxious to throw her weight around, as usual.' He studied the map. The reference she had given was at least two days away, and he still wanted to get closer to the German lines and see what could be accomplished. She would indeed have to be patient.

Next day they moved back to the road which, east of Derna, was even more crowded with both locals and troops. 'I would say our friend is preparing another offensive,' Ali said.

'He'll have to hurry,' John commented.

Then there was the usual blaring of horns and they had to leave the road. But the traffic was mostly coming the other way now, trucks loaded with wounded men. 'He did,' Uluma suggested. 'Hurry.'

John studied the trucks, counting and calculating. There were several of the vehicles, each perhaps containing some twenty men. Supposing there had been, as was usual, one death to every three wounded, the indication was a total casualty list of perhaps two hundred men. That did not indicate either a very big battle or a heavy defeat. Could Rommel have broken through at Alamein? In which case all the information he was gathering, and the risk he was running, both for himself and his friends, might be worthless. Was that why Margo had been recalled from leave and come charging out into the desert to take over? Take over what?

The ambulance convoy continued on its way, but they were not allowed onto the road again. Now everyone seemed to be waiting for something, and an hour later they found out what it was. Another convoy came along, this time mainly outriders and command cars. In the centre of the convoy, riding in an open car, John recognised Rommel himself. He was slumped in his seat, and the man beside him, who wore a red cross on his sleeve, was bending over him, both talking and giving the field marshal attention. Then they were gone in a cloud of dust.

Rommel, wounded? Or perhaps... John recalled the impression he had gained a few months earlier, that the field marshal had been ill. Whatever the cause, he was being taken away from the front line for treatment. 'Let's get out of here,' he told Ali.

They drove the camels back onto the road, and were again scattered by a blaring of horns. They were forced back into the now very noisy onlookers, as more command cars came rumbling through, these heading east. They stared at the SS insignia, Major Buelow and Freda Schultz.

'That woman,' Uluma exclaimed. 'And that bastard...'

'Right,' John said.

'You should have let me kill her, at the least.'

'I'm glad I didn't,' John said. She could be the answer to a prayer, he thought.

Ali glanced at him. 'You know those people.'

'They're the ones who duffed up Uluma.'

Ali licked his lips as he gazed at the expression on Uluma's face. 'What will you do?'

288

'Their headquarters are in Tobruk. That is only a few miles away.'

Ali frowned. 'You mean to go there? You said it would be too dangerous.'

'It is now a risk worth taking. Buelow is a senior SS officer in North Africa. He will know all of Rommel's dispositions. So will Fraulein Schultz.'

Ali stroked his chin. 'Can you round up some aid?' John asked. 'Just as a distraction, really.'

'I will see what I can do. You mean to kill these people?'

'I mean to kidnap them. For information.'

'This is very dangerous.'

'It could mean the winning of the War.'

Ali looked at Uluma. Halil as usual did not seem entirely sure of what was going on. Uluma grinned. 'You will give them to me,' she said. 'I will make them tell you what you wish to know.'

What a way to wage a war, John thought, as they retraced their steps into the town. But, fought at this level, away from roaring guns and blazing tanks and deeds of derring-do, it had to be done. And even the roaring guns and blazing tanks had not been a particularly clean business. While the information he might be able to obtain...

They reached the town just on dusk, and there were the usual checkpoints and inspection of papers. But the Italian soldiers were agitated; John guessed they had learned of Rommel's illness, perhaps even seen him being driven through. Of course he remained a temptation, but there was little chance of catching up with him now.

They found an open space – the town had been so thoroughly bombed and shelled over the preceding year that there were many of these, as John well remembered – and pitched their tents while Ali went off to see how many of his cousins he could round up. Halil cooked their evening meal over a small fire, while Uluma sharpened her knife. 'We play this my way,' John told her. 'No cutting up unless I say so.'

She grinned. 'Until we get them into the desert,' she said.

'Not even then, unless I say so.' She continued to grin.

Ali returned, accompanied by a dozen men, all very determined-looking Arabs. 'These are all your cousins?' John was astounded.

'Or my cousins' cousins,' Ali explained. 'They all hate the Italians. And now they hate the Germans too. And they are glad to be serving with the great Warrey.'

'What of their families? The Germans will almost certainly take hostages, and shoot them too.'

'They are already leaving. They will

rendezvous with us in the desert.'

'Can they leave the town at night? What about the checkpoints?'

'This is not a problem. The women will offer themselves to the Italians, and there will be no trouble.'

John scratched his head. But he had set the ball rolling, and there was nothing he could do to stop it now. They checked their weapons, and again he was surprised; the Bedouin were very well armed. While he and Ali each had tommy-guns, and there was every prospect of obtaining some more.

Halil also headed for the desert, with the camels. John would have preferred Uluma to go with her, but he knew there was no chance of that. 'Will she also have to offer herself?" he asked Ali.

Ali gave one of his grins. 'She is good at that.'

They mounted a watch on the SS Headquarters, noting the time of changing the sentries, and the sentries' patrol habits. Then their plans had to be changed; at nine o'clock, Buelow and Freda left the compound in a command car. Buelow was in uniform, but Freda had changed into a frock; both were very jolly. John sent one of the Arabs on foot behind them; in the darkened and empty streets he could run through the shadows as fast as the car could travel, having as it did to avoid bomb craters and piles of rubble. He returned half an hour later to tell them that the Germans were at a restaurant by the water. 'They have played into our hands,' Ali said.

The Arabs crept forward, going to ground in the shadows when they were passed by an Italian patrol, moving silently towards the water. When they were within sight of the restaurant, which while officially blacked out was showing a great deal of light, John halted them. 'Now, remember,' he said. 'We wish the German officer and the woman, alive.'

They grinned as they nodded – he had not said anything about any of the waiters, or anyone else who might be dining. John checked out the building as best he could from a distance. There was only the one entrance, guarded by a bouncer; in the forecourt were several parked cars, at least two German; their drivers were smoking cigarettes and chatting.

The restaurant itself was a single-storeyed building, jutting out over the sea on stilts. 'How deep is the water?' he asked Ali.

He enquired of a cousin. 'It is not deep,' Ali said. 'Perhaps five feet.'

Deep enough, John thought, to discourage careless jumping in. 'Right,' he said. 'We attack with everything we have. But remember: Buelow and the woman alive.'

'It shall be done,' Ali said. 'You have but to give the signal.'

John looked at his watch; it was a quarter to nine. There were another nine hours of darkness left, long enough for them to make their escape. 'Well,' he said. 'There is no time like the present. Let's go.'

Ten

The General

The Arabs were widely dispersed, and it took a few minutes to alert them all. 'When I open fire,' John said.

He checked his magazine, looked at Uluma, who did the same. Now the adrenalin was flowing, and he knew hers was as well; he could only hope she was as much under control. But it was still necessary to be on a killing high. And to lead!

He stood up, drew a deep breath, and ran forward, firing into the cars and their drivers. The German chauffeurs turned round with startled exclamations. One fell immediately. The second drew his revolver, but was then hit by several rounds and tumbled over backwards. The other drivers ran for shelter, screaming their fear. They had acted just in time, for as John's bullets, supported by Uluma's, slashed into the vehicles first one petrol tank went up, then another, then the whole bank of parked cars was a blazing bonfire. John could only hope the two Germans had been killed outright, otherwise they were being roasted alive.

By now he was in the forecourt. The bouncer had run forward. Then he saw the men charging at him, and ran back. Several rounds sliced into him and he fell on his face. John leapt over him and raced at the door. By now the diners and the restaurant staff had been alerted by the din and the fire. Waiters appeared in the doorway and hastily disappeared again. German officers also appeared, pulling Lugers from their holsters and opening fire, but being met with such a hail of bullets that several fell and the rest scattered for shelter. One had the presence of mind to kick the doors shut, but John shoulder-charged the thin panels and they burst open again. Bullets whanged about him; he had no idea which were being fired by the Germans and which by his own people following him inside. Women screamed and with their civilian partners dropped to the floor. Random shots smashed into plates of lobster and crab, green salad and sliced tomatoes, glasses and bottles of hock and Chianti. Tables over-turned, and were held up as ineffective shelters by those beneath them.

But John had already concentrated on a table in the far corner, where Buelow and Freda had been seated. The major had leapt to his feet at the first firing and loosed off several shots at the door, but realising that he and his friends were outnumbered, he had dropped to the floor again, hiding behind the table he had overturned. John ran at it, holding his fire, reached it and kicked it over. Buelow was not there but John saw him crawling through the doorway immediately behind where the table had been.

Freda lay on the ground, screaming her head off. 'Take her,' John snapped at Uluma who was at his shoulder. That brought an even louder scream from Freda. 'But don't hurt her,' John shouted over his shoulder, hurling himself into the darkened corridor down which Buelow had vanished. He blinked in the gloom, saw nothing. There was a door on his right, and he threw this open, revealing a storeroom. He stepped inside, standing still while drawing deep breaths, attempting to listen as he did so.

The noise continued to be tremendous from the restaurant itself. But he was sure Buelow would reveal himself if he were here. When, after a few seconds, there was no movement, he stepped back outside and went on down the corridor, to emerge onto the balcony overlooking the sea. This was full of men and women who had escaped the gunfight in the restaurant and hurled themselves over the rail. Buelow was almost certainly amongst them, but in the darkness it was impossible to tell which one. And

John had no taste for firing into a mass of helpless people, most of whom, he reckoned, were restaurant staff, and therefore probably as Arab as his supporters. And they had Freda.

So he ran back, through the kitchen. There had been shooting in there as well, and a great deal of disorder, with platters and pots and pans and their contents scattered about amidst several dead bodies. Two of the Arabs were busily stuffing themselves with food. 'Out,' John said. 'We must get out.'

He wasn't sure whether or not they understood him, but they cheered and ran behind him. The restaurant itself was the most complete shambles John had ever seen, but here again the Arabs were triumphant; only one of their number had been hit, and the rest were busily looting the dead and dying. Uluma had Freda standing against a wall, one hand twined in the front of her dress, the other pressing her revolver into the German woman's midriff. She was smiling and talking, no doubt uttering all manner of bloodthirsty threats, John supposed. 'Ali!' he shouted.

'I am here, Warrey.'

Ali had secured a gold watch, which he was proudly strapping to his wrist. 'We must get out of here,' John told him. 'Listen!' In the distance there was the wail of a siren. 'Set this place alight,' John commanded.

'Make sure it burns. Then get your people out. We have to disappear before the Italians figure out what has happened.'

'Or the Germans,' Ali grinned, but he shouted orders in Arabic. Bottles of alcohol were shattered on the floor, tablecloths and napkins impregnated.

'Come on,' John told Uluma.

'I think she needs to be gagged,' Uluma said.

Freda continued to pant. 'Please,' she said. 'Please–'

John nodded and Uluma rolled up a napkin and stuffed it into Freda's mouth; Freda made no effort to resist her – she was both shocked and terrified. Uluma turned her round, tore a tablecloth into strips and bound Freda's wrists behind her. John had the impression that she regarded Freda as her own personal trophy. He was going to have a problem there, but for the time being ... Ali was already striking matches.

He grasped Freda's shoulder and hurried her to the broken doors leading onto the forecourt. Here the vehicles were still blazing; the dead bodies remained scattered about. Behind them the restaurant gradually burst into flames. 'Come,' Ali said. He embraced his cousins who would find their own way out of the town, then led John and the two women down a side street.

Now the entire waterfront was a mass of

fresh noise, wailing sirens as both police and firemen hurried to the scene, and shouts and shrieks from a gathering band of civilians. John reckoned they had bought some time. The authorities would not know for sure what had happened until they could put out the blaze and get into the restaurant ... or until the people in the water got ashore.

Ali led them down a succession of alleyways. The noise around them grew, but it was still concentrated on the waterfront. Freda stumbled and one of her shoes came off, she made a high pitched moaning sound, but Uluma and John hurried her on. 'What do we do at the checkpoint?' Ali asked, panting.

'We play it by ear, but we need transport.'

Ali nodded. A few minutes later they reached the outskirts of the town, heading due south, and the checkpoint. 'Halt!' ordered the sentry.

But John had already spotted the truck waiting behind the little post. He opened fire. So did Ali, while Uluma hurled Freda to the ground before stepping on her to keep her there as she too fired. The first guard fell immediately, the other three died as they emerged from their little hut. John stepped past them to look inside by the light of the kerosene lamp on the desk; the radio was chattering, but he didn't have time to work out what was being said. 'The truck,' he said. 'Uluma, collect up all the canteens and rations. And whatever spare magazines you can find.' Uluma got to work.

John picked Freda up and slung her into the back. Uluma, heavily laden, crawled in behind her. Ali got into the front beside John as he started the engine and sent the vehicle roaring down the track. 'That was very efficient,' Ali said, admiringly.

'Uluma and I have done it before,' John reminded him.

But he reckoned they had even less time now than the last occasion he had broken out of Tobruk. Behind him there was still a blaze in the night sky, but if by now the Italians were closing all exits, they would very rapidly deduce that something had gone wrong with the checkpoint they had just left, if only because it wouldn't be acknowledging their commands. On the other hand, planes would not be able to find them in the darkness as he was not using lights, which meant that the truck seemed to find every pothole in the track. 'Where are your people waiting?' he asked.

'They were to go as far as possible. Maybe fifteen kilometres.'

'And you can find them?'

'When it is light, I will find them,' Ali said, and grinned. 'Or they will find me. But they may shoot at the truck.'

'There won't be a truck,' John said.

He was watching the kilometre gauge. When they had driven twelve kilometres from the checkpoint he braked to a halt and got down. 'We ask this woman questions now?' Uluma said hopefully.

'Later,' John told her.

They dragged Freda out. He suspected she had had a busy and possibly unhappy time, for her dress was more torn than he remembered and her face was bruised. 'Mmmm,' she protested. Mmmm...'

'Soon,' John promised her. He looked at his watch: it was coming up to midnight.

'Why are we leaving the truck?' Ali asked.

'Because the aeroplanes will spot it at first light. By then we can be ten miles away.'

'My people will not be able to find us in the dark.'

'We shall have to find them tomorrow.' He took off Freda's gag, gave her a drink of water.

'Please don't give me to that woman,' she begged.

'That depends on how successful a chat we have. Right now, let's move.'

'I cannot walk,' she protested. 'I have no shoes.'

'Neither does Uluma,' John pointed out. 'You'll just have to grin and bear it.'

He took his bearings from the stars, using the navigational knowledge he had accumulated during his yachting days, setting off as near due south as he could estimate. They plodded slowly over the stony desert, Freda giving little yelps every time her bare feet encountered something sharp. By first light John reckoned they had certainly made half-a-dozen miles from where they had left the truck. 'Now,' he said, 'we need somewhere to hide while we rest.'

Ali found them a wadi with steep sides, which meant that they could be in the shade on one side or the other, wherever the sun happened to be. They were all very tired and Freda's feet were bleeding. John made her take off her torn dress and tore it even further, into strips of cloth which he bound round her feet. Uluma sniffed. 'I do not see why you care for her so,' she commented. 'She is going to die anyway.'

She was very interested in Freda's underwear, which in the North African heat consisted of a single camisole; nor was she wearing stockings. Ali was equally interested; Freda was a buxom young woman at both thigh and breast, and her obvious embarrassment, the manner in which she kept trying to conceal herself, increased her attractiveness. 'She is a prisoner of war,' John pointed out, addressing them both. 'And she has things to say to us.'

'We ask her now?' Uluma said eagerly.

John considered. Now was as good a time as any, he supposed. Freda's morale had to be at a very low ebb. He gave her a drink of water and they ate some of the Italians' iron rations.

'I will go now,' Ali announced, 'to find my people.'

'Can you do this?'

'Of course.'

'And bring them back to us?'

'Of course,' Ali said simply, and plodded off.

John watched him go, only hoping that the boy's confidence was not misplaced. 'Now,' he said, taking his notebook from the pocket of his jibbah. 'As we have a few hours to kill, tell me things.'

Freda glared at him, blinking. 'Just how short-sighted are you, anyway?' he asked.

'I can see you,' she snapped.

'And that's all you need to see. Firstly, the field marshal. What is the matter with him?'

'I do not know.'

'Freda,' John said earnestly. 'Uluma is very keen to get at your bits.'

Uluma was sharpening her knife.

'The field marshal is ill,' Freda said.

'What with?'

'I do not know. I think he is just worn out.'

'And where is he going into hospital?'

'He is returning to Germany.'

'Is that a fact? So who is in command of the Afrika Korps?'

'General von Thoma. But the overall commanding general is General Stumme.'

John frowned while he wrote down the names. While he had heard of von Thoma, the name Stumme was new to him. 'What command has Stumme held before this?'

'I do not know. He only arrived last week.'

'Arrived at Mersa Matruh?'

'No. Arrived in North Africa.'

'Let me get this straight,' John said. 'Rommel is being returned to Germany for hospitalisation, and he has been replaced by a general who has not fought in North Africa before?'

'So?' Freda asked. 'Your General Montgomery has not fought in North Africa before, either.'

'Two tyros,' John agreed, writing. 'Okay, Freda, you're doing very well. Now, strengths. How many men has General Stumme got?'

She shrugged. 'A hundred thousand, maybe.'

'How many of those are German?'

'Maybe half.'

'Now, tanks.'

'I do not know about tanks.'

'Freda, please.'

Uluma, who had been listening carefully,

picked up Freda's right leg and began examining her toes, sticking out from the rough bandages John had applied. Freda tried to withdraw the leg and Uluma pulled it straight again. 'I cut these off, eh?' Uluma said. 'And then I cut her tits. I put them in my little bag.'

Freda gasped.

'I think she's quite serious,' John remarked.

'About six hundred,' Freda panted.

'All German?'

'No. About half.'

'But not all that half are Mark III. I saw some Mark IVs in Benghazi.'

'There are some Mark IVs,' Freda said. 'The field marshal put in for a regiment, but was told they were needed on the Russian front to relieve Stalingrad. There is only a squadron here.'

John wrote. 'I see. Right. Now, those anti-tank mines I saw in Benghazi, moving up to the front.'

Freda hesitated and Uluma gently massaged the little toe, the knife poised. 'I should point out that you will find walking very difficult without toes,' John said.

'General Stumme is to stand on the defensive,' Freda gasped. 'Until Field Marshal Rommel can return, and until his forces can be augmented sufficiently for another attack. Those mines are to be placed over our entire front, to depths of several miles. There is no way your people can get through them.'

'I see. Now, field commanders.'

Freda licked her lips, and gave another little tug on her foot. Uluma was still holding her toes. 'Come along,' John said.

'Planes,' Uluma commented. She had been watching the sky, and now John saw the two aircraft, flying quite low over the desert. But they were in shade.

'Nobody move,' John said. 'We'll talk again in a moment.'

Freda had also seen the planes and her face was twisting. He could tell what she was thinking. If she could get out of the wadi and wave her arms ... but that would certainly mean her death. Just in case she was suicidally inclined, he nodded to Uluma, who tightened her grasp on Freda's foot. The planes droned on. 'They will have seen the truck,' Uluma said.

'So they'll know we're somewhere close,' John agreed. 'As long as they can't see us, there is nothing they can do about it.' Nor, he was happy to observe, had they dropped any lower to indicate that they might have spotted Ali. 'You were telling me about dispositions, Freda.'

Freda sighed. 'The Fifteenth Panzer Division and the Italian Littorio Division are holding the north flank, by Sidi Abd el Rahman.'

John wrote.

'The Twenty-First Panzer Division and the Italian Ariete Division are at Gebel Karakh. The Ariete has suffered severe casualties in the recent battle. General Navarrini commands the forward positions. He has General Ramcke's Parachute Brigade on his left, in the extreme north. There also some Bersaglieri. The Italian Trieste Division and the Ninetieth Light Division are in reserve.'

'And in the south?'

Another sigh. 'One Hundred and Sixty-Fourth Division holds what is called Kidney Ridge. The Trento Division holds Miteirya Ridge, and the Bologna Division holds Ruweisat Ridge. These are all Italian forces, but they have some German paratroopers with them. General Orsi and the Tenth Corps holds the front before Ruweisat Ridge, the Brescia Division is in Bab el Qattara, and the extreme right is held by the Pavia Division.' She paused for breath.

John finished writing. 'Freda, you have been magnificent. General Montgomery may well give you a medal.' He looked at Uluma. 'Now what I need to do is get back to our people just as rapidly as possible.'

Uluma nodded. 'The sheikh will soon return,' she promised.

To John's surprise, and relief, she was right.

Ali was back that evening with his people. The planes had continued to fly overhead most of the day, but had apparently been unable to discover the Bedouin, who were a small group and had had ample time to take shelter, while John and the two women had remained totally concealed.

But it had been a very long day, with Uluma watching Freda like a hawk, keeping the German woman in a state of constant terror, and himself anxious only to get back to the Army with his information. He had to be patient. It took them a week to get down to Sheikh Mamun's oasis where Margo was waiting for them. 'You disobeyed my orders,' she said furiously.

'I had already been given my orders by Commander Jones,' John riposted. 'And I was carrying them out.'

'Jones had no business sending you on this mission,' she declared. 'He did it behind my back because I was out of Cairo. I have made a strong report. The operation should have been mine.'

'I'm sure you have made a report, Margo,' John said. 'But, with respect, I don't think you could have carried the operation out quite this successfully. It involved a good deal of violence and death.'

She continued to glare at him for some seconds, then looked at Ali, who gave one of his reassuring grins. 'Warrey is a great warrior,' he said.

Margo snorted. 'And just what did you learn about Rommel's dispositions?'

John tapped his notebook. 'A great deal that will be of use to General Montgomery. When can we get out of here?'

'We can call an aircraft to come for us at Ali's oasis; the strip has been rebuilt.' She looked at Freda, who had been given a haik to wear and looked quite respectable. 'And who is this person?'

'A German lady who has been the source of most of my information,' John explained.

'You'd believe a traitor?'

'She's actually a prisoner of war.'

'And what are we supposed to do with her?'

'I will take care of her,' Uluma said.

Margo looked at her, and then at John. 'I don't think we can permit that,' John said. 'The pair of them don't actually like each other.'

'Well, we can't take her back to Cairo with us. I doubt the aircraft will have sufficient capacity.'

John scratched his head. 'You may leave her here,' Mamun said. Everyone looked at the sheikh. Mamun spread his hands. 'I will take her into my harem. She will be quite safe.'

'You can't be serious!' Freda shouted.

'Do you treat your women well?' John asked.

'Of course. They are happy.'

'He beats them,' Uluma said gleefully.

'Oh, my God!' Freda moaned. 'You cannot give me to an Arab. That is against the rules of the Geneva Convention.'

'To which of course you adhere on every occasion,' John commented.

'Oh, you ... you...'

'If you swear, he will probably beat you right away,' John said. 'I think this is a very equitable solution to our problem.'

Freda was removed, screaming and shouting, and they resumed their journey south. 'Do not treat her too badly,' John told Mamun.

'She will give me many handsome children,' Mamun assured him.

'I'll bet she will.'

'I hope he beats her every day,' Uluma grumbled. 'You should have given her to me.'

That evening, to John's surprise, Margo sat beside him as they ate their evening meal. 'So,' she said, 'you have had another great success.'

'I reckon I have,' John agreed.

'Murdering people.'

'Killing some of the enemy.'

'And are now going home to greater glory.' She brooded into the darkness. 'Ali has

311

asked me to stay in the desert, and be his wife.'

'Ah. He did mention the idea. Does it appeal to you?'

'Don't be absurd. Quite apart from, well ... he's an Arab. And I am old enough to be his mother.'

'Security,' John suggested. 'Surely you're not too old to be a mother for him.'

'You are quite obscene,' she remarked and walked away. But she had mentioned it. He wondered.

A week later they regained Ali's oasis, and the next day a Lysander touched down on the airstrip. 'Little!' John said, shaking hands. 'Good to see you again.'

'They sent me because I know the area,' Little explained. 'I brought Major Cartwright down.'

'You come back?' Uluma asked, winningly,

John smiled at her, and kissed her, to her obvious delight. 'As soon as I can,' he promised.

'When you have won the War,' Ali said, embracing him. 'But if we can help you–'

'Don't worry, we'll call on you.'

'You've made quite a hit with those people,' Margo commented as they took off. 'I assume that uncouth creature is your mistress?'

312

'We were partners,' he told her, wickedly.

Margo snorted. 'Those notes you took,' she said. 'You'd better let me have them.'

'What for?'

'To present to General Montgomery.'

'I'll do that.'

'I am the senior officer in charge of this operation,' Margo said. 'It is my responsibility to give the information to the general.'

'No way. I collected them and I am going to hand them over.

'I am going to put you on a charge,' Margo said. 'Insubordination and deliberate disregard of the orders of your superior. I am going to have you sent back to England in disgrace.'

'Your play,' John agreed.

'Everything all right back there?' Little called over his shoulder. 'Cairo in half an hour.'

Margo seemed determined to carry out her threat, and hurried off in search of Jones as soon as they landed. But John also hurried, summoning a command car to take him up to Alexandria and then army headquarters behind Alamein. He was astonished at what he saw. Although the evidence of a recent and fairly desperate battle was all around him, as the Allied Army had held their ground most of the tanks were being

313

repaired, as were the various defensive positions that had been shot up or overrun. The real difference was in the men. The whole area was a buzz of confident activity. Some soldiers were bathing in the sea, some were running up and down the beach, some were painting dummy trucks and tanks, while others were even drilling; they made him feel tired just looking at them. When he recalled the low morale evident everywhere the last time he had visited this army...

He was driven to the little group of caravans and wireless trucks that composed the headquarters, and shown into a heavily built, bluff man who he knew to be General de Guingand, Montgomery's chief of staff. 'Captain Warrey, sir.'

De Guingand frowned at the sunburned figure in the crushed uniform standing before him. 'Warrey? That's familiar.'

'Intelligence, sir.'

'That's it. Jones mentioned you. Said he'd sent you behind the enemy lines on a recce.' De Guingand looked John up and down. 'I had a feeling he didn't really expect you to come back.'

'I have the information Commander Jones suggested would be useful, sir.'

'Have you, by jove. Let's have a look at it.' He observed John's hesitation, and smiled. 'But you'd rather give it to the army commander yourself. Can't blame you. Wait a moment.'

He knocked and entered the inner compartment, returned a moment later. 'The general will see you now. Ah ... brace yourself.'

John drew a deep breath and stepped into the inner room. Montgomery was seated behind his desk, and had apparently been looking at reports. Now he raised his head, and John found himself looking at an almost birdlike profile, so sharp was the nose. But the eyes were equally sharp, and there was every suggestion of mental strength in the mouth and chin. 'That uniform is a disgrace,' Montgomery commented.

'Captain Warrey has just returned from behind enemy lines, sir,' de Guingand explained. 'He has with him information which he believes may be vital.'

Montgomery leaned back in his chair. 'At ease, Warrey,' he said. 'One of Jones's people, are you?'

'Yes, sir.'

'The Commander has a high regard for you,' Montgomery remarked, not apparently convinced himself. 'What is this information?'

John took out his notebook. 'I have here the exact dispositions of the Axis forces, sir, and their approximate strengths.'

Montgomery held out his hand, and John

gave him the book. The general studied the notes for several seconds. 'Six-mile depths of minefields?'

'Yes, sir.'

'That's not entirely like Rommel, from what I've seen, and heard, even if it is possible,' Montgomery said. 'You mean he has no intention of attacking again?'

'Not right now, sir. Field Marshal Rommel is no longer in North Africa.'

Now Montgomery's head came up with a jerk. 'Explain.'

'The field marshal has been taken ill, sir, and has been returned to Germany for treatment.'

'Ill? Ill with what?'

'I am not certain, sir. My information is that it is sheer exhaustion.'

Montgomery stroked his chin. 'And his replacement? Do you know who that is?'

'General Stumme, sir. General Stumme was sent to North Africa to replace Field Marshal Rommel, as soon as the Field Marshal's condition was realised. General Stumme has no previous experience of North Africa.'

'You are certain of this?'

'Yes, sir.'

'Now, these tank figures. Are they accurate?'

'I believe they are, yes, sir.'

'You have here that there is only one

316

squadron of Panzer Mark IVs. I was given a much higher figure by Intelligence in London.'

'Again, sir, I believe my figures to be accurate.'

'Let us hope they are.' Montgomery got up and went to the huge map pinned to the inner wall. With John's notebook in his hand, he inserted some more pins, each with a different coloured head.

De Guingand and John stood at his shoulder. 'That looks fairly straightforward, sir,' the chief of staff remarked. 'He has concentrated all of his Axis forces in the north, and has left the south held mainly by the Italians, with inferior armour. So...'

Montgomery gave a dry smile. 'We attack in the south. It is never a very good idea to do exactly what your enemy wishes, Francis.'

'But if we go in the north—'

'It will be a long and hard slog. I never supposed it would be otherwise. But it is the only way to win. What we shall do is feint in the south, and put our real punch into the north.'

'We still need to find a way through those minefields.'

'Yes,' Montgomery said. 'A long, hard slog.' He turned. 'Just supposing this Stumme, or whoever is in command at the time of the coming battle, is bold enough to launch a counter-attack, give me your estimate of how long he can sustain it.'

'I do not believe the Afrika Korps has sufficient petrol, or tanks, to undertake more than one very brief attack, sir.'

Montgomery gazed at him for several seconds, then he said, 'I shall hope that estimate, too, is accurate. You've done a splendid job, Captain Warrey. I shall mention it. Now I would say you are due for some R and R.'

'With respect, sir, I would very much like a place in the battle.'

'Would you, now. But you are not a front-line soldier.'

'I have served with the Seventh Armoured, sir, on three occasions.'

Montgomery returned behind his desk and sat down.

'Captain Warrey was with Blanchard when they checked that attempt by Rommel to turn the Qattara position, sir,' Guingand said.

'Is that so? Very good, Warrey, if that is what you would really like to do, you will be seconded to Colonel Blanchard's regiment. However, that will be after you have had your rest and recreation.' He gave one of his cold smiles. 'There is time,'

De Guingand escorted John outside. 'I do not wish to miss the battle, sir,' John said.

'You won't,' de Guingand assured him.

'We are a long way from being ready.'

'But ... I would have thought time was essential, sir. If Rommel recovers and returns, and is provided with fuel and tanks, my estimation will be entirely incorrect.'

'You are suffering from what we call the Eighth Army complex, Warrey. Field Marshal Rommel is, from what I have read and heard, a brilliant tactical soldier. He is not a god. General Montgomery is not the least afraid of him, and one of his main duties since arriving here has been to convince every man in this army that no one need be afraid of him. That includes you. But of course, if he is not there, our task is made that much simpler. What the general *is* afraid of is starting off on another half-baked offensive without the strength to maintain it to the end and to defeat any counter-attacks Rommel may attempt. Or Stumme. We have men and material pouring into Egypt every day. We are receiving tanks from the Americans, Grants and Shermans. They are quite powerful enough and sufficiently well armoured to deal with even Panzer Mark IVs. Planes are arriving every day. The general does not intend to attack until we have double the Axis strength.'

John remembered how Wavell's early campaigns, so successful in both concept and execution, had been ruined, not only by

319

lack of adequate reserves but because so many of his men had been siphoned off to fight, unsuccessfully, in Greece. And how far more recently, Auchinleck had been desperate for more men and more tanks, and hadn't received them. How times changed. 'And London is happy with this, sir?' he asked.

De Guingand smiled. 'No, London is not happy with it. But it is the way the general intends to play it. That is a confidential remark, by the way.'

'Yes, sir.'

'So go and play for a while. You'll receive your orders long before the balloon goes up.'

'Thank you, sir. I should mention that my superior officer intends to place me on a charge for disobeying orders and for insubordination.'

De Guingand raised his eyebrows. 'Commander Jones?'

'No, sir, Major Cartwright.'

'Major Cartwright! Good God! Thank the lord you didn't mention this inside. If there is one thing Monty loathes it is the idea of women in the firing line. As for this so-called major ... oh, I know she's been useful in the past, but employing her in the desert... When you return to Cairo, go to see Commander Jones and tell him you have explained the situation to me. I do not wish

to hear anything more of *Major* Cartwright.'
John saluted.

Poor old Margo, he thought, as he was driven to the railway station to catch the train down to Cairo. But with her continually abrasive temper she had it coming. He wondered what they would do to her? Or with her?

It was dusk by the time he reached Cairo, utterly exhausted. Amazing to remember that only twelve hours ago he had been in the desert saying goodbye to Ali and Uluma. He hoped they prospered.

'Captain Warrey?' The clerk was astonished. 'I'm afraid, ah...'

'I didn't expect you to keep my old room,' John said. 'Any one will do.'

'Ah ... the hotel is full, sir.'

'Eh?'

'All these new people' the clerk seemed quite put out. 'We have some of your spare gear in store...'

'Thanks. So where do you suppose I should spend the night?'

'Well, I could telephone around–'

'Forget it,' John said. It was suddenly occurring to him that if Margo didn't know where he had gone, she couldn't have him arrested ... until he had seen Jones first. He went outside, called a taxi. All he wanted to do was sleep for a month. Rest and

Recreation, the generals had told him. He knew where he could obtain that on a big scale.

He paid off the taxi two blocks short of his destination. That way no one would be able to find him until he was ready. He delved into a liquor store, bought, at a most exorbitant price, a bottle of Scotch, and walked the streets, looked at curiously by the passers-by, knocked on the door. Arsinoe blinked at him. 'Warrey? Oh, Warrey!' she shrieked, as usual draping herself around his neck and up and down his chest.

'Sssh, we don't want the whole world to know,' he told her, carrying her inside and closing the door. 'Don't tell me you're alone?'

'How I am going to have company?'

'Well—'

'That asshole came back after you had left. He said I owed him time. Well, I pay my debts, eh?'

'Do you?' John sank into a chair.

'I make coffee, eh?'

'I have my own.' He put the bottle on the table.

Arsinoe peered at it. 'This is alcohol.'

'We don't all have your hang-ups. That is medicinal.'

Arsinoe unscrewed the cap, sniffed. 'It is

forbidden by the Prophet.'

'So are a lot of the vices you practice. Are you going to pour?'

She pouted, but obeyed, half filling two coffee cups.

'Mud in your eye.' He raised his.

'There is something in my eye?'

'It's an old English saying.' He drank, and felt immeasurably better.

Arsinoe also drank. 'Brrr. It makes my head spin.'

'It's intended to. Now, sweetheart, what I really want is a bed.'

'Oh, yes,' she said enthusiastically. 'Upstairs.' And then frowned. 'You no stay at the hotel?'

'No. Actually, I'm on the run.'

'Eh?'

'The military police,' he explained.

'Oooh!' Her eyes were round as saucers. 'You have committed a crime?'

'Only in their eyes. And it will only be for a day or two.'

'You stay here, for a day or two?' She was utterly delighted.

'What I'm mainly interested in is sleep.'

'Sleep,' she said. 'You sleep. Afterwards.'

Afterwards was a long way away. It was now three years since Arsinoe had first tried to get him into bed. He had resisted her for a variety of reasons, but perhaps the main one had been that he had known that once he really got to grips with Arsinoe it was going to be a very difficult matter to get free of her again ... or even to wish to get free.

In between there had been so many temptations ... Rosalind Carson, her sister, that sad MacLean, even Margo. Not to mention Uluma in a maniacal sort of way.

Now he knew he had been right, both to wait, and to be afraid of her. Arsinoe was all things a man might want, all at the same time. She was soft and cuddly, she was vigorous and demanding. She kissed softly, and then would nip his flesh with her razor sharp teeth. She smelt delightful, yet exuded an oddly attractive aroma of yesterday's cooking. Her breath had only the faintest hint of garlic in it.

Her hands moved all over his body with practised dexterity, her body slid behind her hands. And she knew what she wanted, what she would have. When he would have entered her from in front she demurred and rolled onto her stomach, raising her delightful buttocks. When he entered her there, she immediately subsided, but with her thighs clenched so tightly that he could not slide out, and then brought her legs together so that he was straddling her.

Aileen would have to forgive him. He knew she would.

He slept heavily, awoke with a start as the bedroom door burst open – two men stood there, armed with sub-machine guns.

Eleven

Alamein

John's first impression was that it was Mustafa and friend, out to avenge his wife's honour. But that of course was impossible: Mustafa did not give a fig for his wife's honour. Even as the thoughts were flashing through his mind, he was hurling himself sideways, carrying Arsinoe with him, so that they both fell out of the bed seconds before the mattress was sliced into a thousand feathers.

They landed on top of the clothes John had recently discarded, and thus on top of his holster. He drew the revolver instinctively, while Arsinoe gave vent to several of the loudest screams he had ever heard. Automatic fire chattered into the wall above his head and he had some idea of how the diners in the restaurant must have felt. Like them he returned fire; unlike them, he was dealing with only two men. One of the intruders gave a shriek and collapsed. The other fired a last burst and ran back down the stairs.

John leapt to his feet; he had only fired

four times, so had two rounds left. He dashed across the room, while Arsinoe took to screaming again. 'You no go!' she shrieked.

John checked for a moment to look down at the man he had shot, who was writhing and groaning, losing a great deal of blood – the bullet had hit him in the abdomen – then ran on to the landing. The street door was open and the second assassin had disappeared. But there was a great deal of noise out there, and he suddenly realised he was naked. He went back into the bedroom.

'They wished to kill me,' Arsinoe shouted, standing up, her back pressed against the wall as if she expected to be shot again at any moment.

'No,' John said. 'They wished to kill me.' He dragged on his clothes. 'Do you have a telephone?'

'What I am going to do with a telephone?'

'Telephone people. Like a doctor for that chap.'

Arsinoe advanced across the room, slowly, and stood above the wounded man. Cautiously she prodded him with her toe, then hastily stepped back as his eyes opened and more blood spread across the floor. 'I think he is dying,' she remarked.

John supposed he would do so happy, looking up at a naked Arsinoe. But then, he might not be dying. In any event, help was at hand. Of a sort. The house was suddenly filled with Egyptians, all shouting and screaming and waving their arms.

'Get dressed,' John told Arsinoe. 'Listen,' he shouted. 'A doctor. We need a doctor. And an ambulance. An ambulance.'

A policeman appeared, with drawn revolver. John realised he was still holding his gun. The policemen levelled his weapon. 'I will shoot, effendi.'

Don't do that.' John threw the revolver on the bed. 'That man tried to kill me.'

'Why?' The policeman's eyes rolled towards Arsinoe, who was hastily dragging on her knickers. He obviously reckoned it was to do with her.

'It's a long story,' John said. 'Fetch a military policeman.'

'You come with me.' The policeman was gaining in confidence now that John was disarmed.

'And what about him?'

'I think he is dead.'

John supposed he could be right; the wounded man was no longer moving and his eyes were sightless. 'So you come, you see,' the policeman said, reasonably. 'You have killed a man. You know this man?' His eyes kept rolling towards Arsinoe, who was now quite decent.

'Never seen him before in my life,' John

said. 'But I have an idea I know something about him.'

'You come,' the policeman said again, feeling behind himself to make sure he had his handcuffs. 'No trouble, eh?'

'You no go!' Arsinoe shouted.

'Seems I must, sweetheart. She will be safe?' he asked the policeman.

'That man will not come back,' the policeman assured him.

'We got the bugger,' Jones said. 'He's Egyptian, but he works for the Germans. Does the name Buelow mean anything to you?'

John nodded. He had spent a long morning in police custody, being asked questions, before he had been able to contact Jones at all. 'He's the joker I was mixed up with when I was taken prisoner. An absolute Nazi thug. I went after him last month, and missed. But I got his girlfriend. She's the one who did all the singing for us. Did this character mention Buelow?'

'He works for him. Major Buelow is in charge of secret intelligence work for the Axis in North Africa.' Jones gave a dry smile. 'My equivalent, you might say. And as you say, he's clearly out for blood. It seems that this Egyptian lady friend of yours, Arsinoe, has been boasting that you were her man, and that you often visited her. So it was a simple matter for the assassins, having received their orders from Buelow, to stake out her house and wait for your next visit.'

'Kind of gives one the creeps,' John admitted.

'Yes, it does. Now, we must find you somewhere safe where you can rest up. The obvious choice would be England.'

'Ah, no. Not right this minute.'

Jones raised his eyebrows. 'You have a wife, don't you?'

'Yes. She's in the ATS, so it is extremely unlikely that she would have leave at the same time as me.'

'These things can be arranged.'

'Thank you. But I really would like to see it out here before I go home.'

'That could take a very long time.'

'I don't think it will. I think this time could be it.'

'I hope you're right,' Jones said. 'I also have a wife and children. But I suspect there is something personal in this. Buelow?'

'I'd like to get him, yes.'

Jones shook his head. 'That's not a good attitude, in war. Personal vendettas, I mean. However ... we have a safe place up-river. I'm afraid, to make it safe, we've also had to make it somewhat military. Here's a train pass and a pass for the camp itself. At least you'll be able to, ah, sleep, without worrying where the next bullet will come from.'

'And is sleeping all that I am likely to be able to do?'

'I'm quite sure you'll find someone with whom you can play cards,' Jones said.

'You're sure I'm not just being quietly arrested?'

'Why should I do that?'

'I was thinking of Margo's report.'

'That has been taken care of.' Jones gave a little sigh. 'So has Margo.'

'Eh?'

'She has spent a lot of her time rubbing people up the wrong way. When she came back from leave and discovered you had been sent back to the Senussi without her, she blew her top. When I told her it couldn't wait for her return, she went storming off to catch you up. Which she did, I believe.'

'In a manner of speaking.'

'Right. Well, Montgomery got to hear of it. He had no idea we were employing a woman as an agent, and it didn't do much good trying to explain that she was an old and trusted acquaintance of the Senussi. Actually, I don't think he cares much for our links with the Arabs in any event. Anyway, the upshot was that he ordered her to be returned to England to do what he supposes women soldiers do best – organising motor pools and duty rosters.'

'Has she gone?'

'I think she leaves tomorrow.' Jones pointed. 'So do you – up-river. And I'd like to see you back here in a couple of weeks, fighting fit.'

'Yes, sir. Am I allowed to see Arsinoe before I go?'

'Do you think that's a good idea?'

'It's a necessary one. She has all my gear, such as it is.'

But first of all he went back to Shepheard's.

'Major Cartwright in?'

The clerk checked the pigeonholes. 'Yes, sir. She's in her room.'

John rode up in the lift, went along to that so well-remembered number, knocked. 'Who is it?'

'John Warrey.'

The key turned and the door opened. John gazed at her tear-stained face. 'Come to gloat?'

'Come to say I'm sorry.'

She stood back, allowed him in. 'Bastards,' she said. 'Do you know how long I have worked for Intelligence? Ten years. Before anyone really thought there'd be a war. Before they gave me a uniform and a rank so I could tell people what to do. Now I'm to be a commandant in some girls' brigade. It's the desert that matters to me. I know the desert. I *belong* in the desert.'

'There's always Ali.'

333

'Oh, don't be obscene.'

'Sorry, just a suggestion. So ... I guess it's goodbye.'

She sat on the bed. 'I suppose you're going on to great things.'

'That depends on the battle. Whenever it happens.'

'And then it's home to wifey.'

'I'd like to think so.'

'Well ... good luck.'

'And to you. Margo ... we made a good partnership, from time to time.'

'From time to time,' she said. 'For God's sake get out of here.' She was crying again.

'You come, you go, you get killed, I get killed,' Arsinoe complained. At least the dead body had been removed, and she had scrubbed away the blood. But as a policeman remained on guard at her door, her activities were obviously going to be curtailed for the next few days.

'Nobody was trying to kill you,' John reminded her. 'And with me away, no one is even going to try to kill me here.' He packed up his kitbag.

'When you come back?' she asked.

'I really have no idea. But I probably will.'

'You come back.' Now she too was weeping, and clinging to him, her tears staining the front of his tunic. 'I like you, Warrey. I like you more than any man.'

'I like you too, Arsinoe. Listen, I'll be back.' He kissed her. 'I always have come back, haven't I?'

She sniffed. 'You come, you go. You no care about me, really.'

'I do,' he assured her. But it was half an hour before he could get away.

As Jones had indicated, the rest camp was very like a prison camp. Nobody was allowed in without a pass, and none of the recuperating officers was allowed out. They played tennis or nine-hole golf during the day, and poker or bridge or chess in the evenings. It was the most boring fortnight of John's life, made more so because he did not belong to any regular unit, and could not talk about either his work or his men; he didn't have any, save for Ali and his people. Out in the desert, waiting.

Most of the people in the camp were suffering from combat fatigue and had very little confidence in Montgomery. 'He wants to have everything just so before he fights,' someone complained. 'You can't have that in war. It's the unpredictable that decides battles. The ability to take advantage of the unpredictable. You'll see, Rommel will cut him up as he cut up Auchinleck.'

John couldn't even counter by telling them that Rommel wouldn't be commanding in this battle. That was top secret. But he was never so glad as when he finally received orders to leave the camp and join Seventh Armoured Division.

This was situated in an area he knew very well, at the southernmost end of the British position, and just north of the Qattara Depression; here they were part of General Brian Horrocks's Thirteenth Corps. John arrived on the morning of 22 October, to find everyone chafing at the bit. In fact, as he knew, the main strength of the British and Allied army lay to the north, while down in the south it was made even more impressive by the immense number of men and tanks and by the presence of the RAF ranging constantly overhead. 'One has to wonder if Monty ever intends to give the go-ahead,' Blanchard grumbled. 'But welcome aboard, Johnnie.'

They sat beneath a large sun umbrella beside Blanchard's tank, drinking tea and remembering the old days. 'Is it true Jerry tried to have you assassinated?' asked Coleman, Blanchard's new second-in-command,

'One of them did,' John said.

Blanchard grinned. 'You're safer here.'

The tank crews went through their drills constantly, did their keep-fit exercises, and oiled and greased their tanks and their weapons, all the next day. Around them everyone else was doing the same thing, Horrocks also having under his command the Forty-Fourth Infantry Division and the First Free French Brigade, which included a regiment of the Foreign Legion. The French were great fraternisers, exchanging bottles of surprisingly drinkable red wine for tins of bully beef. 'This war may be revolutionising the entire eating habits of Europe,' Blanchard remarked.

The general himself visited them that afternoon, inspecting the crews before joining Blanchard and John for a cup of tea. 'All still quiet, sir?' Blanchard asked.

'For the moment. I've a message for you, though,' the general said. 'Tonight is the off.'

Blanchard's head jerked. So did John's. At last!

'It's full moon, you see. Twenty-one forty. Our job down here is to make the enemy think we're the main thrust,' Horrocks explained. 'But we know there are minefields to a depth of several miles in front of us.' He glanced at John, 'I'm told you brought in that information, Warrey.'

'I got lucky, sir.'

'Well, let's hope you stay lucky. The infantry and engineers will go in first, to clear a way through the fields. The armour will follow. However, it is not our business either to suffer heavy casualties or to draw in any of our reserves to dig us out of a hole. We probe, and we suggest we're serious, but we pull back at the first sign of real opposition. Understood?'

'Yes, sir,' Blanchard said, glumly.

Horrocks grinned. 'Of course, there is always the unpredictable in war. If we were to find the way open, by any chance, we shall of course seize it. Good luck, gentlemen. I shall be in close contact.' He got into his command car and was driven off, while darkness came down with invariable desert suddenness.

'What do you reckon?' Blanchard asked.

'That tomorrow is going to be a long day.'

'Yes,' Blanchard agreed. 'We'd better see if we can get some sleep.'

There was little chance of that with only a few hours to go. The men stood around their tanks muttering to each other, drinking tea and eating their suppers, watching the moon rise to contrast dark shadows with areas of brilliant light, while across the desert there spread a slow rustle of anticipation and sound. Then precisely at twenty to ten the entire sky was lit up as something like a thousand British guns opened fire. The noise was utterly deafening, so great indeed that it affected the senses, had one or two men reeling.

But everyone knew what he had to do

and the tanks were immediately manned, while around them and in front of them long lines of tin-helmeted infantry and sappers moved forward, the French Foreign Legion on the left, the British on the right. Still the guns boomed and now the western skyline was also lit up by the mass of explosive bursts. As with most first-time observers of a major bombardment, John found it difficult to believe that anyone, or anything, could survive such a weight of shells, but his military reading reminded him that man's capacity for surviving bombardment had been proved time and time again.

It was just before dawn when they received the order to advance. The cleared path was well marked with luminous cords and pointers, but as they rolled slowly forward they could see to either side the scattered bodies of those gallant men who had died to create the opening. Now they came under fire from the enemy and blazed away with their own guns. But progress remained slow, and now their own tanks were on the receiving end, some being halted with smoke and flames belching from them.

It was a startling dawn with great plumes of smoke rising into the sky in the distance, both to the west and to the north, but also from close at hand where the tanks had brewed, with planes wheeling and snarling overhead, nearly all British, with the sky amazingly blue above the vapour trails, and with a steady stream of wounded men coming back from engaging the Italians. 'Hot stuff,' Blanchard commented. 'Who said the Eyeties can't fight?'

John wondered where Umberto was in all this

At midday the orders came to pull back and consolidate what they had. Which wasn't very much. But at least they could have breakfast and brew up the inevitable cups of tea. General Horrocks appeared. 'We've done what we were told to do,' he said. 'We'll try again tonight. How many tanks did you lose, Blanchard?'

'Five, sir.'

'And the crews?'

'I'm afraid so.'

Horrocks nodded. 'It's going to be rough. The Legion has lost Colonel Amilakvari. We've some prisoners, Warrey. Have a chat with them.'

The Italian soldiers were completely shell-shocked. John found an officer whose hands were shaking as he tried to drink his tea. 'It was so sudden, so unexpected,' he muttered. 'And then, General Stumme–'

'What about General Stumme?' John asked.

'He's disappeared,' the Italian moaned.

'He's been killed?' John's brain was tumbling.

'No, no. I do not know. When the bombardment began and he realised there was to be a battle, he tried to get up to the front, but ran into one of your advanced patrols, Australians I believe, and came under fire. His driver turned off to escape, and the general fell out of the car. It came over on the radio just before your men got through.'

'Have they got through?'

The Italian officer shrugged. 'The first line.'

'Didn't the driver go back for the general?'

'I believe so, but in the darkness and the firing he could not find him.'

John hurried off to give the news to Horrocks, who immediately radioed it to HQ. They already knew, but in fact Stumme or no Stumme, the initial assault had been held all along the line. The minefields were the Germans' principal defence; finding a way through them was proving more difficult than had been anticipated. Thirteen Corps attacked again the following day, and again the day after, and made no progress, while losing more tanks and men. The only positive news was that General Stumme's body had been found; he had apparently suffered a massive heart attack. That meant General von Thoma was now in command of the Afrika Korps, but from the British point of view this was hardly an advantage, as Thoma had been an aide to Rommel and was an experienced desert fighter.

And on the morning of 26 October, they learned that Rommel had returned from Germany, once again to take command.

'I hope Monty knows what he's doing,' Blanchard growled, surveying his battered regiment as they breakfasted the next day. Three days of hard fighting had produced only casualties, with not an inch of ground gained, and morale was suffering, especially as the news from further north was even less encouraging, heavy losses again having produced no results.

That evening Brigadier Harding came down to chat to the tank commanders. 'They need us further north,' he said. 'We're certainly not doing any good here. One regiment will remain. Blanchard, you'll move your men out and up to the map co-ordinates you'll be given.'

'How is the battle going, sir?' Blanchard asked.

Harding gave a wintry smile. 'No one ever thought it was going to be easy. Warrey, the army commander wants a word.'

John was driven north in a command car to where Montgomery's caravan was situated, surrounded by HQ troops. It was a hive of acitivity, but the faces were mostly glum. 'Warrey!' De Guingand himself escorted him into the inner office.

Montgomery looked as perky as ever. 'Those estimates you brought in have proved very accurate, Warrey.'

'Thank you, sir.'

'Now, you said that Rommel had about six hundred tanks, of which half were Panzers.'

'Yes, sir.'

'You also estimated that he had fuel for only perhaps one major counter-assault.'

'Yes, sir.'

'Well, he has launched that assault, and we have held him. We have also shot up a large number of Panzers. What is your estimation of his next move?'

John hesitated, looking at the map. 'He will hold, as long as he can, sir.'

'Even when he is down to less than a hundred tanks, and no fuel?'

'I believe he will hold, sir, as long as he can stop us breaking through.'

Montgomery considered for a few moments, then nodded. 'Very good. Seen any of that action you wanted?'

'Yes, sir.'

'But you'd like to see more, eh? Rejoin your unit. But stay alive. I may need you later on.'

'Which is as close to a compliment as you'll get,' de Guingand told him as he was returned to his car.

By now rumours were seeping down that GHQ in Cairo, and even more so, the Cabinet in London, were unhappy with the way things were going. This was exemplified by a visit from General Alexander. But Montgomery was going to fight his way; he did not anticipate that Alexander would do an Auchinleck and remove him in the middle of the battle. The probing attacks and the attempts to find a way through the minefields continued for the next week. The troops had very little idea what was going on, save that they and their comrades, and in the case of the armour, their machines, were being cut down with relentless monotony. John, with his knowledge that Rommel's position had to be reaching the final stages of precariousness, was better off than most, and he shared his knowledge with Blanchard, but it was still soul-destroying, to move forward behind the various infantry formations to which they were attached, to be engaged by enemy armour, and to be checked time and again by the discovery of a fresh minefield.

They lost track of time, existed from sunrise to sunset, sunset to sunrise, eating whenever they could, perpetually thirsty, filthy and unwashed and unshaven. Until suddenly they were through. No one was quite sure how it had happened, save that it was obviously the result of the relentless, expensive probing. But the message came back from the sappers: All clear.

Blanchard levelled his glasses at the desert in front of him, as did John. They could make out vehicles moving, some miles away, and columns of dust. 'He's getting out,' Blanchard said, and reported by radio to Harding. 'Advance,' Harding ordered.

'Hallelujah!' Blanchard shouted, and thumbed his mike. 'Squadron will advance.'

'Destination, sir?' someone asked.

'Just go,' Blanchard said.

The tank engines roared and they raced past the cheering infantry and sappers, sending their own pillars of dust clouding into the sky. They raced up to the Axis strongpoint at El Aqqaqir, passing on their way burned-out tanks and, inevitably, the scattered bodies of blackened men, some of whom had been lying unburied on the sand for several days. And, too, they encountered columns of men, mainly Italians, walking slowly towards them, some with their hands in the air, reminding John of 1940. But these men were resentful as most of the wheeled transport which had been available had been commandeered by the Germans to move their own men out. The tanks ignored them – they would be picked up by the infantry coming behind.

They had to stop that evening to allow

their logistical support to catch up with them as they were nearly out of fuel. Blanchard reported his position but was somewhat abashed to be told in reply that he had gone further than he should, and that he must stand fast and wait for the rest of the army to catch him up. 'One needs to bear in mind the possibility of an Axis trap, or counter-attack,' Harding told him.

Blanchard looked at John, who shook his head. 'Not a chance now.' That evening it began to rain.

In the beginning this was great fun. Men just stood away from their tanks and allowed the water to flood their filthy bodies; some stripped right off and cavorted about like schoolboys. Even Blanchard and John allowed themselves to be soaked, while on a more practical note, Coleman had the cooks collecting as much of the water as they could.

However, when at midnight it was still pouring, it ceased to be quite as enjoyable; they could feel the desert beneath their feet turning into a huge swamp. 'Is this supposed to happen?' Coleman asked. He hadn't been in North Africa as long as either John or Blanchard.

'Not really,' Blanchard said. 'It does rain, from time to time. But this is a damned inconvenient time for it to happen.'

'Must affect the enemy as much as

ourselves,' Coleman suggested.

'I suspect he has less gear to get through it,' John said.

Next morning they were in a morass. More armour arrived, along with truckloads of infantry, the wheeled vehicles slithering to and fro on the muddy tracks; even the tanks were difficult to steer. But the pursuit was resumed. Rommel had already turned back to make a stand at Fuka, some sixty miles west of Alamein, but had then had to pull out again, as two squadrons of the Royal Dragoon Guards, using armoured cars, had got behind his lines and were shooting up everything in sight. 'We need to be up there with them,' Blanchard complained.

For the next week they slowly advanced, while the rain continued to pour down, and the entire countryside seemed to be turning into a quagmire. They passed growing numbers of abandoned vehicles, neither shot up nor bogged down, but simply lacking fuel. They took increasing numbers of prisoners, but as before, these were mainly Italian. They had not caught up with the Afrika Korps, or what was left of it, which was steadily withdrawing to the comparative safety of Tunis, where there were huge Axis forces concentrated.

'They don't really have a hope,' Blanchard said. 'Listen to this: yesterday the Americans and the British landed in Morocco. A huge army! We've got him from both sides.' The tank crews gave a hearty cheer.

There could be no doubt that Alamein had been a great, if largely unspectacular, victory. It had been won by resolute men pressing ahead regardless of casualties, and equally by the determination of their commanding general. But the real victory, everyone knew, would be achieved when the Afrika Korps had been destroyed or driven out of Africa, and hopefully, Rommel had been captured. And that still had not been accomplished.

Meanwhile British armour was becoming subject to the weather. Blanchard stood with his hands on his hips glaring at the mechanics who were working as best they could in the still teeming rain. John, his cap strapped under his chin and wearing a poncho-type raincoat, stood beside him. 'Well?' Blanchard demanded.

'There's a bearing gone, sir,' said the sergeant.

'Well?'

'We can repair it, but it'll take time.'

'Well?'

'Maybe twenty-four hours.'

'Twenty-four hours?'

'Takes time, sir.'

'Fucking hell,' Blanchard said. 'I'll have to

catch you up, Roddy,' he told Coleman.

He grinned. 'We'll look out for you. You coming with us, Johnnie?'

John hesitated. Almost his entire war, shootingwise, had been done at Blanchard's side. A figure emerged through the rain. 'Excuse me, sir, but there's a wog here asking for you, Captain Warrey.'

'I'm sure you mean a Bedouin, corporal,' John said.

'Ah, yes, sir. Claims to be some kind of sheikh.'

John splashed through the mud. 'Ali!'

'Warrey!' They embraced, watched with interest by the tank crews.

'You mean you know each other?' Blanchard had also come up.

'My oldest friend, virtually,' John said. 'What are you doing here, Ali?'

'My people wish to be in at the death, eh?'

'Where are they?'

'Not far from here. I have news.'

'Yes?'

'Of Rommel. He is not far.'

'Well, we figured that. You mean you know exactly where he is?'

'He wishes to make another stand. It will be at Tobruk. You still wish this man?'

John looked at Blanchard. 'I wish him,' Ali said. 'He killed my father.'

'And you can get to him?' Blanchard asked.

'There is no order any more.' Ali waved his hand. 'People come and go everywhere. I have been to Tobruk. Rommel will go to Tobruk. An hotel is being prepared for him.'

'Shit,' Blanchard commented. 'If we could nobble Rommel...'

'I have an idea the sheikh is thinking of something more permanent than nobbling him,' John said.

'Is he really a sheikh? He looks a little young.'

'Right on both counts. Can you really get to him, Ali?'

'Oh, yes,' Ali said.

'How long will it take you to reach Tobruk?'

'We travel fast, across the desert. Your trucks and tanks and the Germans travel slow because of the rain.'

John nodded. 'Right. I'll come with you.' He explained to Blanchard.

'Now hold on just a minute,' Blanchard said. 'We'll need authority.'

'This is an intelligence job,' John pointed out. 'I am an intelligence officer. We haven't time to ask for authority. Just pretend I wandered off into the desert.'

Blanchard scratched his chin. 'I'll wait for you in Tobruk,' John said.

'Warrey!' Uluma shrieked, throwing herself into his arms. 'You came back. I knew you

350

would come back.' John and Ali had ridden their camels through the night and the rain to reach the Bedouin encampment, which was only some twenty kilometres from the Allied advanced posts, and about level with the Germans. Save that the Germans, and the Italians, were all concentrated on the coast road, trying to take advantage of the cloud cover that was protecting them from the RAF.

There were some fifty Senussi, and some of them John recognised as his allies in the raid on the Tobruk restaurant. But there was also Mamun, apparently determined to be in at the kill, now that it appeared the Axis forces were well and truly beaten. With him were some of his women, including, to John's amazement, Freda. And of course, Uluma. He did not suppose there was any possibility she would have stayed behind. But Freda...?

'You may speak with her,' Mamun said. 'As you know her so well.'

She remained hidden behind her yashmak, her eyes as myopic as ever, but even her forehead was pink. 'So, how are things?' John asked.

'How should things be?' she asked. 'I am the sheikh's woman.'

'And life is acceptable?'

She tossed her head. 'I am his favourite. He wishes me all the time.'

'Even in Tobruk, killing Germans?'

'He says I am to interpret.' What? John wondered. 'Besides,' she went on, 'in Tobruk I will be able to obtain new glasses. So the sheikh says.'

'And the best of luck.' He went off to find Uluma and Ali.

'Now we have won,' she said, 'we kill all the Germans, and all the Italians, too.'

'Rommel,' Ali said. 'He is the one we want.' He waved his people into action, and they mounted their camels and rode to the west, while the rain continued to fall and every step was a splash. All their clothes were soaked through, but no one cared, and their rifles and tommy-guns were well greased to keep out the water. 'How is Major Cartwright?' Ali asked.

'She has returned to England,' John said.

'Ah. When the War is over, perhaps I go to England to find her.'

'I'm sure she'd enjoy that,' John agreed, mentally rolling his eyes.

Two days later they saw Tobruk. It had stopped raining but the ground was still a morass, out of which the half-destroyed buildings rose like creatures of the swamp. Now they were once again in the presence of the enemy, although it was difficult to regard them as enemies any longer. There were few vehicles moving on the road, but a great many scattered to either side. Some had clearly just run out of fuel, but most had been strafed by the RAF and were burnt-out shells.

Those vehicles that did have fuel and were still moving were packed with men, both inside and out; even the tanks were covered with men, all desperately trying to get away. Of those who could not find places on the tanks or in the trucks, some trudged along to the west, heads bowed, many of them lacking rifles. Others had just given up and sat by the roadside. They looked without interest at the Arab group – Ali having told his people to conceal their weapons – although one or two cursed at them. There were no officers to be seen; what order there was was being maintained by hard-bitten NCOs. 'We could kill all these people,' Uluma said.

'And be killed ourselves,' John said. 'Our business is Rommel.'

As before, he wanted a prisoner. They made their way towards the burning town, keeping off the road, taking shelter as did everyone else whenever a RAF plane soared overhead, but with the clouds still low this did not happen very often. At last they came across a lone German soldier. He had been wounded in the leg; his pants were split open and a bloodstained bandage was wrapped round his thigh. He had obviously been trying to walk into Tobruk and had just run out of strength. Now he sat on the edge of a wadi, some fifty yards from the road, head hanging between his knees, but looking up with a start as the Arabs surrounded him. 'Do you speak Italian?' John asked. The man stared at him. 'We need Freda,' John decided.

She was brought forward. 'Careful what you say, now,' John said. 'Remember you're here to interpret, not give anyone ideas.' She sniffed. 'Ask him where the field marshal is.'

Freda asked the question, and the man – he was hardly more than a boy – raised his head to stare at her. Then spoke volubly.

'*Nein, nein,*' Freda said, and replied.

'What is he asking?' John inquired.

'He recognises me as a German,' Freda explained.

'Does he know where Rommel is?'

Freda asked again. The boy shrugged, but made a reply. 'Well?'

'He says he thinks the field marshal is still in the town.'

'Right. If he's still there, he must be thinking about another stand. Let's get in there before the barricades go up.'

'And this one?' Ali asked. 'If he knows that we have a German woman with us–'

'Did you admit you were German?' John asked.

'No. I told him I am a Bedouin,' Freda said. 'A Berber,' she added, in explanation of her fair skin.

'Then we'll chance our arm,' John said. Ali looked doubtful, but the wounded man was left unharmed.

Tobruk was still a few miles away and it was nearly dusk before they reached the outskirts of the town. Here there were already machine-gun emplacements, and several tanks as well, with motorised artillery, overlooking the road. The soldiers coming up the road were being stopped at a checkpoint and checked before being allowed in. 'I do not think they will let us through,' Ali said. 'We must try somewhere else.'

They turned aside and trekked through the gathering darkness, round the outskirts of the town, territory John knew very well, but always overseen by the machine-gun nests and the half-concealed tanks. 'He certainly means to fight,' John commented.

Then there was another checkpoint where the road came out of the desert. John saw the Italian flag waving above the post. 'This is our best bet,' he said, and waved the group forward.

'Halt!' came the shout.

John waved again, and the Arabs obeyed; they were now some fifty yards from the post. 'What do you wish?' the lieutenant in command called.

John went forward, his burnous pulled across his face. 'We wish to enter the town, effendi.'

'You cannot. This is a military area.'

John made a pre-arranged signal with his hand, behind his back, and the Arab men came forward. The women remained at a distance, ready to go to ground. 'We have relatives in the town, effendi,' John said.

'Then you will have to wait to see them,' the lieutenant said. 'My orders are to admit no Arabs.'

'Well, then,' John said, drew his revolver, and fired. The lieutenant went down without a sound and before his startled men could understand what was happening Ali and his people had also opened fire. The skirmish was over in a matter of seconds. Ali waved his women forward and led his men towards the town, John at his side.

Now a siren was wailing and they could hear the roar of engines as men were rushed to the scene of the incident, where seven men lay dead or dying on the ground. 'This way,' said Ali's cousin, who lived in the town,

They ran down a side street, then another, before ducking into a ruined house to pause for breath. The din quite close at hand was tremendous. 'They will certainly come after us,' John said.

Ali nodded. 'We must get on.' He turned to Freda, 'Where will Rommel be?'

She looked, as usual, totally shocked by what had just happened, what she had seen. 'He has headquarters, by the sea.'

'Lead us there.' She licked her lips, and swallowed, then nodded.

John had a sudden uneasy feeling. 'She means to betray us,' he whispered to Ali.

'How can she do this?'

'How can she not do this? She is a German, and a Nazi. These are her people. Rommel is her god.'

'What must we do? I cannot kill her. She is my uncle Mamun's woman.'

'I think you should tell him.'

'He will not believe me. He is very much in love with her.'

'All right,' John said. 'But I will remain at her side, and if she starts anything, I shall kill her.'

Ali was aghast. 'You cannot do that. You cannot kill Mamun's woman. That would give him the right to kill you.'

What a shitting mess, John thought. 'Are you telling me that as Mamun's woman she is inviolate?'

'Only Mamun may kill her,' Ali said.

'And he won't believe she will betray him.' John gave up. 'Let's go.' But he stayed immediately behind Freda as they crept out of the building; Mamun was beside her.

Uluma was behind him. But even Uluma seemed to have accepted that Freda was beyond her immediate reach.

Ali's cousin led the way, directed by Freda, and they actually avoided any contact with the Germans or Italians, even if they had from time to time to crouch in the shadows as patrols hurried by. But all the men at the checkpoint were dead, and the defenders had no way of knowing whether any enemy had actually entered the town or had merely shot up the outpost and gone back into the desert. The little group crept forward and reached the Gestapo headquarters. Here the policemen were packing up. Three trucks and four command cars waited in the yard, while the trucks were being loaded with both files and supplies. They had no intention of taking part in Rommel's last stand.

John glanced at Freda, saw the strain in her face as she saw her erstwhile comrades – there were women secretaries as well as men helping with the loading – preparing to escape. She licked her lips and suddenly her expression changed. John followed the direction of her gaze ... and saw Buelow just emerging from the building.

Twelve

The Victors

'Fritz!' Freda screamed. 'Help me!'

Buelow's head swung round even as the Arabs began firing, realising that they had been betrayed. Mamun grasped Freda round the waist and hurled her to the ground where she continued to scream.

The Gestapo guards returned fire, while retreating into the building. One of them had been hit and lay on the ground shouting for help. One of the Arabs had also been hit, but he was dead. 'The bitch!' Mamun bellowed. 'The bitch. I will cut out her heart.'

'Later,' John snapped. It was very necessary to finish this business as rapidly as they could, because the Gestapo would certainly be calling for help. 'Grenades,' he said. Two were thrust into his hands. 'We need several.'

'I will come with you,' Ali said.

There was no time to argue. 'Cover us,' John said, and ran forward, tommy-gun spitting.

The firing had died down for the moment.

Now the Germans opened up again and John had to hurl himself to one side, pulling the pin and tossing a grenade as he did so. He was jarred by the fall but did not think he had been hit, while the grenade had landed close to one of the trucks where it exploded. Under cover of this John reached the gate, joined by Ali, who had also tossed a grenade into the forecourt. One of the command cars went up but the Germans were spraying the vehicles and beyond with automatic fire, and a further advance was for the moment impossible.

The rest of the Arabs now moved forward, firing as they came. Two were hit and went down, but their companions did not lack courage and surged on. John and Ali threw two more grenades, as his people, who now included several of the women, led by Uluma, crouched beside them. 'We will need a big gun to smash our way in,' Ali panted.

And that they did not have, while from behind them they could hear the sound of sirens and the roar of engines. It was going to have to be a frontal assault, supposing any of them could survive that. The alternative was simply to melt away and regroup. But with Buelow so close ... he had to do the sensible thing, John knew. 'We must get out of here,' he said.

'I want that man,' Uluma snarled, her lips

drawn back from her mouth.

'I'm sure you'll get him one of these days,' John told her. 'But it won't do you much good if he gets *you* again.'

As he spoke, there was a sudden flurry of movement in front of them. The Germans were certainly not going to lie down and die. They had manned the two of the trucks and now came driving out of the yard, through the flames, sub-machine guns chattering away. The Arabs were taken entirely by surprise and threw themselves left and right, but several were hit. John flung himself down, firing as he did so, looked up and saw Buelow, only feet away from him, as the truck slewed sideways and braked. He levelled his revolver, but checked as Uluma ran forward, screaming her hatred, waving her knife. His heart seemed to skip a beat as he realised she was about to die, and then he stared in consternation as Buelow leaned out of the truck, slapping sideways with the barrel of his sub-machine gun.

The blow struck Uluma on the side of the head and she gave a little shriek and dropped her knife as she fell. But still Buelow did not shoot her. Instead he leaned from the truck, dug his fingers into her haik and plucked her bodily into the vehicle. Then the engine was gunning again and the truck raced forward. Ali stood beside John and levelled his own tommy-gun, but John slapped it down. 'You'll kill Uluma.'

Ali glared at him. 'Do you not suppose they mean to do that?'

John sighed. 'Let us hope not. They seem to regard her as a hostage for their safety. We'll catch up with them, Ali. Right now, we have to get out of here.'

Ali could see that to remain would be suicidal, and he waved his men back after tossing a few more grenades in the direction of the remaining Gestapo transport, then threw some more inside the building. They heard screams from inside; Buelow had abandoned his wounded in his determination to get out. But the dying men could not be rescued now. The Arabs recrossed the street and gained the shelter of the buildings opposite.

Here John found Freda, who had been left lying on the ground, her wrists and ankles tied. She had stopped screaming, from exhaustion, but now she panted. 'Help me,' she begged.

Help you, John thought, when Uluma is probably being tortured right this minute? He felt utterly exhausted, more mentally than physically. He had led these people into this inferno. Now ... he looked at Mamun. 'She will die,' the sheikh said.

John swallowed. Freda's shriek had caused the catastrophe that had overtaken them. Yet as a presumably civilised British officer he had to do the best he could. 'Not here,' he said. 'The enemy are too close.'

In fact an armoured car was already coming down the street, machine-gun blazing. But this attracted return fire from a tank coming the other way, and the Arabs seized the opportunity to get away. 'Bring her,' Mamun told one of his sons, a big man, who unceremoniously threw Freda over his shoulder.

'Utter a sound and I will cut your throat,' he told her. Freda continued to pant but she kept silent, no doubt still hoping to be rescued.

While John wondered what on earth he was to do? He had known that she would betray them. He had known that the only fate she could expect was death. But it was the thought of how she was going to die... He was a British Army officer. These men were nominally under his command. He could insist that Freda's life be spared ... but would they obey him in such a domestic matter?

They crept through the tumbled ruins, going to ground whenever they saw a German or an Italian patrol. Behind them the firing had died down as the armoured car and tank had established that they were on the same side. But that there was a possibly large and certainly determined enemy force all around them could not be denied; now the whole town was filled with grinding noise. 'They are pulling out,' Ali said, and grinned. 'We made them do that. They think we are the British.'

He was undoubtedly right. Every main street was filled with armour and with men, moving to the west. There was no hope of finding Rommel, at least in a position where he could be killed or captured. Or of immediately getting after Uluma. 'What are we to do?' Ali asked.

'Sit tight for the moment,' John said. 'Once the Germans and Italians go, the British will move in.'

'Now we can deal with the woman,' Mamun said.

'Ah ... technically, she is a prisoner of war,' John pointed out.

'She is my wife, who has betrayed me,' Mamun said. 'She will die for it. The law is mine.'

'Ah...' John desperately tried to think, hampered by Freda's little moaning sounds. 'Just what did you have in mind?'

'She must be placed in a strong sack, together with a dog, a cat and a rat, and hoisted from the ground, and left there until all movement ceases.'

Freda gave a shriek of purest terror, which ended abruptly as someone hit her in the stomach. 'I see,' John said. 'Where is this sack?'

'I do not have a sack,' Mamun said.

'There's a point. Well, do you have a dog, a cat, or a rat?'

'I can obtain them. And a sack.'

'But not while this town is running wild with enemy troops, I think we will have to put her fate on hold for a while.'

'Burn her,' Mamun said enthusiastically.

'Yes, we will burn her. I will push a flaming stick up her ass.' Freda gave another stifled shriek.

'I meant, she will have to wait,' John said severely. 'I understand and appreciate your laws and customs, Sheikh Mamun and I have no intention of interfering with them. But now I am speaking as your commanding officer. The woman's execution must wait until the Germans and Italians have entirely evacuated the town. I wish this understood.'

Mamun considered him for some seconds, then nodded. 'Perhaps it will be best. Once the enemy have gone, we will be able to let her scream as she dies.'

'Absolutely,' John said. 'We wouldn't want her to die without screaming. Now let's see what's going on.'

He split them up to seek various vantage points and report back: they knew the town far better than he did. He stayed with Freda and the women, just to be sure. He didn't trust them where the German woman was concerned. Correctly. 'You mean to free that bitch,' Halil growled.

'Me? Have I not said–'

'You are a liar,' Halil declared. 'You will delay her execution until the soldiers get here, then you will let them deal with Mamun. You are a traitor to my people. And you have let the Germans take Uluma. She was like a sister to me.'

'As it happens, I am not your people,' John said. 'And what you have just said amounts to insubordination. Watch your tongue, or I will have you whipped.'

'You?' she enquired contemptuously. 'You have not the spirit for it.'

Right that moment, he did. He dug his fingers into her thick hair and brought her face close to his. Halil gave a little squeal, but it was mostly pleasure. And too late he remembered that she was fully armed, her weapons including her fearsome knife. But she was showing no signs of using it. 'I like it when you hold me,' she said. 'I would like it when you beat me, too.'

'For God's sake–'

To his relief, Ali appeared beside them. 'The Germans have all gone,' he said. 'Only the Italians are left.'

John frowned. 'They still mean to hold the town?'

Ali grinned. 'I do not think so. These are mainly policemen. But the Germans have taken all the transport. Listen, Warrey, this is our big chance. My people wish to attack these policemen, eh, and destroy them. They have suffered very much and very often at the hands of these people. Now they wish to be avenged. With the Italian policeman is their commander, Colonel Umberto. They wish to hang him.'

John frowned. 'Umberto has ill-treated your people? Personally?' He couldn't believe it.

'I do not know if he has done this personally,' Ali said. 'But his men have certainly done so. On his orders.'

'More likely he was just obeying orders himself,' John muttered. Once again he was in a dilemma. He had to maintain and retain the trust of the Arabs. But he could not allow Umberto to be cut to pieces, or hanged; the man was an old friend, and he had helped him to escape two years before.

'We will call on them to surrender,' he said.

'That is not what we want. They are packing up now, and then they will attempt to leave the town on foot. When they have left their headquarters they will be easy pickings. We will have them all.' Halil clapped her hands.

What a mess, John thought. But again, he was the man on the spot. Voluntarily. To get even with Buelow. 'We will call upon them to surrender,' he said again. 'And put them under guard until the British Army gets here.'

Ali considered him with the same expression Mamun had worn a few minutes earlier. Then he shrugged. 'And if they do not surrender?'

John sighed. 'Then I suppose we will attack them.'

'I will summon my people,' Ali said.

'But we are going to do it now,' John said.

Ali frowned. 'They have a strong position. It would be better to wait until they leave.'

'We will do it now,' John told him.

Ali assembled his people; there were now some sixty of them and John guessed that he had recruited from amongst the Tobruk Arab population, emerging from their underground shelters now that the fighting had ceased. The town was still filled with noise. There were several fires out of which timbers were falling and stone and plaster crumbling; there were quite a few shots and screams as the Arabs sought revenge on their Italian taskmasters, and there was a distant but growing rumble as the Allied Army came closer.

John wondered if they would get there in time to prevent a massacre. But he could not save the lives of everyone in the town. He could only concentrate on certain objectives.

The Arabs moved forward until they reached the square on the far side of which was the Police Station. Oddly, John realised, he had never been in there. When he had been taken prisoner the first time, it had been in Benghazi. And the second time, while it had been here in Tobruk, he had been taken straight to Gestapo headquarters, which was one of the buildings still burning.

It was now quite close to dawn and there were no lights showing in the Police Station. But even in the gloom they could tell that there was a considerable amount of activity in there. And now the first men emerged, carrying knapsacks as well as haversacks and water bottles, rifles slung, ready for a long march. John drew his revolver and fired a single shot. He had meant it as a warning, but instantly the Arabs opened general fire. One of the Italian policemen spun round and crashed to the ground. The others darted back into the building and returned fire, but they had no idea at whom they were aiming, and it soon died down.

'Cease fire,' John bawled. 'Colonel Umberto!' he shouted. 'You cannot leave Tobruk. If you attempt to do so you will be killed. This is John Warrey speaking. If you and your men come out of the Station unarmed and with your hands in the air, you will be taken prisoner, unharmed.'

Sufficient of the Arabs spoke Italian to start a ripple of muttered discontent.

'Warrey?' Umberto called. 'Are you responsible for this mayhem? I should have known.'

'Let's say I'm calling the shots today, Umberto,' John said. 'I do not wish you to be harmed. Please be sensible and surrender.'

'And can you control your friends, Giovanni?'

'Yes,' John said, praying he was right.

'I wish time to consider this.'

John looked at the luminous dial of his watch. 'You will surrender by five o'clock,' he said. 'That is in half an hour.'

Umberto did not reply. 'We should have let them all come out,' Ali grumbled. 'And *then* called on them to surrender.'

'They will surrender,' John assured him.

How he wished they would, and that the British would arrive. Then he could get on after Buelow. And Uluma ... whatever was left of her. A single shot cut across the morning. The Arabs sat up straight, peering at the Police Station and the men who began to file out, behind a white flag. 'Remember,' John said. 'No one is to be harmed.' But he had a leaden feeling in his stomach. A single shot... Umberto was a man of honour.

The Arabs saw that the policemen were

unarmed and stood up, their guns thrust forward. At that moment they would obey him, he was sure. 'Place them under guard,' he told Ali.

The Arabs surrounded the twenty-odd policemen, pushing them together, muttering threats, but not prepared to act on their own; they could hear the growl of the British armour approaching along the road. John went into the station itself; Umberto had not been amongst the prisoners. Heart beating most painfully, he went up the stairs and quickly found the colonel's office. And Umberto. His old friend lay on his back, his revolver on the floor beside him. Only by his uniform was it possible to determine who it was; by placing the muzzle to his temple before squeezing the trigger, Umberto had blown his head to bits.

'Well, Warrey, another coup,' said General Montgomery. Monty was in very good spirits, as he should be; the rain had stopped, at least for the moment, the enemy had evacuated Tobruk, and he could now get on with his pursuit. 'I understand it was your entry into the town with the partisans that forced the Germans to pull out.'

'I wouldn't go so far as to claim that, sir,' John said. 'But I think we gave them a suggestion that the place was untenable, with an Arab uprising on their hands.'

'Excellent. I think you could probably do with another break.'

'With respect, sir, we haven't got Rommel yet.'

Montgomery frowned at him. 'We are going to do that.'

'I think he may need a few more prods.'

'And you think you can catch up with him before we do? That's a tall order.'

'Not so tall, sir. He is short of both transport and fuel. That means a large part of his army is on foot. He seems prepared to abandon the Italians where necessary, but he is certainly not going to abandon the Afrika Korps, I would estimate that he will make another stand at the first position he feels he can hold. Now, sir, the roads are still very bad, and there is still rain about. Our armour is not going to be able to travel very fast either. Whereas I and my Arabs, using camels, can cross the desert.'

'You cannot take on the Afrika Korps with camels, rifles and tommy-guns, Warrey.'

'In direct confrontation, no, sir. But if we can get round behind them, we can cause an awful amount of trouble.'

'Hm.' Montgomery stroked his chin. 'I imagine you could. You'll suffer casualties.'

'My people are prepared for that, sir.'

'Very good, Warrey. It is a brilliant idea, if it works. I'm appointing you brevet lieutenant colonel for the rest of this campaign. Raise as many men as you can in a hurry, and see what you can do.'

'I'll need weapons and ammunition, and dynamite, sir.'

Montgomery nodded. 'Requisition whatever you need.'

'God, I wish I was coming with you,' Blanchard said. 'Can't you twist the old man's arm?'

'I had to twist it as it is,' John said. 'And the fact is, William, that the desert is so torn up by that rain I doubt even tracked vehicles could get through. Whereas camels will have no problem.'

'Well ... we'll be coming along the road, just as hard as we can,' Blanchard promised.

John rode off to where Ali and his people had encamped. There was a British outpost just north of the harka; the men there were looking haggard. 'There have been some pretty unearthly sounds coming from down there, sir,' the sergeant said. 'I supposed it might be a German they had got hold of, and went down to have a look, but I was told it was a domestic matter.'

'Yes,' John said.

'Will you sort it out, sir?'

'If I can.'

He walked his camel down the slope

towards the black tents. He was quickly seen and a great shout went up. 'Warrey! Warrey is back!'

Ali came forward to greet him. 'What news?'

'We have been given permission to strike at the enemy's rear,' John said.

'Oorah!' Ali shouted.

His men took up the cry. 'Oorah!'

'Now tell me what has been happening here,' John said.

'We have been waiting for you,' Ali said, innocently.

'You have executed Freda.'

Ali shrugged. 'Mamun was determined on it. And she deserved it.'

'How was it done?'

Another shrug. 'He told you how it would be done.'

John brushed him aside and strode into the midst of the tents. Halil ran forward to grasp his arm. 'Now we are avenged,' she said. 'Uluma is avenged.'

He brushed her aside also, and gazed at Mamun. 'Now we go back to war,' the sheikh said.

'Where is she?' John demanded.

Mamun waved his arm. 'You do not wish to see her, Warrey. They have buried her.'

'Together with the dog and the cat and the rat?'

Mamun grinned. 'The dog ate the rat.'

John felt sick. 'She was my prisoner. I took her prisoner. And I promised her her life.'

'But then you gave her to me,' Mamun pointed out.

'I did that to save her life, not so that she could be tortured to death.'

'A man, or a woman's, fate is written,' Mamun said. 'Who can go against Fate?'

John glared at him for several seconds. But there was nothing to be done now. And was Mamun not right? Freda's fate had been inescapable from the moment she had accompanied Buelow into Uluma's cell. It would have been most merciful to execute her out there in the desert, the very first time, instead of tying her up, so that she could escape and make one or two more futile grabs at life. But then, did that not also apply to Buelow? 'Let's move out,' he said.

He now commanded a sizeable harka, some seventy men, well-armed and eager, and a score of women, no less anxious to get at the enemy. At least there were no children. Sadly, several dogs had accumulated at the encampment, and these had to be shot; he could not risk their barking alerting any enemy.

He spread his map before Ali and Mamun. 'The enemy are pulling back along the road,' he told them. 'They may make a stand at Derna, but there are no port facilities there. I would expect them to be thinking of Benghazi as their best defensive position, especially as the Eighth Army can only get at them along the road. We will cross the desert south of the Jebel al Akhdar, and reach the coast south of Benghazi.'

He showed them what he had brought with him, and they gazed at the dynamite in wonder. 'Our business must be to blow up the road here,' he said, prodding the map. 'You will see that there is a bridge over a wadi. If that goes, their transport will be held up. That is our primary objective. But we are also to cause as much disruption as possible. If we can make them believe that a large Arab army is concentrating south of Benghazi, they may well determine to surrender.' He grinned. 'To Montgomery rather than to us.'

'We will kill them all,' Mamun said.

'We will take them prisoner, if we can,' John corrected. But he knew that a little bit of frightfulness, to begin with, would be even more encouragement to the Italians, at least, to call it a day.

They rode out that night, although as there were no Axis planes left to overfly them, there was no danger in daylight travel. By dawn, the camels maintaining a steady ten miles an hour, they had covered 120 miles, and while his people – as he now had to consider them – knelt in prayer, John climbed up a nearby dune and used his binoculars. This was the same territory he had covered with the Seventh Armoured Brigade back in 1940, when General O'Connor had launched his brilliant counter attack that had all but destroyed the Italian Army. Nothing had changed. To his north the mountains rose in serrated splendour, glowing in the rising sun. For the rest there was nothing but desert. But he knew that roughly a hundred miles away was the fortified town of Beda Fomm. As with the tanks two years previously, he needed to bypass the town: he had neither the men nor the firepower to engage in a pitched battle.

Prayers over, and a meal, he led his small force forward again for another few hours. By then he estimated they were within seventy miles of the town and called a halt. Here they would sit out the midday heat and from here they were well placed to pass the town in darkness. 'We're going to fight a great battle,' Ali said, sitting beside him.

'Hopefully not,' John said. 'Our aim is to discourage the enemy from fighting another great battle.'

Ali considered this. Then he asked, 'Do you think Uluma is still alive?'

'I wouldn't count on it. Unless Buelow still has a weakness for her.'

'Will you avenge her?'

'I intend to, if I get the chance,'

'You should give him to our women. Give him to Halil.'

'I think we have had enough of that,' John said.

But Halil kept staring at him. He had an uneasy feeling that if he did not give Buelow to her, she might take him instead. He hoped the SS officer was good and dead. And Uluma? She would have died spitting her defiance to the end.

As the sun began to set, the harka resumed its journey. At midnight they saw lights to the south-west. They might be on the losing side, and no doubt they had been strafed by the RAF, but the people of Beda Fomm were endeavouring to get on with their lives. And at dawn, with the town behind them, they saw the sea. Again, *déjà vu*. Only this time, instead of Blanchard and Plassey and Layton and all his other friends in the Armoured Brigade, he was in command of a bunch of the most bloodthirsty people he had ever known. 'We move down now?' Ali asked, at his shoulder.

John studied the coast road through his binoculars, and began to wonder if the Germans did intend to make a stand in

Benghazi. The road was filled with a steady line of vehicles and another line of infantry, marching along, rifles slung, shoulders humped in dejection. Then the RAF roared overhead and the men on the road scattered, while bombs exploded and vehicles burned. 'They will leave nothing for us,' Ali grumbled.

'We will move down at dusk,' John told him. Ali snorted in disgust. But he cheered up when John outlined what they would have to do. 'As it seems the road is in constant use,' John said, 'probably by night as well as day, we will have to mount a holding action while the dynamite and detonators are laid.'

'We will kill them all,' Mamun said, repeating his favourite theme.

'You will do as I tell you,' John said. 'Sheikh Mamun will take the main force to a position ... here.' He stabbed the map with his finger. 'He will seize his opportunity, cut the road, establish a block, and hold off the enemy until the charges are laid. Understood?' Mamun rubbed his hands together.

'You understand,' John said, 'that if there is considerable traffic on the road there will be casualties. Perhaps heavy.'

'It is written,' Mamun said.

'But you should only need to hold for a short while. Ali, pick six men to cover me while I lay the charges.'

'Or women,' Ali grinned. 'Halil wishes to come with us.'

'Or women,' John agreed.

'What action will we take against an attack from the south?'

'I think any enemy force that has crossed the bridge will be inclined to keep on going, no matter what is happening behind them,' John said. 'But if any of them do come back, you and your men, and women, will have to hold them off until I am finished. The signal for completion will be a Very pistol flare shot into the sky. Understood?' The Arab leaders nodded.

'Now let's assemble the machine-guns,' John said. This was done, and they settled down to wait. Evening prayers were said and a meal eaten. It was a dark night, which was ideal for their purpose. Once again John spent a long time studying the road with his glasses. There was definitely still traffic down there – he could tell from the dimmed headlights – but it had slackened with darkness.

At eight o'clock he told Mamun to go and the sheikh led his seventy men and women down the slope to the right. They stayed on foot, leading two camels, on the back of one of which was the precious machine-gun; the other animals were left with their minders. John let them get clear, then led Ali and Halil and their small party forward, also carrying their machine-gun. They approached within half a mile of the road, undetected by the traffic, growling by at a steady pace, but there were definite gaps now.

John studied the bridge. Although setting explosives had been included in his training, he had never actually done it. But it seemed straightforward enough. An hour passed and he studied his watch. Mamun must be in position by now, he thought, and almost at the same moment there came a burst of firing.

Ali rose immediately and his people followed him. Now the firing from the north was general, bugles were blowing, and traffic was roaring. To the south the convoys continued to move as John had expected. But now there was a big gap in the stream, as Mamun's people took the road.

John raced down the hill, the haversack containing the dynamite banging on his back. He wondered what would happen were that haversack to be hit by a bullet? There probably wouldn't be enough of him left to cremate.

They reached the wadi, leapt in and made their way along it to the underside of the bridge. Now there was no traffic at all above them and John was able to work in comparative ease, Halil holding the torch for him while he bound the lengths of dynamite in place. But now at last one of the commanders who had already passed the bridge stopped to wonder what was happening behind him. About a quarter of a mile away they could see two of the trucks beginning to move to and fro as they turned on the road.

Ali waved his men forward, and moved down the road, staying to either side so as not to reveal themselves. John continued to work as carefully and methodically as he had been taught, while conscious all the while of the sounds of battle to either side. Halil grinned at him encouragingly. She appeared to be absolutely fearless, or she had the comforting philosophy of her people: it is written.

The last stick of dynamite was in place; now it was a matter of attaching the detonators and then the line. 'We move back now,' he told Halil and picked up the fuse box. She nodded and they crept out from under the bridge.

Now they could see the road; it had only been a few seconds since Ali had moved his people down, but the trucks were coming back at speed. The Arabs were firing at them from the shelter of the ditch, but lacked the firepower to stop them, although even as John looked one of the trucks careered sideways and toppled over. But the men inside were leaping out, firing their rifles as they did so.

'Over there!' John ran a further fifty feet up the wadi, but that was as far as he dared go. The Germans had definitely broken through Ali's people and were at the bridge, more men disembarking from the remaining truck. Most of these were already moving across the bridge to take Mamun in the rear, but one or two were inspecting the bridge itself, obviously suspicious of the holding action. He could spare no more time to retreat further. He connected the leads. 'Lie down,' he told Halil.

She obeyed and he pressed the plunger, dropping to the bottom of the wadi himself as he did so. The explosion was louder than he had expected because they were so close. A rush of hot air seemed to envelop him and Halil gave a little shriek as she was rolled away from him by the force of the blast.

But the bridge had gone up, and was descending again in a thousand splinters; in their midst were the remains of several men. John recollected that he had forgotten to signal – he had not had the time. He drew the Very pistol from his belt and sent a flare arcing into the darkness, than looked for Halil.

She was sitting up, her haik torn to ribbons. There was blood on her face and beneath her nostrils, but she seemed to be all right. John grabbed her arm. 'Come on.'

'We must kill them!' she shouted.

'All in good time.' He peered over the edge of the wadi. Now some more of the people already across the bridge had returned, summoned by the huge explosion. Those already at the bridge who had survived the blast were standing around looking dazed. There was no sign of Ali or any of his people. To the north Mamun's party was still engaged in a virtual toe to toe battle. The machine-gun continued to blaze away and grenades were being thrown, men were shouting and shrieking and rifles were cracking. 'Pull out, you fool,' John growled, and fired another Very cartridge.

'We go to them,' Halil announced.

'We pull out,' John corrected. 'They had their orders.'

He led her back up the hill for a couple of hundred yards. Then they lay down to study the situation beneath them. There was now a huge crowd milling about the shattered bridge, orders were being shouted, engines continued to roar. But the shooting had largely stopped, save for the odd stray shot. And closer at hand dark figures were stumbling through the gloom towards them.

Two men carried Ali. They laid him on the ground before John. His eyes were open but his body was a mass of blood. 'You did it, Warrey,' he said. 'You blew the bridge.'

'You did it, Ali,' John said. 'You made it possible for the bridge to be blown.' Ali smiled and his eyes closed.

Mamun stood above him. 'Now is his family quite destroyed. I am the sheikh of all his people.' It was not a point to be disputed at that moment, although John had to wonder what Uncle Osman was going to make of it. 'We have killed many of the enemy,' Mamun said.

'And your own people?'

Mamun shrugged. 'Some have died. But how better may a man die than in battle against the infidel? And we have taken prisoners.' Hell, John thought, here we go again.

He went to where Salud and his cousins were holding four very frightened German soldiers. They appeared to be unharmed at the moment, but had certainly been roughly handled. 'Now we have sport,' Halil said.

'These men are prisoners of war,' John said, and stared at Mamun. 'I hold you responsible for their safe delivery to the British Army.'

'Where is the British Army?' Mamun enquired.

'It'll be along. Let's get out of here.'

Some sort of order was being restored on the road, although a huge bottleneck of traffic was forming north of the broken bridge. Come dawn, and the RAF, they would be blasted out of existence. The Arabs withdrew to where their camels waited. John estimated they had lost about a third of their numbers; he could only hope it had all been worthwhile. Meanwhile...

'Do any of you speak English?' he asked the prisoners. 'Or Italian?'

'I speak Italian,' replied one of the Germans in that language.

'Then you can answer some questions.'

'Yes, yes,' the man agreed, eagerly, like his fellows, terribly conscious of being surrounded by the Arab women staring at him.

'Firstly, tell me of Field Marshal Rommel. Is he in Berighazi?'

'I do not think he has got there yet, sir. He is with the rearguard.'

Maybe they would get him after all, John thought. 'I am also seeking the whereabouts of the SS commander named Major Fritz Buelow,' he said.

'Yes, yes,' the soldier said. 'Major Buelow is in Benghazi.'

'Still? Well, hooray. Tell me, has he a woman with him?'

'A woman? Yes, I think he has a woman.'

John had a suspicion this man was going to say yes to every question asked, but then he added, 'This is an Arab woman. A prisoner.'

'That's right,' John said. 'Well, glory be.'

386

He told Halil. 'Uluma is still alive?'

'That's what the man said.'

'We go into Benghazi and get her?'

John shook his head. 'I don't think we can chance that. It would be a shame to have come so far and done so much and wind up against a wall.'

'You do not care about her,' Halil declared, as angrily as usual. 'She is my friend.'

'And she means a great deal to me, too,' John assured her. 'But getting ourselves killed isn't going to help her. If she's still alive, then I would say Buelow means to keep her alive, at least until he can be certain of his own safety. I would also say that he means to get out of Benghazi before it falls to the British. We will wait, and watch, and choose our moment.'

At first light John and Halil, accompanied by Salud and several of his cousins, moved back down the hillside to a vantage point from which they could overlook the road. They gazed at a scene of even greater chaos than suggested in the darkness. Sappers were busily repairing the bridge, while traffic was backed up out of sight to the north. Quite a few of the retreating soldiers had preferred to abandon their transport and proceed on foot, crossing the wadi and plodding down the road to El Agheila, which remained a very long way away.

John studied them through his glasses, but they seemed to be a disconnected lot. He was quite sure that Buelow would wait for transport and would also maintain an escort. As for Rommel... Halil touched his arm and pointed and he looked up at the bombers and their fighter escort appearing out of the dawn sky. Within a few minutes they were both bombing and strafing the road. Work on the bridge was abandoned as men hurled themselves towards shelter, but a good number never made it and remained sprawled about the road and the wadi. Halil clapped her hands in glee.

The attack lasted about fifteen minutes and then the road was merely a mass of debris, movement further complicated by the fresh craters that had appeared everywhere. Mamun joined them, accompanied by most of his people. 'We go down again now?' he asked.

'No,' John said. 'Why waste our lives when the aeroplanes are doing the job for us.'

'Then what do we do?' the sheikh demanded, disgruntedly.

'We wait,' John told him.

The RAF returned again that afternoon, but this was a brief raid. Most movement on the road had ceased; the Germans were waiting for darkness and the planes had more important work to do further north. John left Salud watching and used the radio. 'The general sends you his congratulations,' the operator said.

'Thank him for me. I have information that Rommel is still on the road to Benghazi.'

'Negative,' the operator said. 'Our information is that Rommel has flown out to Tripoli, to organise the defence there.'

'Ah,' John said. 'Do you expect Benghazi to be defended?'

'Not in any force,' the operator said.

'I would like permission to enter the city as soon as is appropriate, with my people,' John said.

'For what purpose?'

'There are some matters to be cleaned up.'

'I think the general would prefer you to continue to use your people against the enemy's lines of communication,' the operator said. 'But I will remit exact orders as soon as I obtain them. Until then, maintain your position. Is your radio continuously manned?'

'No,' John said.

'Very good. Call back in four hours time and you will receive your ongoing orders. Out.'

John returned to the Arabs, who were still peering down at the chaos on the road. 'We go in now?' Mamun asked again.

'No,' John said. 'We await orders.'

'Who gives these orders?' Mamun demanded. 'We should give our own orders.'

'That's not how things work in the Army,' John pointed out.

Halil clutched his arm; her fingers were like talons. He turned his head to look in the indicated direction. Order was being restored on the road beneath them by German and Italian military police. A new line of vehicles was being formed up and work was recommencing on the bridge. And supervising the work, walking up and down as he gave instructions, was a man in a black uniform. 'We go now,' she said.

John chewed his lip. Once the bridge was repaired, and it would not be long now, Buelow would be across it and on his way to Tripoli – and no doubt a plane back to Germany. But to go in now would be to disobey orders and risk heavy casualties. 'That is the man who kidnapped Uluma,' Halil told Mamun.

'Now we go.'

'Wait. Who is your best shot?' He knew he would not qualify.

'Yasud,' Mamun said.

The young man grinned. 'Can you pick off Buelow from here?' John asked.

Another grin. 'What about Uluma?' Halil asked.

'Buelow first,' John said.

Yasud levelled his rifle, took a couple of deep breaths and squeezed the trigger. Buelow swung round and fell over the side of the road into the ditch. The Arabs screamed with delight, only to groan as the black-clad figure re-emerged, crawling out of the ditch, hatless, but very much alive.

'Shit,' John muttered. 'You'll have to try again.'

Then realised he was speaking to a void. For the Arabs had left shelter and were racing down the slope, firing their rifles and tommy-guns, hurling their grenades. The German soldiers had been taken by surprise by the sniper's bullet. Now they were even more surprised by the charging Arabs. Hastily they attempted to return fire, but several had already been hit.

John drew his revolver and ran behind his so-called command. Bullets were flying in every direction, but very few of them were aimed, at least from the German side. Men were collapsing all over the road, and now the Arabs were into them, firing at close quarters and wielding their knives too. 'Warrey!' Halil was shrieking his name as she fired at close range into the man immediately in front of her. He fell to clear the way to Buelow, who was still shouting orders and waving his revolver.

But now he saw John, and instead ran to his jeep ... in the back of which was Uluma;

her wrists had been bound, but she was just wriggling free. John fired, and Buelow fell, struck in the leg. But he dragged himself up just as John was hit by the cannoning body of a fleeing soldier who had been brought down by a shot from Yasud. He regained his knees, saw Buelow sliding behind the wheel of his car, leaving a trail of blood, and raised his gun again. But it wasn't necessary. Buelow hadn't noticed that Uluma had wriggled free, and now he uttered a shriek of pain and surprise as a bayonet was thrust into his back, again and again. Uluma's eyes gleamed. 'He was bad to me,' she said.

Salud embraced John. They stood on the slopes above the road outside Benghazi. The bridge had been repaired and now the road was again filled with moving vehicles, but these were all Allied. The rumour was that the Germans had even evacuated Tripoli and were retreating as fast as they could to Tunisia where there were large Axis forces, but these were already under attack from the Americans in the west. 'Is it really done?'

'Bar the shouting.'

'What will happen to my people now?'

'I wish I knew, old friend. For the time being you will have to come under British military law, until the future is sorted out.'

'You will stay?'

John shook his head. 'I don't think I will

be able to do that.' He squeezed Salud's hand. 'It has been a privilege to fight with you.'

'To win,' Salud grinned.

'When you come back?' Uluma asked.

John sighed. 'I do not know. Perhaps I will not come back.'

Her lips pouted. 'And you not take me?'

'I'm afraid that's not possible.'

'Because of Buelow? He was nothing. He gave me no pleasure. Only pain.'

'Of course not because of Buelow, Uluma. But I have my own woman to return to, and still a war to fight.' He held her hands. 'I shall not forget you.'

Her teeth gleamed. 'We had good times together, Warrey. You are a great fighting man. But you will not take me.'

'I've explained...'

A tear trickled out of her eye. 'No one will take me now, because of Buelow.'

'Of course someone will take you. I'll have a word with Salud.'

He could only hope the word had some effect. Leaving the Arabs was the most difficult thing he had ever had to do. They were barbarous when it came to fighting, but utterly faithful. They had died at his behest – he would carry to his grave the knowledge that he had caused the deaths of

Ali, Ali's father, Ali's grandfather and of countless others. All to secure a victory he was not at all sure the British and their allies knew how to use. 'You have done a magnificent job, Warrey,' Montgomery said, shaking his hand. 'There is both a DSO and a bar to your MC waiting for you. Not to mention promotion to major.'

'Where, exactly, sir?'

'In England. I'm sending you home. You've earned a break.'

'And the war here, sir?'

'Oh, that's just a cleaning-up operation, now. They can't hold out forever. Even Rommel knows that: he's gone home. Arnim commands in Tunisia. But he's on a hiding to nothing. So, when you've had your rest, I'll look forward to having you back on my staff, when we go...' The severe face actually broke into a grin. 'To wherever we're going.'

Cairo was a hubbub of excited triumph. Mustafa opened the door to him. 'Warrey!' he shouted.

John embraced him. 'About the money for the car,' Mustafa said, anxiously.

'Forget it,' John told him. 'I have come to say goodbye.'

'You go? Again?' Arsinoe burst into their midst to hug and kiss him. Mustafa looked embarrassed.

'I'm afraid I must.'

She pulled her head back to look at him. 'You come, you go. When you come again?'

'Ah ... I'm not sure about that.'

'But you come again?'

'Who knows,' he said.

How does one turn one's back upon the past? Only by looking resolutely to the future. Aileen had a week's leave soon after he returned to England. 'You look battered,' she commented.

'Too many cocktails at Shepheard's,' he agreed.

She looked splendid in her uniform, even if he still couldn't relate to her bobbed black hair, when he remembered the luxuriant tresses that had swept her shoulders before the War. 'And you're to get the DSO,' she commented. 'Lucky for some. I'm so glad. I'm so glad you're home, unwounded, after the last time. They kept you out of the firing line, this time, did they?'

'In a manner of speaking. I'm in Intelligence, remember?'

'And did you bring off any great political coups?'

'I made a lot of friends,' he told her.

The publishers hope that this book has given you enjoyable reading. Large Print Books are especially designed to be as easy to see and hold as possible. If you wish a complete list of our books please ask at your local library or write directly to:

Magna Large Print Books
Magna House, Long Preston,
Skipton, North Yorkshire.
BD23 4ND

This Large Print Book for the partially sighted, who cannot read normal print, is published under the auspices of

THE ULVERSCROFT FOUNDATION

THE ULVERSCROFT FOUNDATION

... we hope that you have enjoyed this Large Print Book. Please think for a moment about those people who have worse eyesight problems than you ... and are unable to even read or enjoy Large Print, without great difficulty.

You can help them by sending a donation, large or small to:

**The Ulverscroft Foundation,
1, The Green, Bradgate Road,
Anstey, Leicestershire, LE7 7FU,
England.**
or request a copy of our brochure for more details.

The Foundation will use all your help to assist those people who are handicapped by various sight problems and need special attention.

Thank you very much for your help.